Praise for
Judgment Day

"High-octane straight from the start. With breakneck action, high-strung suspense and characters you can't help but root for, *Judgment Day* is an irresistible read."

—TOSCA LEE, author of *Demon: A Memoir*

"The Queen of High Octane Suspense has done it again! Wanda Dyson takes us on a roller-coaster ride worthy of a whiplash warning. High suspense, romantic tension, and even comic relief will keep you riveted and turning pages as fast as you can read. It's all in there!"

—BONNIE S. CALHOUN, owner and publisher of *Christian Fiction Online Magazine*

"*Judgment Day* is packed with action and adventure. Private detective duo Marcus Crisp and Alexandria Fisher-Hawthorne are fascinating and keep the story rolling with their wit, sarcasm, and teamed-up tactical skills reminiscent of many favorite action-adventure movies. Dyson has penned a great suspense with strong Christian themes in *Judgment Day*!"

—RONIE KENDIG, author of *Dead Reckoning* and *Nightshade*

"From page one I couldn't put this book down. Suzanne is a highly flawed individual in the fight of her life. When she's forced to call in Alex and Marcus to unravel who's trying to frame her, they instead unravel an evil plot that ends with harvested organs. The pacing is tight, the characters people I want to know, and the plot so intricate I literally could not stop reading. Two thumbs up for those who love tightly written suspense with a very light twist of romance."

—CARA C. PUTMAN, author of *Canteen Dreams*
and *A Promise Forged*

"*Judgment Day* is Dyson's best suspense to date! The current event woven expertly into the fast-paced plot kept me turning the pages. For a fabulous, edge-of-your-seat, keep-you-up-late novel, *Judgment Day* is not to be missed!"

—ROBIN CAROLL, author of *Deliver Us from Evil*
and *Fear No Evil*

JUDGMENT
DAY

Also by Wanda Dyson

Fiction
Abduction
Obsession
Intimidation
Shepherd's Fall

Nonfiction
Why I Jumped, coauthored with Tina Zahn

A NOVEL

JUDGMENT DAY

WANDA DYSON

WATERBROOK
PRESS

JUDGMENT DAY
PUBLISHED BY WATERBROOK PRESS
12265 Oracle Boulevard, Suite 200
Colorado Springs, Colorado 80921

All Scripture quotations, unless otherwise indicated, are taken or paraphrased from the New King James Version®. Copyright © 1982 by Thomas Nelson Inc. Used by permission. All rights reserved.

The characters and events in this book are fictional, and any resemblance to actual persons or events is coincidental.

ISBN 978-1-4000-7475-4
ISNB 978-0-307-45812-4 (electronic)

Published in the United States by WaterBrook Multnomah, an imprint of the Crown Publishing Group, a division of Random House Inc., New York.

WATERBROOK and its deer colophon are registered trademarks of Random House Inc.

Library of Congress Cataloging-in-Publication Data
Dyson, Wanda L.
    Judgment Day : a novel / Wanda L. Dyson. — 1st ed.
        p. cm.
    ISBN 978-1-4000-7475-4 — ISBN 978-0-307-45812-4 (electronic)
    1. Women television journalists—Fiction. 2. Private investigators—Fiction.
3. Corruption investigation—Fiction. 4. Murder—Investigation—Fiction. I. Title.
    PS3604.Y77J83 2010
    813'.6—dc22

                                        2010024546

Printed in the United States of America
2010—First Edition

10 9 8 7 6 5 4 3 2 1

—

Shannon Marchese, Jennifer Peterson, Nicci Jordan Hubert, and Jessica Barnes. This one's for you.

It was never about avoiding judgment day.
It was all about surviving it.

—JOHN CONNOR in *Terminator 3: Rise of the Machines*

Prologue

Friday, April 3. Baltimore, MD

Running away from home had sounded like the best idea ever when she was planning it, but now that sixteen-year-old Britney Abbott was tired, hungry, and out of money, it felt more like the biggest mistake of her life. She climbed down off the bus, slung her backpack over her shoulder, and wondered where she was going to sleep for the night.

If only her mother hadn't married that jerk. He was so strict. According to Ronnie, Britney couldn't date, couldn't stay over at a friend's for the night, and she had to be in the house no later than seven every evening. None of her friends had to live like that.

Last Saturday night her mom and Ronnie went out to dinner, leaving her home alone with the usual litany of instructions: You cannot have anyone over. You will do your homework. You will be in bed by ten. You will not spend the evening on the phone with your friends. And you will not—I repeat, not—leave this house; I am going to call and if you aren't here to answer the phone, you will be grounded for a month.

Fifteen minutes after they left, Ronnie-the-Predictable called. She answered the phone. An hour and a half later, she was gone.

She looked around at the crowds dispersing in several directions. The smell of diesel fuel overwhelmed her empty stomach and it growled in protest. Everything looked the way she felt—worn-out, dirty, and depressed.

"Hey, you okay?" A girl stood against the wall near the exit from the bus station. Torn jeans, pink T-shirt, high-top sneakers, leather jacket, and numerous rings and studs from ear to nose to lip.

"Yeah, I'm cool."

"You look hungry. I was just going over to Mickey D's. You wanna come?"

"No money."

"It's okay. I think I can buy you a hamburger and some fries."

Britney was hungry enough to be tempted and wary enough to wonder why the girl would make such an offer. "Me?"

"Yeah." The girl walked over. "My name's Kathi. I came to Washington about five months ago. A friend of mine was supposed to be on the bus, but either her parents caught her trying to run away or she changed her mind."

"You're a runaway?"

Kathi laughed as she shoved her hands deep into the pockets of her jacket. "Look around, girl. There are lots of us. We come to DC to get away. Some stay, some move on to Chicago or New York."

Britney felt relieved to know she wasn't alone. "Okay. I'll take a hamburger. Thanks."

Kathi linked her arm in Britney's and led her down the street toward the Golden Arches. "What's your name?"

"Britney."

"Well, let's get you something to eat, and then you can crash at my place."

They chatted as they ate their food and drank their sodas, and with each passing minute Britney liked Kathi more. She might look a little tough, but Britney supposed that living on the streets, you had to be. Her appearance aside, Kathi seemed friendly and generous.

They were about a block past McDonald's when a woozy feeling interrupted their conversation. When she stumbled, Kathi steadied her. "You okay?"

"Just lightheaded."

"Tired, more than likely. It's not far to my place."

But Britney's body felt heavier with each step. She struggled to stay awake. She had never felt this way before in her entire life. Not even after staying up for two straight days studying for a math test.

"I don't feel so good."

"We're almost there," Kathi told her. "Just down this way."

Britney didn't like the dark alley or the dark van parked there with the motor running, but she couldn't find the strength to resist Kathi's pull on her arm.

As they passed the van, the side door opened and a man stepped out. "Too bad she's such a looker."

"Yeah, well," Kathi replied. "You get what I can find."

The man picked up Britney and tossed her into the van. Britney tried to call out, tried to resist, but she could no longer control her arms or legs. She could only lie there and let the fear grow and build until the scream inside felt like an explosion in her head.

The man duct-taped her arms and legs. Then he placed a piece over her mouth. "Don't worry, kid. This will be over real soon."

1

Wednesday, April 15. Outside Washington DC

Suzanne Kidwell shoved her tape recorder in the cop's face, smiling up at him as if he were the hero in her own personal story. "We have two girls missing now, and both were students at Longview High. Are you looking at the faculty and staff at the school?"

The officer puffed a bit, squaring his shoulders and thrusting out his chest as he hiked up his utility belt. "You have to understand that we haven't finished our investigation, but I can tell you that we found pornography on the principal's computer. I'd say we're just hours away from arresting him."

She lightly traced a glossy red nail down his forearm. "I knew I came to the right man. You have that air of authority and competence. And I'll bet you were the one who sent those detectives in the right direction too."

He dropped his head in one of those "aw shucks, ma'am" moves. "Well, I did tell them that he had been arrested about ten years ago for assault."

"And they made a man like that the principal. What is this world coming to?" Before he could comment, she hit him with another question. "Has he told you yet what he did with the girls?"

"Not yet. He's still insisting he's innocent, but it's just a matter of time before we get a confession out of him."

"Thank you so much, Officer. You're a hero. Those girls would be dead without you."

He blushed hard as she hurried off, lobbing him another dazzling smile as she calculated her timetable. It was nearly four, and she had to be ready and on the air at six, scooping every other network in the city.

———

At the station, she ran up the stairs to the second floor and jogged down to Frank's office. "Is he in?" she asked his secretary.

"Sure. Go on in."

If there was a dark spot anywhere in her job at all, it was Frank Dawson. The man delighted in hassling her. Professional jealousy, no doubt. She knocked on his doorjamb. "Can I talk to you for a minute?"

Like Frank, the room was heavy on shine and light on substance. Awards and diplomas covered all the walls. Pictures of Frank with politicians, presidents, and the wealthy, beautiful, and powerful were displayed prominently on all the bookshelves. His desk dominated the center of the room, covered in paperwork, tapes, and files.

"Sure."

Suzanne took a deep breath, clutched her notes, and strode into his office. "You know the two local girls that went missing recently?"

He glanced up at the clock, a subtle reminder that she should be getting dressed and into makeup. "I think so."

"Well, I've been doing some digging, and they have a suspect."

"And this is your business exactly why?"

"Because I scooped everyone else. I talked to one of the officers working the case, and he told me that they have a suspect, they're interrogating him now, and they expect to announce his arrest momentarily."

"And what does this have to do with me?"

She stared at him for a long moment. "I want to go on the air with this late-breaking news."

He scratched his chin. "Your show is already scheduled, Suzanne. Corruption in the horse industry."

"I know that, and I can still do that. I just need five minutes at the end of the show to cover this. We've got the scoop! How can we not run with it?"

Waving a hand, he said, "Fine. Go with it. I sure hope you have all the facts."

"I have them straight from the mouth of the police. How much more do you want?"

"Fine. Do it."

Grinning, she rushed back down to wardrobe and makeup in record time, entering the studio with mere minutes to spare.

Suzanne looked over at one of the assistants. "Where's my microphone?"

As someone rushed to get her miked up, the director walked in. "We have a job to do, people; let's get to it. We're on the air in two."

She straightened her jacket as the assistant adjusted the small microphone clipped to her lapel. "It's fine. Move."

The cameraman finished the countdown with his fingers. Three…two…one. She fixed her expression.

"Good evening, ladies and gentlemen." Suzanne turned slightly. "I'm Suzanne Kidwell. And this is *Judgment Day*."

Suzanne took a deep breath while the station ran the introduction, taking a moment to straighten the notes in front of her and sip her water.

When the director pointed at her, she launched into the ongoing corruption and abuses endangering horse owners.

The camera shifted for a closeup. "And before I close tonight, I want to give you a late-breaking report. Just like you, I've been horrified by the tragic disappearance of teens here in the tristate area. But what made me truly sit up and take notice was that within the last two weeks, two young girls—seventeen-year-old Jennifer Link and sixteen-year-old Britney Abbott—were reported as runaways. Same neighborhood, same school, both runaways?

"Now maybe that could happen, but I was skeptical. I did some digging. And I'm happy to report that the police have arrested Peter Fryer, the principal of Longview High School."

Suzanne changed her expression from a touch of sorrow mixed with concern to outrage. "I spoke to the lead officer, and he told me that evidence against the principal included child pornography on Fryer's computer. In spite of being arrested ten years ago for assault, Peter Fryer was hired on as the principal of Longview just four years ago. He is still denying any involvement, but the police assured me they have their man. I will keep you posted."

She angled her body. "As long as there are people out there who betray our trust, there will be *Judgment Day with Suzanne Kidwell*. Good night, America. I'll see you next week."

As soon as she got the signal that she was clear, she pulled off her mike and stood up, grabbing her water as she left the studio.

She rushed down the hall, and when she reached her office, she sank down into her chair and kicked off her shoes. She barely had time to curl her toes in the carpet before her phone rang.

She picked it up. "Great job, Suzanne." It was Frank.

"Thanks, boss. I knew you'd be happy."

"The phones are ringing off the hook. The other stations are scrambling to catch up to us."

Smiling, she leaned back. "They'll be eating our dust for a while now."

"You'll stay on this?"

"All the way to conviction."

2

Almost two weeks later—Tuesday, April 28

I heard the principal committed suicide."
Suzanne looked briefly over at her boyfriend, Dr. Guy Mandeville, and then back at the road. "He just couldn't handle the
scrutiny."

"So you're finished with that story?"

"As far as I know, it's over. They got their man, even if he did
take the coward's way out. Why?"

"Why what?"

"Why do you ask if I'm finished? Normally, you barely notice
the stories I'm working on."

As Suzanne took her foot off the gas, the car suddenly acceler-
ated, shooting forward and throwing her back against the seat.
"Whoa!" She stomped on the brake and breathed a heavy sigh of
relief when the car responded.

Guy released his grip on the dashboard. "What was that?"

"That's happened twice now this week. Just accelerating by it-self." She turned the wheel and pulled into the parking lot of her station. "It's scaring the daylights out of me."

"That's dangerous, honey," he replied as she eased into a park-ing space and shut the engine down.

"I just haven't had time to get it checked out."

Guy climbed out of the car and pulled out his car keys. "Take my car. I'll drop yours off at Pete's shop on my way home. I don't want you driving this home tonight."

She would have taken him up on that offer even if her car was working perfectly. The chance to drive his Porsche? No contest. Sidling up to him, she wrapped one arm around his neck and re-warded him with a kiss on the lips. "You realize that you may never get your car back."

Toying with a lock of her blond hair, he just smiled. "Marry me and you can drive it anytime you want. Or better yet, I'll buy one for you as an engagement present."

Slipping her keys into his hand, she leaned into him. "I'm thinking about it. Seriously."

"Then say yes."

She sobered. "I just don't know if I'm ready, Guy. There's still so much I want to do before I settle down and get married."

He stiffened slightly, obviously trying hard not to let his dis-pleasure show. "You can be married and still chase your dreams."

"Why the rush?"

"It doesn't take me forever to know what I want."

She glanced at her watch. "I have to go. We can talk about this later."

He wrapped his arms around her, letting his nose come down to touch hers. "I love you, Suzanne. I want to marry you and spoil you rotten. I want to give you everything you ever wanted."

"Except the time to decide what's best for me." She bit her lip as the words tumbled out. "I'm sorry."

He leaned in and kissed her tenderly. "Don't forget we have reservations for dinner at eight."

"Call me when you're ready and I'll pick you up." She ran a finger down his cheek. "It'll give me a little more time with the Porsche."

———

Guy stood and watched Suzanne until she disappeared inside the building. If only being his wife could be enough for her. He loved her passion for her work, but it was a double-edged sword.

With a glance over at his new Porsche gleaming in the afternoon sun, he folded himself into Suzanne's car and adjusted the seat to make room for his long legs, reset the radio to a classical station, and fastened the seat belt. His cell phone rang just as he pulled out of the parking lot.

"Hi, Dad."

———

Willard Mandeville tucked the phone under his chin as he poured himself a drink. "Where are you? I just called the hospital and they told me you were out to lunch."

"I'm on my way back now."

He slammed the bottle of Scotch down on the counter. "You were with that woman again."

"Dad, I've made my feelings clear on this. I love Suzanne and hope to marry her. You're going to have to accept that."

"She's just after your money." It sounded weak, but he was running out of arguments. He loved his son, but the boy could be as stubborn as his mother. *Man.* Guy was a well-respected surgeon, intelligent and ambitious. But a fool when it came to women. Suzanne Kidwell was interested for one reason only. To see what dirt she could dig up on the Mandeville family—and there was no way Willard was going to let her destroy their lives.

"If that were true, she'd already have a ring on her finger."

"You proposed to her?" Willard sank down in the brown leather chair near the window, his mind scrambling for another argument against this woman.

"Yes. Several times."

"Guy, this is a mistake. She's an overly ambitious reporter who doesn't care who she hurts. I guarantee you she's going to do all she can to make us her next big story."

"But that's not the reason you called."

"No." Willard took a drink from his glass. "Your mother wanted me to ask if you could drop by this evening for dinner. She's having Pierre make that beef dish you like so well."

"I appreciate it, but I already have other plans."

"Listen. Bring Suzanne for dinner. I know I haven't been the most accommodating. The thought of a reporter in the family… well, it's disconcerting, to say the least. But if you are determined to marry her, I'm going to respect your wishes." *And with any luck, she'd be dead before she arrived.*

"I understand, but Suzanne can be trusted. Anyway, her car has been acting up—accelerating when it isn't supposed to. I'm taking it over to Pete's as soon as I'm done with this afternoon's surgery. Suzanne is on the air until seven. There's no way either of us can be there by five for dinner. And you know Mother hates to have dinner late."

Willard dropped his glass. "You're driving Suzanne's car?"

"Yes, why?"

He ran a hand down his face as his heart began to race. "Well, if it's acting up, are you sure that's wise? Perhaps you should just pull over and call Pete. Have him send a tow truck to pick it up. You don't want to get into an accident."

"It's okay. I'm just a few miles away."

"Guy, listen to me. I have a bad feeling."

"What else is new?" Guy laughed. "I'll talk to you later."

"Guy—"

At that moment, the car jerked and then lurched forward. Guy dropped the cell phone and slammed his foot on the brake. It didn't slow down. It didn't stop. It went faster. He checked the sideview mirror and when he saw it was clear, jerked the wheel, changing lanes, barely avoiding the back of the SUV in front of him.

Cursing under his breath, he tried again to get the brakes to respond. His speed hit sixty. Then sixty-five. Somewhere in the distance, he could hear his father shouting his name, but he had no idea where his cell phone was. And until he got the car under control, he wasn't going to worry about it.

He kept pumping the brakes as the car continued to pick up speed. Seventy. Seventy-five. He whipped through traffic, weaving in and out, barely missing three car bumpers and a motorcycle. Sweat beaded on his forehead. He didn't bother to wipe it away. Eyes jumping from rearview mirror to side mirror to windshield, he fought to maneuver through the bridge traffic, desperately hoping to get to the other side so that he could drive the car into a ditch.

Eighty.

Eighty-five.

He approached the end of the bridge, nearly going airborne as he reached the small ledge where the pavements met.

He saw the red light ahead.

And the traffic stopped, waiting.

No option but to plow into the back of a line of cars. Until he remembered a nearby park.

He swerved to the right, hit the curb, bounced.

He saw the trees and aimed the car between two of them, hoping the grass would slow him down. Glancing at the speedometer, he realized he wasn't slowing enough.

The car was like a demon with a mind of its own and hellbent on destruction.

As he approached the opening between the two trees, he realized he'd miscalculated. He wasn't going to make it.

The thought was erased by a flash of memories. He tried to grab one and hold on to it, but they raced through his mind.

The front bumper scraped the tree and began to buckle. Releasing the wheel, he folded his arms over his head, trying to protect his face.

Suzanne.

The airbag exploded. His head snapped back.

The car whipped sideways into the other tree, then shot forward into a concrete monument and flipped.

Guy didn't feel the sensation of being airborne.

He didn't feel the impact when the car landed upside down.

He didn't feel the heat when it burst into flames.

3

Tuesday, April 28

Suzanne checked her watch again as she left the studio. Guy still hadn't called. Well, it wouldn't be the first time that an emergency surgery had pulled him away at the last minute. Unlocking the Porsche, she climbed behind the wheel and took a moment to just inhale the sweet smell of new leather mixing with the subtle musk of Guy's cologne.

Just the right mix of wealth and privilege.

Now she had to decide what to do. Go to the hospital and wait for him? Or go to the restaurant and make sure they didn't lose their reservations? But she couldn't recall what restaurant they were going to.

As she stuck the key into the ignition, she noticed Guy's briefcase on the passenger floor. Strange. If he was going straight to the hospital, he would have needed it. So why hadn't he come back for it? Well, he'd have the reservations logged in his day planner, that she knew for sure.

She pulled it up on the seat. It was locked. Pulling the keys out of the ignition, she checked through the ring. Bingo!

Inside she found his laptop and a stack of patient files. Setting them in her lap, she pushed aside some of the loose papers scattered on the bottom. Travel receipts. Gas receipts. And a thick envelope.

Underneath the envelope, his leather-bound day planner. Flipping through the pages, she saw several notes that made her forget about dinner. Cryptic notes—initials and dates and locations—nagged her instincts.

Struggling to make sense of it, she went back to the patient files and started reading. This couldn't be true. Her heart pounded, accelerating wildly as her hands began to shake. Surely Guy couldn't be this evil. She would have known something.

Reaching over, she picked up the fat envelope, knowing what she was going to find, hoping she was wrong. Biting her lip, she ripped it open. Cash. Lots of it. Hundreds of fifty and hundred dollar bills. She couldn't even begin to estimate how much money spilled into her lap. Many thousands, for sure.

Her cell phone rang and she jumped. Taking a deep breath, she answered, "Suzanne Kidwell."

"Ms. Kidwell? This is Cecelia at Dr. Mandeville's office."

She had only met Cecelia Forbes two or three times, but there was something in her voice that made Suzanne's heart jump. "What's wrong?"

"It's Dr. Mandeville. He died this afternoon."

"Guy? Dead?"

"I need to meet you somewhere. We need to talk. I have a feeling I'm next."

Suzanne sat up, one hand gripping the steering wheel. "Next for what?"

"To be killed."

4

Wednesday, April 29, Washington DC

Marcus Crisp stepped into the restaurant and glanced around. It was one of those places that the elite liked to frequent and the working-class Joes—like himself—knew they weren't welcome.

The maître d' gave him a snooty once-over, taking in Marcus's hundred-dollar suit, Sears tie, and Payless dress shoes. "May I help you?"

"I'm here to meet Mr. Hawthorne."

"Of course. Right this way."

When Marcus arrived at the table, Randolph Hawthorne didn't bother to acknowledge his guest and kept chatting away on his cell phone. He was just trying to put Marcus on the defensive, like those men that have chairs in their offices that are shorter than their own as a subtle power strategy. Such tactics failed with Marcus. At six-foot-six, he was hard to ignore.

Marcus ordered an iced tea and used the time to look around the room, studying the people who were politely dismissing him.

He'd dealt with enough of their type, both as a police detective and currently as a private investigator, not to take their attitudes personally. They couldn't help themselves. They had been taught from birth that they were better than everyone else, and then worked hard their whole lives to make sure everyone else believed it.

Marcus didn't, but he was more than willing to leave them to their delusions—until they began to believe the laws didn't apply to them.

Hawthorne finally ended his call and reached across the table to shake Marcus's hand. "I appreciate you agreeing to meet me."

"Well, you made it sound important."

Hawthorne was the father of Marcus's partner, Alexandria Rachelle Fisher-Hawthorne. Marcus may not have been one of Hawthorne's biggest fans, but he cared enough about his partner to keep things civil.

Hawthorne picked up his menu. "Well, let's order some dinner, shall we?"

Marcus would have preferred to just get to the matter at hand, but he didn't have any plans for the evening. No harm in letting the man run the show for a while.

After finishing one of the best steaks he'd ever eaten, Marcus leaned back and allowed the waiter to bus his plate. "I'm going to take a stab in the dark and assume this meeting is about Alex."

Hawthorne dabbed the corners of his mouth with his napkin and then set it back in his lap. "I thought it was time you and I came to terms about her future."

"I don't see where I have anything to do with her future. She's a grown woman and makes her own decisions."

"We both know that as long as she's with you, she's not going to come home and take over the family business."

He made it sound like Alex had to come home and run the family bakery. In reality, Fisher-Hawthorne was a dynasty worth billions. And Marcus knew that Alex wanted no part of it.

Marcus folded his arms and leaned forward, resting them on the table. "I'm not keeping Alex from anything."

"You are a very intelligent man, Marcus."

"Thanks."

"And ambitious. So let's get down to brass tacks. You've managed to take several unfortunate circumstances in your life and make the most of them. But no matter how much I may admire you as a man, you are not the kind of man my daughter should marry."

Marcus was blindsided by the man's frankness. "Marry? What are you talking about? Alex and I are business partners."

"Oh, please." Hawthorne waved a hand. "My daughter is enamored with you, and as long as she thinks she has you, she's not going to give up this ridiculous job of hers and come back to Boston."

"Enamored with me? She's my best friend and my partner. That's it." He took a deep breath and edged forward. "She was a great lawyer and she's a great investigator. It's what she wants to do with her life. If I wasn't around, she'd just keep going."

Hawthorne shook his head. "I don't believe that. Alexandria was raised to understand her obligations to the family. She is my only child. I want the best for her. I won't have her throwing all that away for some romantic adventure with a man."

"Romantic adventure? Do you know where your daughter is at this moment? Comforting a mother whose sixteen-year-old daughter ran away from home and is now missing. Trying to reassure that woman that she will do everything in her power to find that girl and bring her home. Do you have any idea what it takes in a person to accept that kind of responsibility?"

The waiter returned with coffee. Hawthorne thanked him. Reaching for the cream, he glanced up at Marcus. "I want to know what it will take to make you go away."

Marcus ignored the coffee and sipped from his water glass. "Are you actually trying to pay me off?"

Hawthorne pulled out a checkbook from inside his jacket pocket and set it on the table, folding his hands on top of it. "I'm willing to pay you half a million. You take the money. You tell Alex you're quitting the business."

Marcus leaned back in his chair. "Sir, I appreciate your love for your daughter, I honestly do, but you obviously don't know me. And you don't know your daughter. Alex would never believe that I just decided to leave the business. And even if I did leave the business, she wouldn't close up the firm and go home."

"*Seven* hundred thousand."

"Sir, you don't get it. Please listen to me. I can't be bought.

Neither can your daughter. If she finds out you're doing this behind her back, she will come down on you like a sledgehammer."

The man actually lifted his chin as if insulted. "I am quite aware that my daughter has a temper. But she would get over it."

"You really are something."

"I don't mean to insult you, Marcus. Just to encourage you to start a new life. Seven hundred thousand dollars can buy a lot of nice things."

Marcus couldn't help but roll his eyes. "You didn't insult me, Hawthorne. You insulted your daughter." Marcus pulled the napkin off his lap and set it on the table. "Thank you for dinner. I'll give Alex your regards."

"You have to understand, Marcus." Hawthorne sounded urgent. "A man will do anything to protect his child."

Pushing back his chair, Marcus stood up. "You're not protecting her; you're controlling her."

As he turned to walk away, Hawthorne jumped to his feet. "Marcus."

Marcus turned. Waited.

"You may not be for sale, but look me in the face and tell me you aren't in love with my daughter."

Marcus stared at him for a long moment. Then he turned and walked away.

5

Guy's funeral was well attended by friends, family, and the media. But Suzanne hadn't shown up to cover it for the local news. Or as Guy's girlfriend. Or even for the sake of appearances. She was there because she was still trying to reconcile what she knew with what she had once believed. They were touting him as a saint, a pillar of society, and a humanitarian. She wanted to stand up and declare him a monster who preyed on innocent young teens.

The funeral hadn't gone well at all.

"Guy's mother actually ordered me to leave. Can you believe that?"

Caroline, the station's makeup artist, clicked her tongue in a show of sympathy and reached for the blush. "Well, they're just grieving the loss of their only child. Not that it's fair to treat you so badly, but you can understand how horrible this must be for them."

Suzanne closed her eyes as Caroline sprayed her hair. "Yes, I do, but I was there to pay my respects."

Caroline tilted her head as she gave one last critical look at Suzanne's makeup and then reached for another brush. "He proposed, didn't he?"

"Yes."

"Well—"

One of the production assistants stuck her head in the room. "Five minutes, Ms. Kidwell."

With one last brush across Suzanne's cheeks, Caroline whipped off the drape around Suzanne's neck. "Sorry about spilling that coffee earlier, but I think you look better in this suit anyway."

"I wore this last Thursday. Someone is going to notice."

"We put a different blouse with it."

"I wanted my new suit."

"I'll make sure it's cleaned and ready for Monday's show." Caroline started packing up her brushes. "I promise."

"Good." Suzanne picked up the jacket and headed over to Studio Three, pushing Mrs. Mandeville's scorn to the back of her mind. Time to go to work.

She pulled open the door to the studio and stepped in as Roy Wilkins, one of the cameramen, walked in behind her.

"I wanted to tell you how sorry I am about Mandeville. He was a good guy, Suzanne."

"Thanks." Suzanne kept her eyes on her notes, struggling to fully concentrate on them.

"Guess you'll miss having his gold card at your beck and call too."

She glared at him. "That was uncalled for."

Roy shrugged. "Just calling it the way I see it. You don't seem too broken up."

"I keep my private life and my professional life separate, unlike some people around here."

"Is that why you always paraded him through the studio every chance you got? Because you wanted to keep things *separate*?"

"Zip it, Roy."

"Oh, and nice job with the principal. I hear you drove him to commit suicide."

Suzanne adjusted her mike. "I was not responsible for that. He decided to end his life rather than face the charges."

"There were no charges, Sugarplum."

"Because he killed himself before they could finish up their investigation."

"Sure, you keep telling yourself that."

Suzanne started to respond with a little venom of her own, but the countdown to air had begun. Swallowing the retort, she turned her attention to the news. She plastered a warm smile on her face. "Good evening. I'm Suzanne Kidwell."

———

An hour later, she was back in her office, packing up to go home. Her cell phone rang. She picked it up off the desk and checked the caller ID. With a silent groan, she considered letting the call go to voice mail. On the fourth ring, she answered the call. "Hi, Mom. This isn't a good time."

"It's never a good time for you. I need to know what time your plane is arriving."

"My plane?"

"You forgot, didn't you? I knew it. Once again, all you think about is yourself."

It took about two seconds for her to realize this was about her sister's engagement party. "Mom, I told you. I can't get away this weekend."

"I happen to know you aren't on the air on the weekends. Well, it's Friday night. You should be catching a plane."

"I have a career. I can't just take off whenever I please."

"A career." Her mother snorted. "You sit in front of a camera and read off a monitor. That isn't a career. It's a job, and one that won't miss you for a day or two. This is important to your sister. I'd think you'd want to be there for her."

Suzanne pressed her lips together and blinked back the tears. Not one question about the funeral or how Suzanne was holding up. No acknowledgment of her respected position as a journalist. "Mom, it's just an engagement party. I'll be there for the wedding."

"You'll be here for her engagement party too. And you'll be here when we go out for the dresses. You *are* in the wedding, you know."

"Elizabeth doesn't need me. She has her maid of honor and the rest of her friends."

"You're going to let her down again, aren't you? I should have known. After all I did to get her to even ask you to be in the wedding, this is the thanks I get."

Elizabeth wasn't even going to have her in the wedding? The knife went in a little deeper. "Look, Mom, I have to go."

"Of course you do." Click.

Suzanne slowly closed her phone. When was she going to accept the fact that her mother would always love Elizabeth more? When would the words stop hurting?

A quick knock sounded on her office door, but before she could respond, it opened and a police officer stepped in. Plain clothes, badge hanging from his belt, and a look on his face that said he wasn't going to be pushed around. Detective, more than likely.

"Ms. Kidwell?"

"Don't you know how to knock? I could have been changing clothes."

"I did knock."

"And then stormed in."

"I need to ask you a few questions."

"About what?"

"Did you give your car to Dr. Mandeville, knowing that it was going to kill him?"

She tilted her head back and met his penetrating gaze. He was serious. "You think *I* killed Guy?" She picked up her pen. "What's your name?"

"Detective Hodge. Michael Hodge. Do you want me to spell it for you?"

"No need," she replied as she wrote it down on her notepad. Unfortunately, it didn't seem to intimidate him in the least.

"I asked you a question."

"No." She reached over and uncapped a bottle of water. "I had no idea it would lead to his death. Had I thought for one second he could have been hurt, I wouldn't have let him take it."

"And yet you did."

It dawned on her then, slowly rising up inside. "His mother sent you, didn't she? She thinks I was responsible."

He didn't answer but she saw the affirmation in his eyes. She made him wait while she took a long drink of water. "Guy asked me to marry him. I had no reason to want him dead. I think we're done here."

Dismissing him with a turn of her shoulder, she walked over to her desk and made a show of flipping through file folders and production sheets. She tried to stifle the indignant tears that formed.

"Then tell me this—who wanted *you* dead?"

"Me?" Suzanne turned around, leaning back against her desk. "Is this a joke?"

"Your car had been altered, Ms. Kidwell."

"Altered? As in what? Someone tampered with my accelerator?"

"Yes, they did. But the car didn't explode because Dr. Mandeville ran into a monument. It was also rigged to explode. So I can't help wondering. Do you have any enemies?"

"There was a bomb in my car?"

"Ms. Kidwell, who wants you dead?"

She had interviewed enough cops in her day to know that they liked to keep their suspects off balance, jumping from one topic to another. Her only recourse was to try and take control and attempt to knock him off balance instead.

"A bomb. Someone planted a bomb in my car? That's crazy."

"I repeat, do you have any enemies?"

"I suppose it's possible. Celebrities do sometimes garner the wrong kind of fans."

"I've seen your show, Ms. Kidwell. You're not exactly a celebrity."

Suzanne felt the little barb sting, and she wanted to bare her teeth and claw at his eyes. "I do investigative reporting pieces. Maybe someone wasn't too happy that I was working to expose their crimes."

He lifted an eyebrow in disbelief. "I will need the files."

Suzanne circled the desk and sat down behind it, her mind racing. Give them the files and run the risk of losing whatever edge she had on breaking a story no one else had even scented yet? No way. She'd worked too hard.

"That wasn't a suggestion, Ms. Kidwell."

Picking up the phone, she connected to her secretary. "Gail? Get me legal on the line, will you?"

Hodge walked over to her desk, folded his arms, and waited until she hung up the phone. "You can call legal, you can call your boss, and you can call the mayor, a senator, a congressman, and a host of lobbyists, but you're still going to have to answer my questions and turn over your files."

"And if I give you my files, what happens to my stories? The information will be all over town before sunrise."

"Maybe. Maybe not. I just want to see if there's anything in there that someone might want to kill to protect."

She pointed to a file box on the floor in the corner. "You can look at them, but they are not crossing that threshold." She didn't tell him the most important files were locked in her desk.

"They'll do whatever I need them to." He shot her a glance she couldn't quite interpret. "I would think you'd be anxious to find out if your life is in danger."

"I don't believe my life is in danger."

"Either someone was targeting you or you were targeting Dr. Mandeville. Which is it?"

"There's no reason for anyone to kill me."

"Oh, I don't know about that. Peter Fryer's wife might argue that point."

"Her husband was molesting young girls."

He picked up a box and set it on the edge of her desk. "No, he wasn't. There was a reason he wasn't charged, Ms. Kidwell, but then, you never bothered to get all the facts, did you? The pornography on his computer? His teenage son did that. The previous arrest for assault? Charges dropped because he hit a man who was trying to steal his wife's purse. The two girls ran away. And that, Ms. Kidwell, is the truth. Unfortunately for Mr. Fryer, you aren't overly interested in the truth."

"I reported what the police told me."

"An officer, one year on the job, barely out of rookie status, tells you what seasoned detectives are doing and you didn't bother to question any of it?" He shook his head. "I can see why you're known for being sensational rather than factual."

6

Friday, May 1

It was almost midnight when Suzanne pulled into her apartment complex and parked. She loved her job, but she hated that all the parking spaces even remotely close to the building were filled by the time she arrived home. A few of the neighbors had their lights on, but most were fast asleep. Oak trees lined the sidewalk, and even though there was a light breeze, they seemed unnaturally still. Shadows appeared to move with menace.

Weaving through the parking lot, she couldn't help remembering that detective. He didn't think much of her. Suzanne knew that she wouldn't get anywhere in life unless she was willing to be a little ruthless, a little mercenary, and had a whole lot of ambition. That didn't sit well with most people. So be it.

But Hodge was unusually antagonistic and hateful. After going through all her files, he had insisted on confiscating three of them, explaining that they warranted a closer look. And then he made her go over her relationship with Guy again, especially every little argument. Well, he could think what he liked. She had nothing to do with Guy's death, and Hodge would discover that on his own soon enough.

Something darted out in front of her, making her stop in her tracks. Choking out a short scream, Suzanne jumped back. A cat stopped, hissed, and then ran off. "Don't scare me like that!"

She took a deep breath to calm her thundering heart and then stepped up on the sidewalk.

Stopping at the mailboxes near the curb, she pulled out her mail and sorted through it quickly before tucking it into her briefcase.

Her heels tapped out a steady beat on the concrete as she approached the front of the building. A dog barked off in the distance, and once again, uneasiness skittered down her spine.

She couldn't wait to get in her apartment, kick off her shoes, and pour a glass of wine. Put on a little soft music. Curl up on the sofa with her work. No ringing phones, no pressure to be somewhere or answer questions—

Her face slammed against the side of the building, and she heard the crack of her head a split second before she felt the pain. Her mind scrambled, but before she could form a thought, a reaction, a shred of understanding, a plastic bag covered her head. Panic, pure and clear, hit as hard as her head against the wall. She dropped her purse and briefcase, trying to reach for the bag, but hands as tight as handcuffs gripped her wrists as she was pressed into the wall.

"Your lover's death?" A man's voice. "That was a mistake. It was supposed to be you."

His words were just disembodied echoes as she struggled to breathe. She'd never felt so helpless in her life.

"Where is it?"

She gasped the word, "What?"

"The briefcase? Where is it?"

She felt something sharp press against her throat and then a little sting. She was sucking the plastic into her mouth now, desperate for air. Her lungs burned. Her heart was pounding louder than war drums in her ears. Black dots danced in her eyes.

"It wasn't in the car with him. Did he leave it with you?"

She shook her head.

The darkness pulled her deeper into the abyss, away from his hissing whispers. She didn't feel her heart beating. She couldn't touch the pain. It drifted away as if she were sinking far beneath deep, dark waters.

"Hey! You! What are you doing?"

She was just starting to embrace the nothingness that loomed around her when the bag was ripped away and her lungs pulled sharply for air. Gasping, choking, she slid to the ground. Her knees scraped on the concrete, but all she could do was breathe. Breathe. Pull in the air. Exhale. Inhale.

The tears came so suddenly, she wasn't ready for them. Sobbing, she wrapped her arms around herself and bent over. He was gone.

"Lady? You okay?"

Hands reached out for her, and she winced as her head snapped back. It was the guy that lived down the hall from her. She didn't know his name.

"Let me help you up. You okay?"

She couldn't find or form the words. Hands trembling, she groped for her purse. He picked up her briefcase, handing it to her when she was on her feet. "You need the police or an ambulance or something?"

"No," she whispered roughly. "I'm fine."

"Your neck is bleeding."

She reached up and touched her throat. Her fingers came away wet with blood. "Just a scratch." She took a wobbly step.

"You sure?"

She didn't bother to answer him as she ran through the door and up the stairs to the second floor. It took three tries to steady the key into the lock. Once inside, she turned on every light in every room, made sure every window was closed—the locks engaged and the drapes pulled tight.

She felt cold.

She couldn't stop shaking.

"It was supposed to be you."

His words rolled around in her head. Over and over. Taunting her. Promising something far worse. She curled up in the corner of the sofa. Pulling the throw from the back of the sofa, she wrapped it around herself, staring at the door.

He knew where she lived. He could come back at any time.

And he wanted something she didn't want to give him.

7

The offices of Crisp and Hawthorne Investigations were located in a plush office building in Bethesda, tucked between the Kenwood and Chevy Chase country clubs. Located on the second floor, the glass door was engraved with the owners' names and led into a serene waiting room. An oasis of competence, success, and peace in the midst of your trouble. Marcus had long ago faced it—you didn't go see a private investigator unless you had trouble.

Down the carpeted halls were the private offices. One belonged to Marcus Crisp. It was still painted the original white the landlord ordered before the space was leased. The desk, bookshelves, filing cabinets, and chairs were all secondhand, mismatched, and industrial strength. They suited Marcus's style—or lack thereof. It was sparse; it was organized; and it was clean enough to make any mother proud.

The other office belonged to his partner, Alexandria Fisher-Hawthorne. It was painted various shades of pink with lilac trim and boasted pricy contemporary furniture and plants on the shelves. Of course, the plants were dead, and you couldn't find the furniture under the various files that never seemed to make it into a filing cabinet, and newspapers and soda bottles that were supposed to be headed for the recycling bin.

Marcus avoided Alex's office as much as possible.

Come to think of it, she didn't spend much time in there either.

If they were working in the building—as they were today—they preferred Marcus's office. Alex sat in a chair, legs propped up on the corner of his desk, notebook in her lap. Marcus hunched over his desk, tapping on the computer.

"So," Alex began as she read over a file. "I talked to the bus driver. He confirmed that Britney disembarked in Baltimore. He said it looked like she was met by another teen, a brunette, and the two of them left together. After that, not a trace of her. I canvassed all the hotels, motels, and restaurants in the area, but other than one of the workers at a McDonald's that said she might—and I do stress the word *might*—have seen Britney come in, but she couldn't remember when, couldn't say if she was with anyone, and has no idea where she might have gone." She lowered the file. "What are you doing?"

"Did you know that we have three clients who still haven't paid us from last year?"

"Yeah—Harrison, the Links, and Meyers and Meyers law. But then, Meyers always drags their feet about paying us. Trust me. Next time they need us, we'll get a check for all past due invoices."

Marcus shook his head, leaning back in his chair. "Do these people think we do this for charity?"

Alex closed the file folder and tossed it over to Marcus's desk. "You mean we get to have all this fun and earn money too?"

Marcus gave a small smile. "If you can believe it…"

"I'm stunned. Beyond words."

"Excuse me." Razz knocked on the open door. Besides being Crisp and Hawthorne's resident computer guru, snoop extraordinaire, and master of disguises, he covered the phones and played administrative assistant when he wasn't hacking into someone's computer or evading the attention of the FBI—who had been trying unsuccessfully to recruit him for years. "Those pictures I took last night are on your computer."

"Anything we should know about?"

"Not that I saw."

"Thanks."

Allister Hoffman owned a chain of restaurants in the Maryland metropolitan area. After being caught by his wife with one of the restaurant bartenders in a less than desirable situation—the bartender was a good-looking twenty-something named Robert—Allister was being drawn and quartered in divorce court. And then just before he was ordered to turn over nearly half a million to his wife, there was a robbery. Lo and behold, the wife's jewelry was stolen. The insurance company, convinced it was a setup by Hoffman to give his wife the insurance money and still have the jewels, hired Crisp and Hawthorne to get to the truth.

While Alex and Marcus had been keeping an eye on Mr. Hoffman last night, Razz had been keeping an eye on Mrs. Hoffman at a charity event in Baltimore.

Marcus swiveled around in his chair and opened the file. One by one, he went through the pictures. Alex came up behind him and leaned over his shoulder. "What are you looking for?"

"As a wise man once said, I'll know it when I see it."

"In other words, you have no idea."

"Exactly."

He went through them all before pushing back from the computer. "I didn't find it."

"Go back a couple of pictures. The one with Mrs. Hoffman and her daughter standing near the buffet table."

Marcus backtracked through the pictures. "This one?"

"Yes." Alex leaned over close enough to point to the daughter on the screen. "See that bracelet she's wearing?"

Marcus picked up the file folder the insurance company sent over with pictures of all the stolen pieces. He flipped through it and found the one Alex was talking about. Enlarging the picture on the screen, he compared them. "By golly, partner, I think you've done it."

He picked up the phone and called the insurance company. "Mitchell? You owe me twenty bucks. The wife has the jewelry."

8

Monday, May 4

Miss Kidwell? Frank will see you now."

Suzanne gathered her files and went into Frank's office. For twenty minutes, they discussed upcoming shows, with Frank shifting the schedule air times and Suzanne arguing why it wouldn't work. Finally, she closed the last file. "That's it."

"Not exactly." Frank leaned back in his chair, one hand drumming on the arm of his chair. "We need to talk about Senator Sterling. You need to drop the story. You have nothing on him."

"I have plenty on him, and I'm not going to just drop it."

"You have one young woman that swears she was having an affair with him and no one to verify her story."

"And if she wasn't telling the truth, Sterling wouldn't be trying so hard to shut me down."

"He isn't shutting you down. I am. His lawyers said they would sue this station if you ran the story."

"Same thing." Suzanne gathered up her files. "I know the senator is up to his scrawny neck in illegal activities, but this girl is the only thing I can hang on him. For now. But I'm going to prove he's dirty if it's the last thing I ever do."

"And it may be the last thing you ever do for this station."

Suzanne let the threat hang for a moment, then turned and walked out of the office.

She fumed for the next three hours as she prepared to go on the air. Just because he was a senator, Sterling thought he was untouchable. So far, he had been. Other than some obscure notes in Guy's book, all she had were the accusations of a young girl who swore that she and Sterling had enjoyed a six-month affair. Suzanne had met with Cecelia, Guy's nurse, but her information had pertained only to Guy's side of the operation—nothing on the senator except Cecelia's knowledge that they'd been partners. Not enough. Not nearly enough.

And the creep who threatened her outside her apartment? She'd bet her last dollar it was one of Sterling's goons.

Now she just had to prove it.

———

As Suzanne finished up her show, she knew she had to go on the offensive. Maybe if she pushed him hard enough, Sterling would make a mistake.

Ignoring the TelePrompter, she took a deep breath. "And before we close the show tonight, I want to share something with you. A young lady came to me because she had just been dumped by her lover and is afraid for her life because he has threatened her. Now, that may not sound sensational until you understand who her lover was." She leaned in as camera three came in for a closeup. "Senator John Sterling. And ever since he found out that I knew about this young woman, he's been trying to stop me—going so far as to pressure this news channel to shut me down. Well, Senator, you couldn't silence Hannah, you can't silence me, and you won't get away with your crimes. Your Judgment Day is coming. Count on it."

Suzanne smiled as she leaned back. "As long as there are people out there who betray our trust, there will be *Judgment Day with Suzanne Kidwell.* Good night, America. I'll see you next week."

"And we're out," the show director said a few seconds later.

Suzanne pushed back from the black Plexiglas desk and removed the lavaliere microphone from her collar. "Leann. Water."

Her assistant ran up and held out a bottle. Suzanne snatched it out of the girl's hand and walked off the set. Leann came running up behind her. "Frank wants to see you immediately."

Nothing she didn't expect.

Suzanne took her time, not wanting Frank to think that she was the least bit intimidated.

"Yes?" she asked as she strolled into his office ten minutes later.

"What do you think you're doing? I told you to back off Senator Sterling!"

"And I told you I wasn't going to." She ignored the visitors' chairs in front of his desk to sink down into the leather sofa in the corner. She crossed her legs, swinging one high-heeled foot. "He's dirty and I'm going to take him down."

"Well, you may be going down first. You know that adoption story you ran two weeks ago?"

"Where the so-called adoption agency was intimidating young pregnant girls and forcing them to sign over their babies? Yes, I remember. What does that have to do with anything?"

"Well, the girls are saying you paid them to say that. And the agency can prove none of those girls ever came through the doors."

Suzanne leaned forward. "You can't be serious."

"Oh, I am. And so is this." He tossed a legal document down on the corner of his desk, forcing her to get up, walk over to him, and pick it up. "That's the lawsuit they filed. You blew it."

Suzanne skimmed through page after page. "No way. Those girls came to me. I didn't pay them a dime. They had the story. They showed me documents from the agency."

"Phonies. You ran with it and never did due diligence. You never talked to the agency, never double-checked their records, never did background on the girls, nothing. You had a rumor and some doctored documents and that's all you needed. Now it's blown up in your face. How many times have we had this discussion, Suzanne? You can't go on the air with half-baked accusations!"

"This is crazy!"

He slammed his fist down on the desk. "No, it's you looking for ratings and never bothering to find out if there's any truth there to work with."

Suzanne threw the document back at him. "You want the ratings, Frank! You salivate over them. I'm number one in my time slot week after week, and don't tell me you haven't been sitting up here celebrating that fact."

"Ratings, I want. Lawsuits, I don't."

"Come on, Frank. We've had threats of lawsuits before."

"Which only proves my point. You're sloppy."

"And how many indictments have there been, Frank? That wasn't me being sloppy. That was good investigative work."

"Yeah, you got lucky on a couple of your stories. You've built the show up with sensationalism, and I don't mind that. What I do mind is when you don't do the legwork to back up all the accusations you make."

"I'll talk to the girls." She started pacing the office. "This is just a mistake."

"You can't. They've all filed restraining orders against you."

"And that doesn't tell you something? I didn't pay those girls off, Frank. This whole thing is a setup." Suzanne's mind was racing. "I'll bet it was Sterling."

Frank slapped the desk. "Everything is about the senator. You have a vendetta, and it's going to cost this network big. It stops here and tonight, do you hear me?"

Suzanne placed her hands on the desk and leaned forward. "I told you he was behind those missing girls, and you didn't believe me. I'm going to prove it, Frank."

"First you said it was the principal of the school, remember? Then while he was in custody, another girl disappeared. And then the principal, fired from his job and an outcast in the community, committed suicide. That's what your wild stories lead to. Now you want to turn around and blame it all on the senator. It doesn't fly, Suzanne. It never has."

"And if I prove Sterling set me up?"

"If you had done your homework," Frank continued, "he couldn't have set you up for anything, now could he?"

"I'm right about this, Frank. You have to believe me. I'm giving you the story of a lifetime."

"No, you're giving me lawsuits and headaches. I'm tired of it, and so is Mr. Briggs. And since he's the boss, whatever he's upset about, I'm upset about." He nodded toward the legal documents. "Setup or not, you were wrong and now we'll have to deal with this. And that's on you."

Arthur Briggs, the owner of CableNet, might keep his offices in New York, but he was known to keep his hand on every aspect of his empire. If someone in Washington sneezed, he knew about it. And if someone was causing problems—in this case, her—you could count on the fact that he was storming the New York office in a rage, demanding to know every who, what, and where. Suzanne sank down in one of the visitors' chairs. "It won't happen again."

Frank picked up the legal document and set it down on his blotter, then folded his hands over it. "One more, Suzanne. One more of these poorly investigated pieces and you're off the air."

"You'd fire me?"

"Mr. Briggs hasn't made up his mind yet. For all that you do for this station, you're also a liability—one we may not be able to afford."

"This is crazy. You couldn't fire me. I have a contract."

"See legal about it. In the meantime, no more shortcuts. I'm serious, Suzanne. I have people breathing down my neck to take you off the air now. This is your final warning."

Fuming all the way back to her office, Suzanne was totally unprepared to find a visitor waiting for her there.

"Mr. Mandeville?"

Guy's father stood, straightening his jacket although it wasn't the least bit out of sorts. "Suzanne. I was in Washington and thought I'd stop in and see you. I caught you at a bad time?"

She shook her head as she crossed the room and gave him a hug. A week after Guy's funeral, he had come to her with an armload of apologies. *"The last thing Guy said to me was that he loved you and wanted to marry you. If he hadn't died, you'd have been my daughter-in-law. I know Guy would have wanted me to look out for you."*

He started by giving her Guy's Porsche. Then he put a call into a real estate broker and got her a fantastic townhouse for thousands less than she would have had to pay.

But the biggest reason she cultivated the friendship was in hopes of getting close to Senator Sterling. She knew Mr. Mandeville moved in those circles and might let something drop about the senator that she could use.

"I'm always happy to see you. How have you been?"

He eased down in a chair, unbuttoning his suit coat. "A luncheon meeting with a couple of lawyers, a dinner meeting with the

CEO of a bank, and then a breakfast meeting with my stock-broker." He chuckled. "I was hoping that perhaps I could tip the scales of boredom and take you out to dinner tonight. If you don't already have other plans."

Suzanne smiled. "No other plans."

"I heard about a new restaurant that just opened a few weeks ago. It's supposed to be incredible."

"If it's the place I'm thinking of, we'll never get in. I heard it's booked solid for months."

"We have reservations, my dear, and I guarantee you the best table in the house."

Suzanne laughed. "I should have known better than to question your abilities."

"Speaking of outstanding abilities, tell me about what you're working on these days. Anything interesting?"

Suzanne walked with him to the elevator. Willard enjoyed hearing about the various scandals she was investigating. "A few. A religious leader who may have bilked his followers out of millions. A local businessman who is getting a little too cozy with the Russian mob."

"The Russian mob can be ruthless. Not to mention very dangerous."

She tucked her hand in the crook of his elbow. "I'll tell you all about it over dinner."

9

Tuesday, May 5

Marcus slammed the file folder down on his desk and then dropped into his chair. He had spent most of the morning trying to get his credit report straightened out. It was like attempting to pull the teeth of a rabid dog.

He suspected that the series of little aggravations in his life were directly from the hand of Randolph Hawthorne, but he couldn't prove it. And he wasn't about to tell Alex that her father was trying to force him out. No doubt Hawthorne was smart enough to realize that he wouldn't tell Alex. He remained clean, and Marcus was forced to run from one issue to another. If it wasn't his credit report, it was some loan officer swearing that Marcus was months behind on a loan that he never took out. Before that, his private e-mail accounts were bombarded with porno spam; he'd had to delete over three hundred e-mails a day just to get to the few that were legitimate. Razz finally took care of that problem.

He picked up the phone and called the Fisher-Hawthorne offices in Boston. "Mr. Hawthorne, please. Tell him it's Marcus Crisp."

"You're Alexandria's partner, aren't you?"

"Yes."

"Mr. Hawthorne is working from home, Mr. Crisp. His wife is ill."

"I didn't know. Have they told Alex yet?"

"I honestly couldn't say. I know they were waiting until they knew for sure how serious it was before alarming her."

"Thanks, I'll try the house."

Marcus hung up the phone and leaned back in his chair. Tell Alex or no? She had a right to know her mother was ill. But what if it were nothing? Marcus frowned. Alex's father didn't stay home from the office just because his wife had a cold.

And if it were his mother, he'd want to know.

He glanced up at the clock. Alex would be wandering in shortly. He would tell her, and if he regretted it later, so be it.

"You look depressed. Someone die?" Alex stepped into his office, unbuttoning her jacket.

"You're early."

"Had trouble sleeping. What's up?"

"Have you talked to your mom lately?"

Alex sat down. "It's been about a week, I guess. Why?"

"Did you know she was sick?"

"My mother? She's never sick."

"I don't know what's going on, but I just called your father's office and they told me he was working at home because your mother is ill."

"Why would you call my father?"

He had just stepped into something that was going to stink the rest of the day if he couldn't dance around it. "I'll explain later. I'm just concerned about your mother."

Alex stood up. "I'll go call. See what's going on."

Marcus waited until she was in her office and dialing the phone to grab his jacket and head out the door.

10

Merry looked around for her fiancé, Paul. He was supposed to meet her and take her to his place. They had met online three months earlier in a chat room. After a couple of weeks of communicating through e-mails, they started calling each other. He was eighteen, had his own apartment, worked as an assistant manager for an electronics store, and said he loved her and wanted to marry her.

Merry was the oldest of five children. Her mother worked two full-time jobs and was rarely home, leaving the care of her siblings to her. She went to school, cooked dinner, washed clothes, gave her brothers and sisters their baths, put them to bed, did her home-work, and woke up early the next morning to get them all ready for school and feed them breakfast.

She was tired of it. If she was going to have to give up her life to take care of home and hearth, she wanted it to be her own. So when Paul proposed, she couldn't have been more thrilled. It didn't matter that they hadn't met face to face. They had exchanged photographs. They had talked late into the night. She knew she loved him. And now, she was going to spend the rest of her life with him.

"Merry?"

She turned around to see another girl, smoking a cigarette.

"Yes?"

"Paul had to work late. I'm a friend of his. He asked me to come meet you. Is this all your stuff?"

Disappointment tugged Merry's lips into a frown. Well, at least he'd been thoughtful enough to send a friend. "Yeah."

The girl crushed her cigarette under the toe of her boot and picked up one of Merry's bags. "He gave me a twenty and asked me to at least feed you. There's a burger joint on the way. Wanna stop and eat?"

"Sure. That'll be great." Merry hefted her bag and started following the girl. "What's your name?"

"Kathi."

———

Alex stepped out of the airport and into the hustle and bustle of cabs, rental-car vans, hotel shuttles, and limos picking up arriving passengers. Her father had offered to send the corporate jet down for her, but she didn't want to wait until it returned from Chicago, and there was a flight from Reagan National to Boston leaving in less than two hours.

She headed over to the taxi stand and caught a cab. The driver didn't seem particularly enthused until she gave him the address. Suddenly he perked up and started calling her *ma'am.*

Closing her eyes, she leaned back, dreading the hours ahead. No one had told her that her mother was ill, seeing doctors, getting worse. And they thought they were protecting her.

Didn't they understand how much worse the shock was?

By the time the cab pulled up to the gates, she had set all the resentment aside and was looking forward to seeing her mother. She climbed out of the cab long enough to punch her security code on the pad to open the gates and then had the cab take her up the cobblestone drive that circled around in front of the double doors and wide, sweeping marble stairs.

As she paid the driver, her father appeared in the doorway, looking tired but happy.

"Alexandria." He threw out his arms. "She's going to be so happy to see you."

"How is she?"

"Resting."

Alex stepped through the doors and inhaled. She loved the smell of this place. The ripe red roses on the foyer table. The subtle hint of lemon wax and jasmine perfume and the rich mixture of old wood and antique silks and velvets.

"She's in the library. You know how she loves that room."

She gave her father half a smile and then hurried down the plush oriental runner to the thick oak doors of her father's study. These doors once seemed so huge to her. Now, they were just regular doors.

She knocked once and then, without waiting for an invitation, opened the door and stepped into the room.

"Alexandria!" Her mother was curled up on the leather sofa, a throw over her legs. Alex couldn't believe how pale and fragile her mother looked.

She reached down and kissed her cheek. "You should have told me."

Her mother waved a hand airily. "No sense worrying until we knew for sure what I might be facing."

"How many things have you and Father hidden from me over the years?"

"Many," her mother smiled softly. "Now tell me how long you can stay."

"Long enough to make sure you're getting the best of care."

"Of course I'm getting great care. You know how Dr. Gehle is. And of course, there is your father hovering over me." She eased up a bit as Alex's father came into the room with a tray holding medicine bottles and a glass of juice. "As you can see."

"See what?" he asked, setting the tray down.

"Alexandria just wants to be reassured that you and Dr. Gehle are taking good care of me."

"No, she doesn't." He reached over and kissed his wife on the forehead. "She just wants to be reassured that you aren't going to leave us anytime soon."

They talked for nearly an hour before her mother nodded off. Alex waited until she was asleep and then glanced over at her father, tipped her head toward the door, and left the room.

As soon as her father shut the door behind him, she said, "Why didn't you call me?"

"She didn't want you to worry."

"Not worry? Her heart is failing, and you don't want me to worry? When did you plan on telling me? After the funeral?"

"It isn't going to come to that."

"She's sixty-three. And she's let this go too long. Do you have any idea what the chances are that she's going to get lucky on the donor list?"

"The doctor has explained it all, Alexandria. I am not a child; please refrain from speaking to me as if I were."

Alex fisted her hand and rubbed her forehead. "I'm sorry. What other options are there?"

His silence said it all.

He led the way to his living room, pouring himself a drink. Alex sat down in one of the leather chairs near the piano. "How long did they tell you she might have to wait?"

"The doctor says the average wait time is about two hundred and thirty days."

"But she clearly doesn't have that long. You said maybe a month or two."

He eased down in a chair and took a big swallow from his glass. "I know."

"There has to be something we can do."

"You and Marcus are the Christians. Pray."

11

Wednesday evening, May 6

Suzanne had four drinks at her favorite local bar, dropped two dollars in the jukebox, brushed off the drunken advances of three men, and then headed home with a pleasant-enough buzz. She dropped her purse on the entryway table and staggered toward the hall closet. Why was it so hard for anyone to believe the senator was evil? Was there anyone in this town that wasn't being paid off or intimidated by the man?

It hadn't taken her long to uncover the fact that Sterling's wife sat on the board of the adoption agency that was suing her. Connect the dots, people.

The room spun, and she let her coat slip down her arms and fall to the floor. She reached out to steady her steps toward the living room.

She managed to flip on the light. A woman sprawled on the floor. Suzanne jumped, then stood frozen for a long moment.

Finally gathering her wits, she slowly approached the woman. How had she gotten here? Was she dead? Suzanne wasn't quite sure. Could it be that last drink, playing tricks on her? No. She hadn't had that much to drink, *had* she?

She knelt down and, using two fingers, poked the woman. "Hello?" What did you say to an unconscious woman?

The woman didn't respond, but she didn't feel dead. Then again, Suzanne wasn't sure what dead people felt like. Weren't they supposed to be cold and stiff or something? She poked again. "Hey! Wake up!"

She began to roll the woman over. A little hiss escaped from her lips. The hiss turned into a scream as she jerked back. "Cecelia?"

Why was Guy Mandeville's nurse unconscious in her apartment?

Suzanne felt a sharp pinprick on her neck. As she was turning to get a look at what had stung her, everything went completely black.

Pounding.

Pounding in her head.

Pounding on the door.

Suzanne shifted on the floor, trying to stand. Her hand slipped on the floor, sending her sprawling. "I'm coming. Relax." What a hangover. And why were her hands wet, sticky, and red?

The pounding started again. Harder this time. Swiping her

hands on the thighs of her jeans, she stumbled to the door and flung it open. "What?"

Police officers. Both tall, both dark-haired. Both looking at her as if she'd just killed someone.

"What do you want?" she asked.

"Ma'am, could you step aside, please?"

Rolling her eyes, she blocked the doorway. "Look, I'm tired and I'm not feeling so hot, so could you come back to sell those charity-ball tickets another time?"

"Ma'am, I'm going to have to ask you to step aside."

When the officer put his hand on his gun, enough brain cells fired to tell her to comply. "Sure. Whatever."

Stepping back, she waved them in. "You want to tell me what all this Gestapo stuff is about? What did I do, insult someone at the bar?"

That's when she saw Cecelia sprawled on the floor. Everything in her went very still and very quiet. It all rushed back and made her lightheaded.

Only this time, there was no doubt Cecelia was dead. A knife stuck out of her back.

"Oh no." This time, when Suzanne passed out, it was out of shock.

12

Thursday, early morning, May 7

Usually, when Suzanne met with her attorney, he soared in looking like an eagle among crows. Ted Holden always dressed in a Brooks Brothers suit with shoes polished to a high gloss. His dark hair, shot with a little bit of gray, was usually combed, styled, and thusly commanded not to let so much as one strand fall out of place. Tonight, he looked like a real human being, and that almost scared her. Jeans, loafers, no socks, and a sweatshirt with the sleeves shoved up to his elbows. His hair looked like he'd just gone two rounds with a windstorm and lost.

"You're telling us that when you came in, there was no knife in her back."

"How many times do we have to go over this?"

"One last time. I need to make sure I have it all. When you arrived home, you saw Cecelia on the floor. And she didn't have the knife in her back? Are you sure?"

"I'm positive." She shifted in the hard metal chair and glanced up at the two-way mirror. She'd been here for over five hours. She'd gone over the story four times already, both with the police present and now alone with her attorney. "I tried to turn her over because I didn't know who it was at first. I was a little drunk, okay? But there was no knife."

"And that's when you felt something sting you."

"Yes. On the neck. I asked them to take a blood sample because I think someone drugged me. I went out like a light, Ted. Out cold. When I woke up, the police were pounding on the door."

"Well, if they didn't test your blood as you asked them to, it will be one more little thing we can use in court."

"In court?" Suzanne leaned forward. "I didn't kill Cecelia. The woman was a sweetheart. She used to work for Guy. And she was helping me with a story I'm doing. I had no reason to kill her."

Ted stood up, tossing his legal pad into his briefcase and clipping it shut. "We'll get to the bottom of this. In the meantime, I'll call your parents—"

"Call my parents? No. Uh-uh. We don't call my parents." Suzanne shook her head, folding her arms across her chest.

"Do you have about a quarter of a million sitting around you can use as bail?"

"Of course not! But I'm not guilty. Why would I have to make bail anyway?"

"Because a dead body was found in your living room. Neighbors called the police because they said they heard a ruckus. The police arrived and found a woman dead and blood all over your hands. Did I miss anything?"

Suzanne shrank down in her chair. "I'm innocent."

"And we're going to have to prove it, but first we need to see what we can do about posting bail. You're being arraigned at ten. With any luck, we can get you out of here tomorrow."

He placed both palms on the table and leaned forward. "And then you know what you need to do?"

"What?"

"Hire the best detective you can find. Give him free rein to tear your life apart. You've made a lot of enemies since *Judgment Day*. It seems that one of them wanted to make sure you paid dearly. Find out who it is and prove your innocence. Make my job easier. Trust me; you don't want to know what it will cost you if I have to take this to trial."

"I don't know any detectives."

"I do. Marcus Crisp is the best there is. I'll give him a call and set it up."

"Marcus Crisp?" *What were the chances?* "Attended George-town? Dropped out and became a cop?"

"That's our man. If anyone can prove you're innocent, it's him."

He's a private investigator now? Great. Could things get any worse? "Is there anyone else we can use?"

"Not if you want your freedom."

He turned and walked out of the room. Suzanne folded her arms on the table and buried her head in them. Marcus Crisp. The last time she had seen him, he was studying law. Then again, she didn't want to think about the last time she'd seen him. That was a very bad night. And she doubted he'd forgotten it either.

What in heaven's name had she done to deserve this? Okay, she'd made a few people mad at her, but that was her job.

The door opened and Suzanne looked up. A particularly hard-looking woman in a uniform stood there. "Let's go."

"Go where?"

"Central booking. And then to a jail cell."

"They're charging me with murder?"

"No, Ms. Kidwell, they want your autograph."

Suzanne stood up. "Wow. Humor. Who would have thought."

"Anything to make your stay more pleasurable."

Suzanne was about to walk through the door when the officer stopped her. "Put your hands out."

Handcuffs. Things just kept getting worse. "I don't need those. I'm not going to grab your gun and disappear into the night."

The woman didn't smile. Suzanne held out her hands with as much attitude as she could, considering how tired she was.

After the cuffs were snapped on, she was led down to booking, fingerprinted, photographed, and forced to hand over her watch, earrings, and necklace. Then she changed into a bright orange jumpsuit. She really wanted to comment on the fashion statement, but her head hurt, her muscles ached, and all she could think about was sleeping for about a month.

Ted Holden had been yanked out of a sound sleep at two in the morning to come down and sit in with Suzanne during the questioning. All the way to the station, he'd planned on going straight home as soon as it was done. He was starting to wonder now if that would be possible.

"You got a tough job on this one, counselor." Officer Berry held out the coffeepot in a silent offer.

"No, thanks." Ted shook his head. "You don't really think she's capable of murder, do you?"

"The woman is a shark. You know it and I know it."

"Not Suzanne. Under all that sarcasm and bitterness beats a warm and compassionate heart."

"Right. If I had a woman that warm and compassionate, I'd get frostbite." Berry smiled as he took a sip from his cup, his crooked teeth peeking out between thin lips. Ted remembered a dog that had smiled like that. Just before he bit.

"It's all a show. Trust me."

The officer shook his head and leaned back in his chair. "Holden, she's got you hoodwinked. You didn't see her. Blood all over her hands, a dead woman on the floor, and she's making jokes about charity-ball donations."

"She didn't know Cecelia Forbes was dead."

"She told us she found the woman when she first came home. Now you're telling me she sees that, takes a nap for a couple of hours, and then forgets?"

"Which reminds me—you didn't do the toxicology, did you? She asked you to check her blood for drugs, and you ignored that possibility, correct?"

Berry looked a little uncomfortable as he lifted his coffee and took another sip. "So what if drugs do show up in her blood? She admitted to being in a bar for four hours, drinking hard. Maybe she did a few drugs as well."

Ted stood up. "Well, we'll never know now, will we? I'll remember to bring that up in court."

"Fine, I'll make sure we draw blood immediately."

Holden smiled. "You take care."

As he climbed into his Chrysler 300, he glanced over at the gray Lexus sitting in the parking lot. If he wasn't mistaken, that car belonged to the DA. But what was he doing here this late at night? Or rather, this early in the morning. The sun was only flirting with coming over the horizon. It hadn't actually made the move.

It bothered him enough to toss his briefcase in his car, lock it with his keyless remote, and walk back into the police station. He found District Attorney Bruce Michaelson in with the duty officer. Trust Michaelson to show up at four in the morning dressed like he was about to walk into court—gray pinstripe suit, white shirt, red tie. Unlike Ted, he sure hadn't rolled out of bed and jumped into anything that closely resembled clothing.

"Michaelson! A little early for you, isn't it?"

Bruce glanced over at him, lowering his head to look at him from over the top of his glasses. It was a calculated move that he often used in court to intimidate a witness. It didn't work on Ted. "Could say the same for you. How's your client?"

"You really came down here in the middle of the night because of a television celebrity?"

"No. I'm down here because one of our citizens has been murdered and her *alleged* killer is in custody. Doesn't get much better than that."

Ted snorted. "In your dreams, Michaelson. You keep counting those votes." Turning on his heel, he walked out. This *so* didn't bode well for Suzanne. Michaelson smelled blood, and he was circling.

He whipped out his cell phone and dialed his assistant. "Hate to wake you, but Suzanne Kidwell was just arrested for murder. Arraignment in the morning. I'm heading for the office. How soon can you get there?"

He was about to climb into his car when a reporter showed up. "Mr. Holden. I understand Suzanne Kidwell has been arrested for the murder of a nurse named Cecelia Forbes. Could you make a statement for us?"

"No comment." He climbed into his car. Then he rolled down the window. "She did not kill Ms. Forbes. But we are going to find out who did."

He frowned as he pulled out of the parking lot and headed for his offices. The media circus was arriving, and from here on out, everything would be performed with three rings.

13

Thursday morning, May 7

Alex pulled her suitcase into her apartment and left it by the entryway table. Emotionally, she was numb. Physically, she wanted to crawl into bed and hibernate. But she needed to shower, change, and get to the office. Sure, Marcus would tell her to stay home, rest, take whatever time she needed, but what she needed more than sleep was the diversion of work.

First stop was the kitchen, where she popped a couple of aspirin for the headache and then headed for the shower.

She and her parents didn't see eye to eye on much. They didn't like her career choice; they didn't approve of Marcus; they hated that she wasn't working at her father's side, preparing to take the helm of the Fisher-Hawthorne dynasty. But she loved them both dearly.

She didn't want to lose her mother. Not yet. She wanted to have one argument after another when they disagreed on everything Alex planned for her wedding. She wanted to see her mother's face when she held her grandchild for the first time. She wanted to fight with her mother when she sent her child to a public school instead of some exclusive, private school her mother picked out.

Driving to the office forty-five minutes later, she allowed herself to cry a little. Just a little. She didn't want red eyes all day.

She was almost to the office when her father called her. "Alex?"

Her heart jumped, knocking the air out of her lungs. "What's wrong?"

"I'm just concerned about your mother. She seems to be resigning herself to dying. She doesn't want to fight."

"I'll call her."

"You need to come home. Move back in here. Help your mother through this."

"I can't just drop my life and run home. For days at a time, yes. But to just leave my business behind? Don't ask me to do that."

"I am asking, Alexandria. In fact, I'm doing more than asking. I'm telling you that you need to do this."

Alex pulled her car over to the curb and shifted to park. "I can't," she said softly. "I love you. I love her, but don't ask me to give up the work I love to move home and be the daughter you want."

"This isn't about you being different."

"Yes, it is. You and Mother want me to move home, marry the man you choose for me, and hit the social page every week."

"Alexandria, that's not fair."

"No, it's not fair, Father. I have a life here. I have a business and friends and a home. And you're asking me to give all of it up to move home."

"Your mother needs you."

Alex tapped her head lightly on the steering wheel. Why couldn't they understand? She finally straightened in the seat, staring out the windshield. "Like I said, I can come home and help out for a while, but I'm not selling my business or my house, and I'm not moving home."

"Your mother may not have long to live, and you're not going to spend her last days with her. Can you live with that?"

———

Cameras flashed as Suzanne was led into the courtroom. She kept her head down. It was bad enough to be hauled into court in handcuffs, but she had to wear the prison jumpsuit without makeup or a curling iron to at least partially improve her appearance. There were circles under her eyes, dried blood under her fingernails. And the reporters would be salivating to get pictures of Suzanne at her lowest moment and blaze it across headlines.

Then she lifted her eyes and her heart sank even further. Her parents. In the front row. With fixed expressions of disgust and disappointment.

Standing when she was told to stand, sitting when she was told to sit, Suzanne barely listened as voices and images whirled around her. Her attorney argued that she was a prominent member of the community. The district attorney argued she had nothing to keep her from running.

Her attorney countered with her ties to her family, her willingness to prove her innocence, an offer to turn over her passport.

Michaelson came back with a bombshell—evidence in Ms. Forbes's home that indicated a bitter rivalry between the two women over the affections of Dr. Guy Mandeville and that the nurse felt Suzanne had killed Dr. Mandeville because he was in love with her instead of Suzanne.

She wanted to stand up and scream at the lies. Surely no one could believe that she had anything to do with Guy's death. Or that she and Cecelia were rivals. It was ridiculous.

Ted gently pulled her to her feet. The judge stood up and left the courtroom.

"What happened?"

"He set bail, but it's high."

"How high?"

"One million."

"Dollars?" Suzanne dropped back down in her chair. "That's crazy!"

Ted leaned over, bringing his head closer to hers. "Please keep in mind that the press is still watching every move you make. Now, this is doable. Your parents only have to guarantee ten percent. They've agreed to put up their house."

Suzanne glanced over at them, wondering why they would bother to help her. Their relationship had never been warm, but after she missed Elizabeth's engagement party to cover a story in Chicago, it had gone from cold to frozen.

"Suzanne." Ted's harsh whisper jerked her attention off her parents and back to him. "Listen to me. I'm going with your parents to settle this up with the bail bondsman. You're heading back to holding. As soon as we get all the paperwork processed, they'll release you. I'll be waiting to take you home. Do you understand me?"

She nodded.

"Good. Now, head up. You're innocent. You're a class act. Show them that."

———

"I don't have much money, but I'll give you whatever you need. Even if I have to pay you for the rest of my life."

Alex pulled a tissue from the box on the counter behind the conference table and handed it to Jean Christopher. "I'm not worried about that right now. Do you have a recent picture of Merry that I can have?"

Jean was forty-two and looked closer to sixty. Her brown hair was streaked with gray and her face, pale and drawn, was starting to show the lines of stress and a life that had been far too unkind. She dabbed at her tears. "I have one in my purse. I didn't mean to put so much on her, you know? But if I pay for day care, I don't have enough to pay the rent or the electric or food. I barely make ends meet as it is."

"Merry was complaining about having to care for her younger siblings?"

"All the time. I knew it wasn't fair and I tried to tell her that it wasn't going to be forever, but she's young and she wants a life. I understand, but what am I supposed to do? I've talked to every agency in the world. They can't find my husband and when they do, he gives them a dance and song about not working, and then he disappears and we start all over again, trying to get child support." She reached into her scuffed black fake-leather bag and pulled out a school picture. "Her hair is shorter now."

The girl in the picture was a little too thin, her eyes a little too sad, and her clothes a little too out of style to make her stand out in any way among her peers. But to a predator, she was perfect—pretty in a fragile way, insecure, frustrated with her life, and no father figure. *Looking for love in all the wrong places,* as the song said.

"You brought me her laptop?"

Jean nodded. "I left it with that young man at the front desk. He said he was going to check it for you."

"He's our computer genius. If Merry met someone online, Razz will find out." Alex stared down at her notes. "Did you ever hear Merry talk about wanting to go to any particular place? Especially when she was really upset. You know, 'one of these days I'm going to run away to New York or Miami and then you'll be sorry' kind of thing?"

Jean shook her head, the tears starting up again. "She was so quiet. Even when she complained. She wasn't the type to get in my face with an attitude. She'd just cry and go off to do what I told her to do." Her shoulders started shaking as she buried her face in her hands and sobbed. "Please. Please find my baby."

Alex leaned over and touched the woman's arm. "I'll do everything I can."

But as much as she wanted to sound confident, she was still haunted by the fact that she hadn't found Britney Abbott.

14

Three hours later, Suzanne was finally free, but she wasn't home. The police still had her house secured as a crime scene. Ted drove her there, and they stayed long enough to get her some clothes and personal items. Then he took her to a nearby hotel and set her up with a rental car. The police had confiscated her Porsche, hoping to find something incriminating.

After Ted left, she took a shower, scrubbing as if she could somehow remove everything she'd ever done. Sadness plagued her. Guy. The attack outside her apartment. Now Cecelia. And jail. She soaked in the hot water. She never wanted to go back to that jail. The smell of urine and sweat permeated every surface, but the smell of despair, hopelessness, and fear—part of which came from her own skin—was so thick it seemed to infect her soul.

After her shower, she didn't have the energy to do anything more than change into clothes and brush her hair.

She stared at her reflection. After all she'd gone through, she now had to appeal for help from her ex-boyfriend, of all people.

Correction. Ex-fiancé. The man she had betrayed back in college. The man who told her never to contact him again. It hadn't been one of her best moments. She'd gone over to Marcus's dorm room to tell him she wanted to break off the engagement, only he wasn't there. His roommate invited her to stick around and wait. They had some wine. A lot of wine. Next thing she knew, they were tangling the sheets, and Marcus was walking through the door, looking as if he'd just been gutted with a rusty knife.

Well, she could only hope that he was over it. After nearly eighteen years, she certainly hoped he was. Either way, she had no other choice but to see him again.

She dabbed some concealer under her eyes, trying to hide the dark circles. Stepping back, she looked in the mirror and frowned. Not one of her better days. She would have preferred facing Marcus at her best, but oh well.

Picking up her car keys, she squared her shoulders. Time to face the music.

15

Are we ready for lunch yet?" Alex swung her feet to the floor and rolled her shoulders. "I'm starving. How about Hunan King?"

"Later. We have a client coming in."

Alex's face hosted a million and one expressions. Marcus enjoyed every one of them. Including this little eyebrow-lifting tilt of the head—her "I smell something fishy in the fridge" look. "Razz didn't tell me about any meeting today."

"It came in a little bit ago. Haven't had time to tell you."

"Uh-huh. You being so busy and all. And just who is this client?"

Marcus picked up his pen and stared down at his appointment book as if he needed to be reminded. "Ted Holden is sending over one of his clients. Murder investigation."

Alex shook her head. "No. Uh-uh. No way, Marcus. We are not taking on Suzanne Kidwell. Have you lost what few brain cells she left you?"

"First of all, I haven't—I mean, *we* haven't—even talked to her, so how can we say we won't take the case? And I have all my brain cells, thank you very much."

"I don't need to remind you that she betrayed you, Marcus. With your best friend, no less. You may have forgiven her, but I haven't. You stomped around campus for months, looking like you were half a step away from killing someone."

"You exaggerate. It was a schoolyard romance. It ended. Big deal. That was twenty years ago."

Alex gave him another one of her looks, but this one made him want to curl up under the desk and hide. "It was eighteen years ago, and you never got over it. You can't even stand to watch her show."

"You underestimate me. I don't watch her show because I don't *like* her show."

"And I don't like the idea of her sweeping in here, flipping that blond hair around—"

"You have blond hair."

"—and sucking you back down—"

"How come you never flip it around?"

"—wrapping those tentacles around your heart."

"Hair like tentacles?" He shook his head. "Okay, there's an image I won't dislodge easily."

Alex jumped to her feet. "Cancel the meeting. Call Ted. Tell him we're just too busy."

Razz opened the office door and stuck his head in. "I've settled Ms. Kidwell in the conference room and served her coffee. Any time you're ready."

Marcus rose to his feet. Alex glared at him. "We are *not* taking her case. Got it?"

"Got it."

Alex disappeared into her office and returned a few moments later, slipping into a dark blue blazer. She was the only woman he knew who could put on a blazer and make a pair of jeans look like an expensive power suit. Then he noticed something else.

"You're wearing your gun? To a meeting?"

"A pound of prevention is worth an ounce of cure."

"That's an ounce of prevention and a pound of cure."

"Not in this case, it's not." She turned on her heel and marched down the hall toward the conference room.

Marcus couldn't help smiling as he watched her—her slender shoulders squared off for battle. His partner. Never underestimate a woman who packed a gun—even if she was only five-foot-five and had a face that could drive Helen of Troy to hide behind a veil.

When they entered the conference room, Suzanne stood up. No sign of the television star today. Her blond hair looked like it had been scraped back with her fingers and secured with a clip. She wore jeans, a silk shirt, and a pair of flats, and most surprising of all, very little makeup—mostly concealer caked around her eyes.

He expected to feel something when he saw her face to face after all these years. Surprisingly, he felt nothing at all. Not even a flinch. No pain. No anger. Nothing. *A miracle. Hallelujah.*

Suzanne glanced at Alex before looking up at Marcus. "I didn't realize you would have your secretary sit in with us."

"I'm not his secretary, Ms. Kidwell. I'm his partner." Alex placed both palms down on the table across from Suzanne and leaned in, letting her jacket fall open. "We work all our cases together." She paused a beat or two and then lowered her voice. "I've always got his back."

She made a simple statement sound like a declaration of war. Marcus wiped his hand across his mouth to hide the smile. When Alex had an attitude going, watch out. Maybe the country should think about sending her over to the Middle East to settle things.

Marcus decided to step in before one of them took a piece out of the other. And he wasn't going to take bets against his partner, regardless of Suzanne's reputation. He took a deep breath. "Suzanne, this is my partner, Alexandria Fisher-Hawthorne."

Suzanne sank down in her chair. It was a subtle admission of defeat, but Suzanne never raised the white flag boldly. "As in the Boston Fisher-Hawthornes? Technology, shipping, hotels?"

Alex pulled out a seat and went from brute powerhouse to social lady in the blink of an eye. She fluttered down into her chair, hands folding delicately on the table in front of her. "The same."

Suzanne looked up at Marcus. "You certainly run in different circles these days."

"I try," he said with a light shrug. "The old circles just didn't seem to be worth the trouble."

Suzanne took the hit like a champ, letting a little smile play along her lips as she settled back in her chair. "Touché."

"So, what can we do for you?" Alex asked, slipping into her

blue-blood New England accent. She had snooty down to a science. "I understand you're in a bit of a quandary."

Marcus dropped down in his chair. *Quandary?*

"You could say that." Suzanne turned her attention from Alex to Marcus. Smart woman. Go for the soft touch. "I'm sure you read the papers this morning."

Marcus nodded.

Suzanne fiddled with the ring on her finger. "I didn't kill Cecelia Forbes. On the contrary, she was one of my sources for a story I'm working on. When I arrived home last night, she was sprawled out on my floor."

"Where were you?"

"At a local bar. Charlie Q's. People know I was there. They can verify that."

Alex nodded. "Go on."

"Anyway, I thought she was dead. When I went to check, someone stuck something in my neck and I passed out. When I came to, there was a knife in her back that hadn't been there before."

Alex jotted notes on her legal pad. "Why do you think someone stuck something in your neck?" she asked.

"I felt this little pinprick just before I passed out."

"So you think you were drugged."

"Yes."

"How long were you out?"

Suzanne shrugged. "I think I got home a little after ten. The police say they received a call about twelve thirty."

"The police were called to your house? You didn't call them?"

"No. Their pounding on my door is what woke me up."

Alex finally turned to Marcus. The ball was in his court for a few moments. He uncapped the bottle of water Razz had left for him. "How did Ms. Forbes get into your house?"

"I don't know."

"Do you have an alarm system?"

"Yes. But I don't know if I remembered to set it before I left."

He took a long gulp of water. "Whose fingerprints are on the knife?"

"I don't know."

"Was the knife from your kitchen?"

"Yes."

Alex started tapping her pencil on her pad. Marcus's cue to back off a minute. He went back to his water.

Alex glanced over at him and then looked at Suzanne. "What exactly do you require of us?"

"I need you to find out who framed me." Suzanne started to cry, and Marcus was surprised to see that she didn't even bother wiping the tears from her eyes. "I didn't kill Cecelia. I'd have trouble hitting a squirrel crossing the road."

Alex merely shoved a box of tissues across the table at her.

"And I don't want to go to prison for something I didn't do." Suzanne finally reached for a tissue and swiped at the tears. Her mascara streaked a bit under one eye. "Ted said the DA thinks it's a closed case. I—we—need to find my enemy fast."

"Which one?" Alex asked quietly, but there was enough implication behind that question to make Suzanne's hands shake.

Point and match, Alex.

"Believe me—if anyone's thought about how many enemies I've garnered, it's me." Suzanne stood up and began to pace a little around the room. "I always knew that exposing people's criminal actions could make them mad, but I never counted on this."

"Still playing the victim." Alex shook her head as she stood up. "I don't have time for this."

"I'm not playing anything!" Suzanne shouted, a new resolve across her face. "I've made enemies. Okay. I get that. Now I need your help or I'm going to prison for the rest of my life for something I didn't do. Now maybe that's okay you with you, Miss Boston Tea Party, but it's not okay with me."

Alex apparently wasn't fazed by Suzanne's anger at all. She tilted her head, giving Suzanne one of her famously searing looks. "It's never okay with me to see anyone go to prison for a crime they didn't commit. At the same time, please don't insult my intelligence by implying you didn't deliberately provoke trouble with your actions on the air."

The two women were locked in a nonverbal war of the eyes that made Marcus want to be anywhere but in this room. He was smart enough, on the other hand, not to interfere.

Suzanne finally dropped back down in her seat. Chalk another one up to Alex. "Fine. You're right. I stirred up the hornet's nest, and now I've been stung. I need your help."

Alex sat back down in her chair, swiveled it to face Marcus and gave him the signal—a tilt of her head and a nod. She would take the case. It was up to him now. He cleared his throat. "Would you excuse us just for a moment, Suzanne? I'd like to talk to my partner in private."

Suzanne barely nodded as she slumped down in her chair looking forlorn and defeated.

Marcus closed the door as they stepped out into the hall. He would never understand women as long as he lived. "I thought you didn't want any part of this."

Alex placed her hand on his arm and gazed up at him, letting her big eyes soften. "Look at her, Marcus. She's being railroaded. Okay, she's not one of my favorite people, but I can't see letting her go to prison just because she broke your heart."

Marcus looked at her earnestly. "She did *not* break my heart, Alex."

"So we'll help her?"

"Well, we don't have all the facts yet."

"The Suzanne we knew in college was selfish and self-centered and a bit of a narcissist, but she wasn't stupid and she wasn't a killer. And can you imagine Suzanne killing a woman over a man? Never happen. The second a man looked at another woman, Suzanne would toss him over and start trolling for a new victim."

Marcus suppressed a smile. "Can we agree to be cautious? I still don't trust her."

"Agreed." She patted his arm. "And don't worry. I'll make sure she doesn't try to get her hooks into you again."

"I am not interested in—"

But Alex wasn't listening to him anymore. She opened the door to the conference room, ready to save the damsel in distress. And protect his honor while she was at it. He sighed. He didn't need his honor protected. There was no way he was going to fall for Suzanne again.

Alex picked up the phone on the conference table. "Razz, could you bring us a standard contract, please? And a confidentiality contract. Thanks." She hung up the phone.

Suzanne jerked her head up. Hope flooded her eyes. "You'll help me?"

"We'll help you. But with stipulations. We have complete access to take your life apart, seam from seam. We go through all your files. We dig through all your records. Any objection from you and we walk away. Understood?"

Smiling, Suzanne rose to her feet, confidence restored. "Understood. At this point, I have no choice but to be an open book."

"Sure, whatever." Alex replied. "But sit back down. We still have to sign the contracts. One of them is standard. We work for you. We get results. You pay us. Simple. The other is not so simple. You keep your mouth *shut*. You will not mention us on your show. You will not talk about us, our work practices, or our methods. Nothing you hear from us, nothing we do, nothing you find out we do, will be exposed."

Suzanne nodded her head in agreement, eager. Too eager. Marcus didn't like it. He used his finger to tap the table. "We're not kidding around here, Suzanne. The reason we are effective for our clients is because we are very good at what we do, but we do not always play by the rules. The minute you tell anyone what we do or how we do it, you've closed our doors. You close our doors, and we will release the legal hounds of hell on your head. Between the two of us, we will tie you up in so much legal hot water, you'll wish you'd gone to prison for murder, you got that?"

"I got it, Marcus. I swear. I need you to help me. I won't betray you."

"Again," Marcus corrected.

Suzanne swallowed hard and some of the light in her dimmed a notch. "I won't betray you *again*."

Alex pulled her gun and set it on the table in front of her. "I won't wait for the lawyers. Got that?"

Suzanne glanced down at the gun and swallowed hard again. From the look in her eyes, she firmly believed that Alexandria would have no trouble firing it in her direction if crossed. "I got it. Loud and clear."

Suzanne had always prided herself on being able to read people— dissect their weaknesses and analyze their strengths within moments of meeting them. Not so with Alex. The woman was a chameleon. She could come across as the quintessential lady of wealth and breeding who wouldn't lower herself to deal with the servants, and the next minute turn all lawyer, hammering the points of the contract with a confidence that even Trump would appreciate, and then switch to a gun-wielding Annie Oakley, threatening to blow Suzanne's head off. Which one was the real Alex?

Back in college, she saw Alex around campus, knew she was in a study group with Marcus, but never knew her well enough to have spent any time with her. And she never would have expected to find the ultrarich Alex Fisher-Hawthorne working as a PI. Or partners with Marcus in the detective business.

But she could respect a woman like Alexandria. Given the right circumstances, she'd like to call the woman a friend.

As for Marcus, the years had shaved away the youth from his face and left a sharp, cynical edge around those intelligent brown eyes.

Alex slid the contract across the table to Suzanne. "Any questions?"

"Just one. How soon can you start?"

Marcus handed her a pen. "We're going to get some lunch while you go and find all your records. I want to know what stories you've done, who you've sliced and diced on the air, and I want to see the research for those shows."

Suzanne's hand was shaking a bit as she signed the contract. "Sure." But she wasn't so sure at all. They were bound to find where she'd cut a few corners—where she'd failed to follow up on all the leads, or didn't necessarily get both sides of an issue before declaring someone guilty. How could they understand the cutthroat nature of the business? You had to be bold or the guilty wouldn't pay. And you wouldn't get the viewers.

"Second thoughts?" Alex asked.

The woman was like a mind reader or something. "None that I can't handle."

It was the truth and seemed to satisfy Alex because she nodded and settled back in her chair.

Suzanne slid the signed contract over to Marcus. "I admit, I'm not thrilled with you guys double-guessing what I had to do to make my show successful, but I'm going to have to live with it in order to find out who is behind this."

Marcus took the contract and scribbled his signature across the bottom of the page. "It's not our job to judge you, Suzanne. But if you falsely accused someone of something, they have a reason to come back after you. And motive means everything. We put together a list of possible suspects, and then we go at it, one by one, until we've crossed everyone off our list. Anyone who isn't crossed off gets a more in-depth examination. Alibis, means, opportunity, associates. We'll have it all by the time we're done."

"Suzanne." Alex twirled a pencil through her fingers. "If you were to give us a list of your top three suspects, who would they be?"

"That's not exactly a tough call." Suzanne had investigated a lot of shady people, but a few definitely stood out. "Reverend Walther Scott. He bilked his viewers out of over five million and then used it to build himself a mansion. And believe it or not, I was just starting a story on District Attorney Michaelson. He has built his career on a tough stand against prostitution, but I was tracking down a lead that suggested he has a mistress stashed away somewhere. A high-class call girl."

Marcus rubbed his face with his hand. "The DA? Did you tell Ted about this?"

"No. I didn't think it would look good for me to point fingers at that time. Should I have?"

Before Marcus could respond, Alex leaned forward. "Did the DA know you were investigating him?"

"I don't think so."

Marcus spun his chair around to face Alex. "That doesn't mean he didn't get wind of it."

"If he did, that might explain why he's so anxious to put Suzanne away," Alex said.

"Self-preservation."

Alex nodded, tapping her pencil on the legal pad. "Distinct possibility. Strong starting point. Hard to prove, though. And I'm not sure I see the good reverend ordering a hit on a nurse, but stranger things have happened."

"Have you ever heard of a man named Louis Barone?"

"Sure," Marcus replied. "Head of the Russian mafia here in the area. Drugs, prostitution, gambling. If it's illegal, he has his fingers in it. We've crossed paths a few times."

"Well, Michaelson's mistress works for Barone."

Marcus whistled softly. "That puts Michaelson in some very unsavory pockets."

"To say the least." Suzanne replied. "But my number one choice is the easiest of all: Senator John Sterling."

Marcus and Alex both turned and stared at her, but it was Marcus that spoke. "You're trying to tell us Senator Sterling killed a nurse for no reason other than to frame you for murder? Have you ever met the man?"

"No, but trust me, he knows who I am. And he's behind all this."

"And why is that?" Alex asked, her voice dripping with skepticism.

Nothing new there. No one ever believed her about Sterling. "I have evidence about something he and Dr. Guy Mandeville were involved in. Cecelia knew about it too. That's why they had to kill her. She was going to help me stop them."

"You have evidence?" Alex eyed her thoughtfully.

Razz eased the door open. Alex and Marcus turned in his direction.

"You might want to turn on Channel Six."

Alex reached behind her and grabbed the remote off a bookshelf. She pointed it at the television mounted up in the corner.

Michaelson, dressed in a gray pinstripe suit and red tie, stood on the white marble steps of city hall. Reporters crowded around him, shoving the microphones closer. "…fingerprints on the murder weapon, I think it's safe to say that we have our killer, and I intend to prosecute her to the fullest extent of the law. The fact that she is a big star on television news is not going to help her get away with murder."

A perky brunette reporter appeared on the screen as Michaelson moved away from the microphones. "And there you have it. To recap, District Attorney Bruce Michaelson just reported that the fingerprints on the murder weapon belong to Suzanne Kidwell. Stay tuned for more…"

Alex muted the television. "Well, this just got interesting."

"I've never known them to move so fast on evidence." Marcus folded his arms across his chest, looking thoughtful.

Alex looked over at Suzanne. "We need all the evidence Michaelson has and we need it now."

16

Thursday, late afternoon, May 7

Marcus could smell the food coming down the hall and had to force himself not to start drooling.

Razz set the bags of Chinese food on the conference table and began to pull out little white cartons. "Veggie spring. Broccoli with garlic sauce. Crispy eggplant. General Tso's Chicken. Beef and broccoli. Rice. Did I forget anything?" He smiled, then tossed out plastic silverware and chopsticks and sat down, pushing the empty bag aside. "So what'd I miss while I was gone?"

"We've just been signing off on some of the other cases so you can go ahead and bill them." Marcus picked up his chopsticks and dug into the eggplant.

"Marcus thinks that Suzanne Kidwell's case is going to dominate all our time." Alex popped open a can of soda. "So he wants everything cleared off his desk before we start. But I'm not putting Britney Abbott and Merry Christopher on a back burner. We can look for them and work Suzanne's case at the same time."

"Fine," Marcus conceded.

"If you want, I can follow up on some of the phone calls," Razz offered. "Check with the local police. See if they've come across anything. Maybe check in with some of their friends again."

"Be my guest." Marcus reached for his water bottle. "But first we need you to get copies of the last two months of Suzanne's shows. Then I want you to get the financials for a few people. Alex has the list. See what you can find."

Alex slid her legal pad over to Razz. "And—"

The phone rang, cutting her off. She reached over and picked it up. "Crisp and Hawthorne."

She looked over at Marcus and the tension growing in her expression was clear. "I understand. Well, my partner and I will take that under consideration. Is there a number where we can—"

She put down the receiver. "He hung up without giving me a number."

"It'll be on caller ID at my desk," Razz offered as he hurried out of the room.

Alex looked over at Marcus. "He made us an offer we can't refuse."

"What offer?"

"Drop the Kidwell case, and he'll give us triple our usual fee."

Marcus made a little noise in the back of his throat. "Some offer. And do we know who wants us off this case?"

"He didn't leave a name."

"Of course not."

"Could be one of our suspects. The district attorney maybe?"

Alex went back to her chicken. "He sure wouldn't want to leave a name."

"But then, neither would the preacher."

Marcus leaned back in his chair, taking his broccoli in garlic sauce with him. "Let me think."

Razz came back into the room.

"Number blocked," Alex preempted.

"You got it." Razz sat down, opened his laptop and while it booted up, went back to eating.

"Logical," Marcus replied. He pointed a chopstick at Alex. "Let's see…have to assume that money is no object with this guy."

"All of Suzanne's top suspects have money," Alex reminded him.

Razz nodded, then looked up from his computer. "Okay, so the blocked call was from a throwaway cell, no name registered to it."

"How did you do that?" Alex asked.

"Trade secret," Razz replied. "Don't ask too many questions."

"So you traced our caller to a throwaway cell, but no way to trace who bought it?" Marcus challenged.

"Even I have limitations, boss. It was a cash purchase at a discount store in Virginia. That's the best I can do."

Alex threw up her hands with a light laugh. "And you call yourself a computer expert. What good are you?"

"I don't know why you keep me around." Razz grinned at her. "Would it help you to know that our caller bought the phone two hours ago?"

———

Suzanne sat down on the edge of the hotel bed and stared at the phone. Never in her life had she felt so alone. She wanted to call her parents. She wanted to hear them say that everything was going to work out fine. That they believed in her. That they loved her.

But she knew all she'd get was a lecture on how she'd let them down. Disappointed them. Again. And if she called her sister, she'd get more of the same. How could you do this to Mom and Dad? How could you be so thoughtless? You never think of anyone but yourself.

But a list of her sins was the last thing she wanted.

Thoughts of spending the rest of her life in prison tortured her. When she closed her eyes, she saw Cecelia's body on her floor.

There was a bar downstairs. She could get a drink and forget everything for a little while. Maybe find someone to chat with.

She got as far as the elevator when she thought about what happened last time she went out and had a few drinks.

Two minutes later, she was back in her room. As she set her purse down on the bed, she heard a beep. Her cell phone. She pulled it out of her purse and dialed her voice mail.

The message was from one of her research assistants. "Suz! This is Gail. I can't believe they think you did this! You poor thing. You must be beside yourself. If you need to talk, I'm here for you." Suzanne swiped at her sudden tears. Someone out there actually cared.

There was another message from her boss. "Suzanne. This is Frank. We'd really like to get your side of the story. Give me a call. We can have you on air at five…or whenever you're ready to come back."

Suzanne deleted the message. She scrolled through the incoming calls until she reached Gail's number and hit redial.

Gail answered on the second ring. "Suzanne! Are you okay?"

The concern in Gail's voice soothed her like cool ointment on a hot burn. "I've been better. How are you doing?"

"Forget me. I'm just so worried about you. How anyone could believe you could kill someone is beyond me. How about I take you out to dinner? Take your mind off these ridiculous charges."

Suzanne sagged down onto the bed. "That sounds wonderful. What time?"

17

Alex opened one of the boxes Suzanne sent over and pulled out an accordion file. "It's going to be a long night."

Marcus, already reading Suzanne's notes on the district attorney, merely nodded.

Alex stared at him for a second. His hair was sticking up where he'd run his hands through it. Frustration. His reading glasses were perched on the edge of his nose, slightly askew. Concentration. His feet were up on the edge of the conference table, crossed at the ankle. Comfort.

Alex jumped as Razz stuck his head in the door. "I'm out of here, guys. I wish I could stay and help, but I need to spend time with Mel."

Marcus waved his hand, never taking his eyes off the page he was reading.

Alex opened a file folder. "Don't worry about it. There'll be plenty left here for you tomorrow."

Razz laughed as he looked at all the boxes. "Can I call in sick tomorrow?" Without waiting for a response, he waved and disappeared down the hall.

Five minutes later, Marcus looked up. "Razz is sick?"

"No. He was kidding."

"Oh." He sighed heavily, tossed the paper he was reading down on the table and took off his glasses. "Well, she's got some rumors, but nothing solid on Michaelson."

"Somehow, I don't think that would have stopped Suzanne." Alex swiveled her chair around. "We need to talk about the elephant in the house."

"Room. Elephant in the room."

"Whatever. We need to talk about it." Alex reached for her soda and toyed with the straw. "Suzanne is positive that Senator Sterling is behind all of this. Do you know how hard it's going to be to bring down a sitting senator if he is guilty?"

Marcus flipped through Suzanne's notes. "I figure we'll cross that bridge when we come to it. Right now, I want to look at her other suspects before I look at the senator."

"So that we aren't prejudiced against the senator from the start, I know that. I'm just saying, if it is Sterling, we're going to have to proceed very cautiously."

"And we will." Marcus looked up. "Someone had to know that Suzanne wasn't home." He blew out a heavy sigh and ran one hand through his hair. "Someone had to be tailing Suzanne. They knew she was at the bar. They knew they could keep her there long enough to lure Cecelia to her house and set it up to frame her for the murder."

Alex dropped her hands. "Someone was at the bar with her. Watching her. Making sure whoever was with Cecelia knew if she left the bar early."

Marcus stared at her for a long moment. "Now we're talking at least two, possibly three, people involved."

Alex tapped her legal pad with her pencil. "I keep thinking about Michaelson. If he's playing with one of Barone's girls, that links him to the mob. Do you think it could be them?"

Marcus stared off into space for a long moment. "Obviously murder has never been beneath them, but this is a little convoluted for their tastes. Now, if Cecelia had been found in the trunk of a car somewhere with a bullet to the back of the head, then yeah. But they're not known for well-orchestrated scenarios like this."

"You've watched too many episodes of *The Sopranos*."

Marcus closed the file folder. "I think we need to start at the beginning. Let's go to the bar and see if we can talk to the bartender. Maybe we'll get lucky."

They were surprised to find a well-dressed man coming in as they were leaving. He had a full head of thick, gray hair, bright blue eyes, and a firm handshake. While his smile was friendly enough, there was an underlying trace of steel and sharp edges that made it clear he was a man of power, wealth, and the expectation of getting what he wanted.

"Can we help you?" Marcus asked.

"I won't take too much of your time. I can see you're on your way out for the day." He glanced around the room and then back to Marcus. "My name is Willard Mandeville. I'm a friend of Suzanne's. I wanted to give you this." He pulled an envelope out of his pocket and held it out.

Marcus slowly took it from him. "What's this?"

"It's a check for a hundred thousand. It should be enough to get you started. I just want to make sure that you give Suzanne the best you have to offer and not concern yourself with the bill. Whatever it costs, I want her to have the best possible investigation."

"That's very generous of you," Alex replied.

Mandeville waved a hand. "If you need more, let me know. My business card is in there and it has my cell phone number. Whatever you need."

"Does Suzanne know you're doing this?" Alex asked.

"Not yet. I will let her know that I'm here for her, open checkbook. I don't want her to worry about money on top of everything else. I don't believe for a second that Suzanne would murder anyone." He glanced around again. "By any chance, could I use your bathroom?"

Marcus pointed to the hall. "Second door on the left. Help yourself."

"Thank you. I won't be long. I know you were leaving."

"It's okay. Take your time."

As soon as Mandeville disappeared down the hall, Marcus handed Alex the envelope. "This is a nice surprise."

Alex folded the envelope and tucked it in her back pocket. "She can use every friend she has right now."

———

Suzanne smoothed her skirt and stepped up to the hostess stand. "I'm meeting someone." She looked around the dining room and then checked her watch. It was just a minute before six. Gail would probably be arriving any moment now.

"Would you like to go ahead and be seated and then your friend can join you?"

"Sure. Can we sit in one of the booths in the bar?"

"Absolutely." The hostess led her to a table and set menus down. "Can I get you anything to drink?"

Suzanne thought for a moment. "Why not? How about an apple martini?"

The hostess nodded and strolled away. When Suzanne saw Gail coming through the door, she stood up and waved.

Gail rushed over and hugged her. "Are you okay?"

"I'm fine."

As soon as they were settled and Gail had ordered an iced tea, she leaned on the table. "I am so sorry this is happening to you, Suzanne. It's not going to be the same at the station without you."

"Thanks."

"It must have been horrifying. What in the world did you think when you found that woman in your house?" She shuddered. "I think I'd go crazy coming home and finding a dead body in my house."

Suzanne's martini arrived with Gail's tea. She took a sip and then set the glass down. She recounted the events from that night, and after several long minutes of talking, she quieted.

"You poor thing," Gail said, leaning forward and touching Suzanne's hand.

Suzanne took another sip of her martini. "Thanks, Gail. It's nice that someone believes me. The police didn't want to hear the truth. They just hauled me down to the station and kept me up most of the night, interrogating me."

"I hope you called your attorney."

"I did. Ted came right down."

"Ted Holden?"

Suzanne nodded as she reached for her drink again. "I gave my statement and then they locked me up. I have to tell you, Gail. There is no worse experience in the world than being locked up in a cell like that. I thought I'd go out of my mind."

"Are you ready to order?" Their waitress stepped up to the table and set a cutting board with bread and butter between the two women.

The girls ordered dinner, chatted a bit about Gail's life while they ate their salads, and then Gail pushed her salad plate to the side. "I just keep wondering how in the world you're holding up. First the adoption agency story, and now this. You have to be ready to kill someone."

Suzanne snorted and reached for her martini. Took a sip. "I

hate Sterling. I know he's the one behind all this." She laughed. "If I'm going to be convicted of murder, I wish I'd killed Sterling. It would have been worth it."

"Suzanne!"

"Kidding. Kidding."

"What are you going to do now?"

Suzanne shrugged. "I don't know. I've hired some investigators to look into the case. They're so good, they could get a serial killer off, so my case should be a breeze. I don't think the police are too anxious to look at anyone but me. So, I'm going to have to prove my innocence. But if I can prove Sterling was the one who framed me? You know what they say—hell hath no fury like a woman on the warpath." She laughed again. "The guilty do not go unpunished. And with the help of these investigators, I intend to make sure the real murderer is convicted."

———

Marcus held open the door and then followed Alex into the bar. He wrinkled his nose as the overwhelming smell of sweat, booze, and cigarette smoke assaulted him. Smoking had been banned for some time, yet the place still reeked.

It was a small local bar with a jukebox in the corner playing something loud and hard and unrecognizable. The patrons didn't seem to care as they hovered over their drinks and conversation. Marcus actually overheard one man say, "Come here often?" He thought that line went out with "What's your sign?"

The bartender was a beefy fifty-something with a friendly smile and efficient hands as he answered questions and mixed drinks at the same time.

"Yeah, Suzanne usually comes in two, maybe three times a week. Ties one on and then stumbles outta here."

Marcus leaned on the bar. "Do you recall if there was someone sitting with her the last time she was here? Or maybe someone who may have been watching her?"

The bartender handed off the shots to a waitress and picked up another couple of glasses and filled them with ice. "Suzanne knows several people in here, and just about everyone knows who she is. People always watch her. Some talk to her."

"But no one who may have looked a bit suspicious?"

The bartender stopped moving for a moment. "Well, maybe. There was a guy sitting in the corner over there. But you gotta understand, I don't have a lot of time to stand around and watch everyone."

"I understand. It's a busy place," Alex said.

"Yeah. I do remember now. What made me notice him is that when she left, he pulled out his cell phone and kind of booked it out of here."

"Have you ever seen him before?" Alex asked.

"Don't think so," the bartender replied and then shrugged. "Hard to swear by that, though."

"Do you recall what he looked like?"

"Big guy. Chunky. Brown or black hair. Lighting in here being what it is makes it hard to be sure. I did notice when he came up to the bar to get a refill that he had one of them pockmarked faces. You know. From acne or something. It was real scarred."

It didn't ring any bells with Marcus. He thanked the bartender. They hung around for another fifteen minutes, talking with the waitresses, but none of them knew as much as the bartender did.

"Well," Alex said as they left. "At least we know we were right. Someone was here watching her."

"Now we just have to figure out who."

———

Suzanne stared in horror as an image of her and Gail at dinner played on the television. Her words had been mixed and edited to say something far different than what she had actually said. She knew how it worked. Suzanne had done the same thing for the sake of a story millions of times. But to have it done to her, and about something like this…

Practically screaming, she picked up her shoe and threw it in the direction of the television. Gail! She set this whole thing up.

Suzanne threw herself down on the bed, sobbing.

Revenge. Oh, was she ever going to make some people pay for this. Gail was smart, but she didn't pull this off alone. Frank was behind it. He had to be.

She sat up, eyes narrowing as she ran through a hundred scenarios in her mind, each one involving making a few people suffer. Really suffer.

———

Marcus turned on the news on his way into the bedroom. He stretched and then sat on the bed. He was exhausted. Leaning forward, he rolled his shoulders. Then sat up straight and went to arch his back.

And froze.

Grainy footage of Suzanne and another woman, sitting in a bar somewhere, laughing, played on the screen. Marcus turned up the volume.

He could just barely make out her face, but he knew it was her. And the sound was clear enough to hear Suzanne recounting her story—or at least part of it, the part where there was blood on her hands—to the other woman.

Then Suzanne reached for her drink. Marcus leaned forward a little further. "I have to tell you, Gail," Suzanne said, "I wish I'd killed Sterling. It would have been worth it. You know what they say. Hell hath no fury like a woman on the warpath."

Marcus's phone rang. He didn't need caller ID to tell him it was Alex. He picked it up. "I don't believe what I'm seeing. I'm seeing it. I'm hearing it. I don't believe it."

"Why in the world would she talk like that?"

Marcus slapped his face. "This cannot be happening."

"It's not," Alex replied. "She's stupid, but she's not that stupid. Look at the footage. It's from a distance and it's poor quality. A hundred bucks says she didn't know this was being taped. And the statements. I think they've been edited to say what they want people to hear."

"Please tell me you're right."

"If I'm not...I will kill her myself."

Then Suzanne said, "You'll see. The guilty do not go unpunished." Marcus dropped the phone.

After retrieving it from the floor, Marcus groaned. "This just went from worse to way worse."

"Yep," Alex replied softly. "It's going to be really, really bad."

"Why does the Father give us these cases?"

Alex's laugh washed over him like a soft April rain on a warm day. "Because He knows He can trust us? Or maybe it's payback for all those years we spent in rebellion."

Marcus hated thinking back to just how rebellious he had been. Especially after Suzanne's betrayal. But all that was long ago. He was a different person now. "Didn't we repent for all that stuff?"

Alex laughed again. "Repentance gets us off the guilty charges, but we still reap what we've sown."

"You know, there are times I really don't like you very much."

"Oh, chin up, partner. We just have to walk Suzanne through the darkest days of her life. Nothing new for us."

"Alex?" He held his breath and then released it slowly. No. He wasn't going to go there. "I'm bushed. I'll talk to you in the morning."

"Night, Marcus." And then she was gone.

18

Louis Barone took great pride in his girls. Each was even more beautiful than the next. Blondes, brunettes, redheads. And they made him a great deal of money.

At least once a week, he would stop by the house and talk to them, make sure they were all working hard and being accommodating to the clientele. But his visits were primarily to examine the books. It's not that he didn't trust Treina to be honest, but a smart man never trusted other people with his money. He didn't get to be a very wealthy man by being a fool.

After checking the books, he went into the front room where he had installed an elaborate mahogany bar he'd found in Kansas that had once graced a well-known saloon and brothel in the days of the Old West. Louis was fond of anything that spoke of an era he wished he'd known firsthand. He found the idea of walking down the streets with a Colt on each hip, shooting down anyone that got in his way, particularly appealing.

The district attorney was already there, and from the belligerence in his voice, had been there long enough to down a few drinks.

"Bruce, my friend. What's this you are upset about?"

"Veta. I want to see Veta."

"You've already been informed that Elizaveta is unfortunately unable to attend to you this evening."

Bruce staggered forward, his face red. "I want Veta."

Louis nodded to one of the girls across the room, a beautiful young girl he'd found in Siberia who was all too anxious to leave her home and homeland.

"Here is Sasha. You see how lovely she is? Such fine blond hair. Like silk. She is most anxious to take care of you until Veta returns."

Bruce glanced over at Sasha with the face of a petulant child.

With a nod from Louis, Sasha leaned against Bruce like a cat. Bruce stared at her and then draped his arm over her shoulders.

Louis breathed a sigh of relief as Sasha led Bruce upstairs. His cell phone rang, and he stepped out of the room to take the call. "Yes?"

The caller went through a litany of fires for Louis to put out, and Louis went through a list of people for the caller to contact. Delegation was the key to efficiency.

He was ending the call when screams sent him running back into the living room. Two of his men were already bounding up the stairs, guns drawn. Louis was quick to follow. By the time he arrived, the men had Bruce pinned to the floor. Sasha was curled on the bed, beaten very, very badly.

"Get him out of here before I must kill him. And Ivan? Take our Sasha to the hospital. Make sure it is understood that your niece was on her way home when she was attacked. She made her way home and you brought her in."

Ivan nodded and then wrapped the nearly unconscious girl in the bedspread and lifted her into his arms.

Louis stood there a moment, breathing deeply. He did not like anyone hurting his girls. Now Sasha would not be working for many days. That would cost him money. And Bruce Michaelson would have to make it up to Louis.

19

Thursday night, May 7

Kathi smiled up at the boy as they left McDonald's. "So you play guitar? I think that is so completely awesome. I've always wanted to play."

The boy chatted on, obviously trying to flirt with her as the drug began to take effect. She kept smiling as she led him to the van. Sometimes she would meet one that she really liked and would have preferred to find someone else, but she knew she had to take what she could get.

This kid Adam was an innocent from the get-go. He had that wide-eyed look that just took everything in but didn't seem to process any of it. He was a lamb on his way to the slaughter.

"I feel funny."

"You're just tired. Stress does that sometimes. It's right down this alley. You can sleep in my bed tonight."

At the thought of maybe getting more than just a night of sleep, the boy staggered forward with eager anticipation. *Sorry,*

Adam, but I got rent to pay and food to buy and you're worth two hundred bucks to me. And even more to someone else.

The van door opened. Adam stopped, weaving in place as he tried to assimilate. "Who are you?"

Kathi slipped her arm though his. "A friend of mine. He stops by from time to time."

Adam didn't seem to like that. He frowned.

"Don't worry. He's not staying. Are you, Sam?"

"Nah. Just wanted to say hi. See if you needed anything."

"A little help, yes. I don't think he finished all his soda."

The man nodded.

"Wass gon on?" Adam's words slurred as he leaned harder into Kathi.

"Nothing, honey." She gave him a kiss on the lips. Sure enough, his glazed eyes fixed on her, and he managed a crooked smile, unaware that Sam was right behind him.

"Ouch." Adam reared back as Sam pulled the needle out of his neck. He took one step backward and collapsed in Sam's arms.

20

Friday morning, May 8

Suzanne woke to the beat of a familiar drummer marching around in her head. Groaning, she rolled over and clutched her temples, trying to stop the incessant hammering. After seeing herself on the television, she had ordered up a bottle of wine from the hotel bar and finished it off in just under an hour.

Now she was paying for it.

The pounding stopped for a second. Okay, maybe if she didn't move, it would remain blessedly quiet.

Then the hammering started again, just as loud and just as determined.

And that's when she realized that it wasn't inside her head. It was the door.

Cursing under her breath, she rolled gently out of bed, and reached for her robe, only to notice that she was still wearing her clothes from last night.

"Okay, okay, I'm coming." Using the wall as a brace, she staggered to the peephole.

Marcus.

She ran her fingers through her hair and then released the security bar and faced him, leaning against the jamb to keep from collapsing. "This isn't a good time, Marcus."

"Tough," he replied as he brushed past her.

She let the door swing closed and followed him into the room, slowly sinking down on the foot of the bed. "What are you doing here?"

"Just checking to see if you've done anything else to destroy your life. Oh, I don't know, maybe called the DA and confessed to double homicide or something."

His eyes were as hard as that hotel bed. Marcus was one of the nicest men she'd ever met, but that moral streak in him didn't allow for much wiggle room across the gray lines in life.

Snatching up a pillow, she hugged it to her body as she folded one leg under her. "I'm sorry. I should have known better than to trust her."

"A reporter?" Marcus pulled out one of the studio chairs and dropped down in it. "Gee, ya think? Then again, maybe you figured you were the only reporter that does stuff like that."

"Stop it. I learned my lesson."

"I'm not so sure. What possessed you to go running your mouth? You know firsthand how these things work. You practically wrote the book on sound bites and smear campaigns."

Tossing the pillow aside, she staggered to her feet, wobbled over to the minikitchen, and started a pot of coffee. If she was going to have to listen to one of his lectures, she really needed a strong drink, but she knew him well enough to know it wouldn't get past the door before he'd be tossing it down the sink. And giving her another lecture.

She looked down, wanting to avoid his accusing gaze. "I just felt really alone. And Gail seemed sympathetic. But she betrayed me. You have no idea how it feels, Marcus."

He leaned back, stretching out his legs, folding his arms across his chest. "No? Hmm, let me think. Surely I've been betrayed by someone I trusted…"

"Stop it, okay? I get it. Why are you doing this to me? Can't you see how hurt I am?"

Marcus softened the slightest bit. "Look, Suzanne. We're working really hard to try and find out who is framing you for murder. You can't just go on the air—"

"I didn't go *on the air*, Marcus. They tricked me. Gail acted like she really cared."

"And you didn't stop to think about anything except what you wanted at that particular moment."

She leaned back against the counter. "Are we talking about last night or that night in your dorm room?"

Slapping his hands on the sides of the chair, he jumped to his feet. "I think we're done here. Good luck with your case, Suzanne. I truly wish you well."

"You did what?" Alex set the can of gun oil on the edge of her desk.

Marcus eased it away from the edge. "I told Suzanne she was on her own. Now, I was thinking about the Holdt case." Pete Holdt and Holdt Industries were suffering massive losses. At least twice a week, shipments of electronics were being hijacked. It was thought to be an inside job. They needed Marcus and Alex to find out who was behind it. And stop it. "We told them we couldn't start on the investigation for two weeks, but I think we could move them up on the calendar. And we can catch up on the Christopher case."

Alex tossed aside the oily rag she was using to wipe down the barrel of her SIG. "You're kidding, right? This is your idea of a joke?"

"She's not going to listen to either of us, and it's only a matter of time before she's knee deep in another episode like last night."

"Our job isn't to keep Suzanne from making a fool of herself, Marcus. She has an attorney for that. Our job is to prove she's innocent of Cecelia Forbes's murder." When she started looking around, Marcus reached over and handed her the little patches she would use to wipe down the inside of the barrel. "Thanks."

"Welcome. Listen, I know you don't agree, but I just think Suzanne is going to be more trouble than she's worth."

He watched her tuck the patch on the end of the wand and slide it down the barrel. He would never understand her fascination with guns. She had nine or ten of them, and he never knew which gun she'd be toting from one day to the next. Sometimes he wondered if it depended on the color she wore or purse she carried.

"We don't take clients based on how much trouble they're going to be. We're hired to do a job." She set the wand down on her desk and when the dirty, oily patch came to rest on the wood surface, Marcus cringed. "Now, if all this is because you still have feelings for Suzanne—"

"I do *not* have feelings for Suzanne. And anyway, it's already done. I told her this morning."

"You called her this morning and told her we were dropping her as a client?"

"No, I went over to her hotel room, started to give her a taste of my displeasure, and when she got snippy with me, I told her it was over."

Alex leaned back in her chair, giving him another one of those looks that made him want to run and hide somewhere. Alaska maybe.

"You went to her hotel room, early in the morning? *Alone?*"

He opened his mouth, realized that whatever came out was going to be most likely wrong and snapped it shut again.

"Marcus, you should have called me."

"I didn't think about it."

"Fine. But next time, call me."

"I will. But there won't be a next time. I told her we were done."

"Well, we're not."

"Why not?"

"Item one: Suzanne would never risk her career over the possibility of an affair. Item two: Someone wants us off this case. Item three: If Senator Sterling is the man behind all this, it's going to take everything we have and then some to get to him. Item four: If we don't take this, Suzanne will go to prison."

"I'm sure there are other investigators out there who can handle it."

"Item five: Someone put a bomb in her car a few weeks back and her fiancé was killed. The police actually suspected Suzanne for a time, but the detective in charge of the case"—she looked over at the open file folder behind her on the credenza—"Hodge, said he suspected that Suzanne was actually the target."

"So, someone wanted her dead."

"They were never able to prove anything." She raised her head and he noticed she had a smudge of oil on her cheek. "The night of Dr. Guy Mandeville's funeral, Suzanne was attacked outside her apartment in Virginia."

"But she wasn't killed."

"Because a neighbor showed up, scaring the guy off."

"Then why the elaborate frame-up for murder? Why don't they just kill her?"

"I've been going over some of Suzanne's files on the senator. I think she has something they want. And they're determined to get it."

21

Friday morning, May 8

The limousine eased out of traffic and sped up as it crossed Key Bridge. The meeting at the White House had taken a bit longer than he'd anticipated, and now he ran the risk of being late for his luncheon appointment at the Pentagon.

Willard Mandeville gazed out the tinted windows. The plan to destroy Suzanne had taken a great deal of thought and money, but it was going to be worth every penny. He'd sent his man to install that bomb in her car because Guy wouldn't see what she was. What she could do to the family. The boy had been so brilliant and so blind. It had been his responsibility as Guy's father to look out for his best interests.

But she had been too smart for him; giving her car to Guy. He didn't know how she found out about the bomb but it didn't matter. She'd only delayed the inevitable. It wasn't about keeping her away from Guy now. It was about revenge.

Anger surged through him, hot and feral. His fingers itched to be wrapped around her slender neck, to squeeze until she was dead. The woman wasn't the least bit sorry for what she had done. Yet. But she would be. He would see to that.

But first, he had to find out where she had hidden Guy's briefcase. There was no doubt in his mind now that she had it. She had to have it. His man had searched her apartment. It wasn't there. Or in the car. So where did she have it hidden? He'd placed small listening devices in those PIs' offices, so anything they found out, he'd find out. And if Suzanne brought them the files, he'd know that too.

And when he was done destroying her life publicly, he was going to have the ultimate satisfaction of looking in her face as she died so that she would know exactly who was sending her on her way to hell.

———

The Chalet was an upscale version of a local burger joint. To cater to the socioeconomic culture of the area, it featured a variety of fifteen-dollar hamburgers and a decadent selection of luscious chocolate desserts. There were two bars—one serving alcohol and one boasting a coffee menu that rivaled the Starbucks down the street. Since Marcus wouldn't go near a hamburger, especially if it cost fifteen dollars, Alex only came here when Marcus wasn't around.

Suzanne slipped into the booth across from Alex. "Okay, I'm here."

Alex slid her cell phone to the side and folded her hands on top of the table. She waited until the waitress stopped by, took their lunch order, and hurried off before explaining the purpose behind their meeting.

"I thought you weren't going to help me," Suzanne started. "Marcus said—"

"Marcus was upset. Rightly so. He'll get over it."

"Where is he?" Suzanne looked around as if expecting him to be lurking nearby, waiting to pounce.

"He drove out to Virginia to talk to Detective Hodge."

Suzanne's face registered genuine surprise. She leaned forward. "Why?"

Alex waited until the waitress set their drinks down and scurried away before continuing. "What are you hiding from us?"

"Nothing."

Too quick, and there was a slight widening of the eyes that told Alex that she wasn't being completely honest. "Talk."

"There is nothing I can tell you that has anything to do with Cecelia's murder."

"How do you know?"

Suzanne stared out across the restaurant, obviously stalling. Finally, she looked over at Alex. "I told you about Sterling. I'm not hiding anything."

"You have something he wants. What is it?"

She seemed to be debating long and hard before her shoulders slumped. "Guy's laptop. And some patient files. They were in his briefcase."

"And why would a senator be interested in your boyfriend's laptop?"

"They were partners. I know it sounds crazy, but they were kidnapping teenagers."

"And doing what with them?"

Suzanne stared at her hands for a moment and then looked back up at Alex. "I'm not positive on that. I think they were selling the girls into prostitution. I can't imagine any other scenario. Maybe sending them overseas. I've heard of that sort of thing. Taking them to a country where they don't speak the language. Keeping them drugged up."

Alex draped one arm over the back of the banquette. "And you were going to mention this when?"

"The laptop has password security. I haven't been able to get into it." Suzanne's cell rang and she fished it out of her purse. "Just one second," she said to Alex. "Hello?"

The color drained from Suzanne's face.

Alex reached over and took the phone. When she put it to her ear, all she heard was "—but it's not going to help you one bit. I set the trap, and you walked into it. The next time we meet, you'll beg me to kill you."

"I doubt it, buster, but if you want to test that theory, why don't you just tell me when and where?" Alex looked at Suzanne. The horror on the woman's face was firmly in place.

"Who is this?"

Alex smiled. "You first."

Click.

Alex looked at the screen but the number was blocked. She handed the phone back to Suzanne. "Don't ever answer a blocked or unavailable number again."

"He said—" She swallowed hard, hands trembling as she took her phone as if it were about to bite her. "He said he was going to torture me for days before he killed me. That he wanted me to feel all the pain I've forced other people to feel."

"He's a bully and a coward. He hides in the shadows because he isn't man enough to walk out here in the light. That's the very essence of darkness—it's afraid of the light."

"He's going to kill me. Framing me for murder wasn't enough. He wants me dead."

Alex leaned over and took Suzanne's hand. "I'm sure a lot of people want you out of their way, but you're still breathing. Don't worry. Marcus and I will make sure you stay that way."

"Are you aware that you can intimidate a person even when you're trying to comfort them?"

Alex smiled and lifted her eyebrows. "Me?"

Suzanne slid her phone down in her purse. "Have you ever killed someone, Alex?"

"No. I've never had to. But if you ever see a man with a notch in his ear, he's one of many who tested my patience."

"You cut their ears?"

"No, I shoot their ears."

Suzanne just stared at Alex as if trying to weight the accuracy of her words. "You're kidding."

"All you need to know is that Marcus and I are not going to let someone kill you on our watch. And when we leave here, we're going to pick up that laptop and those files." Alex leaned back as the waitress set a tower of beef and bread in front of her. "Now, this is a burger."

———

Sitting at his kitchen table with a mug of herbal tea at his elbow, Marcus went over the initial crime reports Detective Hodge had faxed.

It was unlikely that Dr. Mandeville was the target of the bomb. Who could have known that he and Suzanne would switch cars after lunch that day? Far more likely that someone planned on Suzanne being killed.

Hodge had interviewed Suzanne's crew, the most interesting of which came from a cameraman named Roy Wilkins. *"She was ambitious—we all got that—but she was cold. Dr. Mandeville was crazy about her, and she paraded him around like a poodle on a leash. She'd whine about needing something, and Guy would get it for her before she had time to fix the mascara from the phony crying jag. He really thought she loved him. She was just using him."*

Marcus tried to push his own bias aside, but it definitely sounded familiar.

Hodge had asked if Roy knew anyone with reason to kill

Suzanne. The answer was no surprise. *"No. She was hard to deal with, but I can't think of anyone that would go so far as to kill her for it."*

When his cell phone rang, he checked the screen. Razz. "What's up?"

"They tore up everything. I couldn't stop them." Through the rush of words, he could hear the panic, propelling him to his feet.

"Are you okay? Are you hurt?" He took the steps up to his bedroom two at a time, his bare feet slapping the highly polished wood.

"The office. The office. It's destroyed. I'm so sorry."

"I'm not worried about the office." He tucked the phone under his chin as he pulled on his socks. "Did they hurt you?"

"A little. I'm fine. Really."

"I'm on my way. Where's Alex?" He shoved his feet down in his boots and grabbed a sweatshirt from the dresser.

"She's out. They came busting in here with masks on and they tore everything up."

"Just lock the doors, call the police, and don't let anyone in unless you know them. I'm leaving now. See you in fifteen minutes."

It took closer to twenty, but Marcus managed to pull into the parking lot before the police arrived.

Razz hadn't been exaggerating. Desks were overturned, papers were scattered all over the floor, lamps shattered, the pictures on the wall torn down and smashed, the seating-area chairs broken, and there was a huge gash in one of the walls. It didn't bode well for the private offices or file room.

"Razz!"

The young man eased out of the supply closet. "Thank goodness you're here."

"Did they hurt you?"

"They just shoved me up against the wall. Banged my head. Not very hard. Then they twisted my arm and told me to tell you to stick your nose in a different case and leave Kidwell alone."

Had to be the same guy who offered to triple Suzanne's fee to stop the investigation. Which meant it was the same person who framed Suzanne for murder. "How many were there?"

"Three men, creatively dressed in black with masks. One of them had a lot of acne on his neck—which was the only bit of skin I could see. They were just thugs, hired hands. I have to assume they were hired by our real culprit."

Marcus recalled the bartender referring to a man with pocked skin. Coincidence? Doubtful.

Razz started picking up the stapler, business cards, and desk blotter. "They said that next time they were going to get personal."

"What in the world happened in here?"

Marcus turned around as Alex stepped over a chair.

"We've just been duly warned off the Kidwell case."

"I see that." Alex looked around, then her eyes stopped. She gasped. "Suzanne's files!"

Razz ran a hand down his face. "Most of it is scattered all over the conference room. But they took everything we had on the senator."

Alex gazed up at Marcus, her eyes narrowing with a dangerous glint. "Well, I wonder who'd want to do that."

"Easy, tiger. Could be someone wanting us to believe it's the senator." He gave Razz's desk a heave and flipped it upright. "I wonder how bad your office is."

Alex's eyes went wide and she ran from the room. A few seconds later, Marcus heard her scream with frustration. "They broke my favorite vase!"

He stepped into the mess of his office. There wasn't much damage they could do to his furniture—industrial strength had its advantages—but they smashed his computer monitor, scattered all his files across the floor, and dumped the contents of his minifridge and then stomped the contents into the carpet. That fruit juice was never going to come out.

He stooped down and started picking up the files. Alex stepped into the room. "Okay, other than some minor damage— like my vase—they did more aggravation than anything else."

"It was just a warning. Back off or it'll get worse."

"Seems terribly inefficient, but whatever. So do you want to back off?"

"Not now, I don't." Marcus handed Alex a stack of paper and continued to pick up more. "I don't like being pushed."

"You let me push you."

"That's different."

"Well, either way, someone's going to have to pay for that vase. It was my grandmother's. I can't replace it."

"I'm sorry."

"Not your fault."

Marcus hefted his desk upright and then picked up his chair. "We've made someone very nervous."

Alex picked up a few pens and set them on the desk. "Did you get a chance to see Hodge?"

"He had something important to do and couldn't meet with me, but he faxed the entire file over. He believes that Suzanne was the target, but he never found out who put the bomb in her car."

Alex placed the stack of papers on the desk and knelt down to help him gather up the rest. Her hand touched the wet, gooey mess from the minifridge. "Yuck. What is this?"

"Fruit juice, carrot juice, water, some leftover broccoli in garlic sauce, an egg roll, and if I recall correctly, two bottles of acai juice."

"This carpet is ruined."

"Yep."

Razz appeared in the doorway. "The police are here."

Alex stood up. "I've got to wash my hands. Marcus, could you handle them until I get back?"

"Sure."

It took half an hour to show the police the damage and explain three times how it happened, and over six hours to put the place in order. Refiling all the paperwork was going to take days if not weeks.

Leaving Razz to work on putting the office back together, Marcus and Alex went to see Suzanne at her office. On the way over, Alex explained about the laptop and patient files, as well as the fact that Suzanne had only given them copies of her research files.

Marcus looked at Alex. "You mean we didn't have the originals?"

She shook her head. "Suzanne hid the originals and the laptop. She couldn't take any chances. She was right, unfortunately."

"Where are the originals?"

"In a bank deposit box."

"Wait," Marcus pulled up to a red light. "Laptop? Did you say laptop?"

"Yes. Guy's laptop. It was in his briefcase, but it's password protected and she couldn't get into it."

"Trust me," Marcus replied. "Razz can get into it."

"I'm counting on it."

They had to wait at the front desk for nearly ten minutes until a young lady with a bounce in her walk and a polite smile showed up. "This way, please."

They were taken up to the fourth floor and then into Suzanne's office. As soon as the young lady left and the door was closed, Alex informed Suzanne about the break-in.

"They took everything?" she asked.

"No. Just your files on the senator," Marcus corrected.

"I told you, didn't I? See? That proves he's behind all this."

"Or someone wants us to think he is. We can't discount that possibility."

"Why won't anyone believe me?"

"We do believe you, Suzanne." Alex touched Suzanne's arm. "But we would be letting you down if we didn't keep an open mind about this."

"I guess that means you want the originals now?" Suzanne picked up her purse. "You do understand: if they steal the originals, it's over."

Alex nodded. "We're ready for them now. We're not going to let them take the originals."

An hour and a half later, Marcus and Alex had dropped Mandeville's laptop off with Razz and then gone back to Marcus's home.

Marcus lived near the Monocacy Battlefield. The house had long since fallen into rubble and been hauled away, but when Marcus inherited the land from his aunt, he spent three years renovating the barn and converting it into a house. The second floor held three bedrooms, one of which was set up as an office, although Marcus rarely used it. Most of the time, he and Alex worked in the kitchen, using nearly every inch of the oversized kitchen table to spread out.

Marcus started going over Suzanne's investigation notes while Alex took notes of her own. "There's no way we're going to be able to just walk in and talk to Senator Sterling," he said.

"I can get my father to help us out on that one. He knows the senator."

"He knows everyone in Washington."

"Well, true." Alex flipped through one of the files on the minister. "Suzanne's investigations suggest that Reverend Scott collected donations to build a five-million-dollar theme park honoring heroes of the Bible, then dropped the idea. Shortly thereafter, he built a five-million-dollar mansion."

"Ouch." Marcus paged through a stack of photos, lingering over a few. "After we talk to Scott, I'd like to see if we can talk to Barone. Suzanne has pictures here of Michaelson and him apparently doing business, which seems to corroborate Suzanne's assumptions."

She looked at the file. "Lenya Bashmakov. It still cracks me up that a man in the Russian mafia comes here and changes his name to something Italian."

"He probably thought it was amusing."

Alex leaned back in her chair, rolling the stiffness out of her shoulders. "I just hate dealing with him. He keeps turning up in our cases like a bad nickel."

"Bad penny. Turning up like a bad penny."

"Whatever. He's made it perfectly clear that he doesn't want to cross our paths again."

Marcus stood, crossing over to the refrigerator and retrieving a bottle of water. "He'll get over it."

"Yeah, right after we ask him if he's in bed with the DA. Sure he will. He has such a forgiving nature."

"He'll just send Ivan after me."

Alex laughed. "And the last time you and Ivan tangled, you came out with two cracked ribs, and I had to notch his ear to persuade him to let you go."

Marcus rubbed his ribs. "Just don't let him get me in another bear hug and we'll be fine."

22

Saturday, May 9

Reverend Walther Scott wasn't one of those pastors who kept the door to his office open all day and his phone number listed in case you needed to call him to the hospital in the middle of the night for a sick relative. Getting into the building was easy; progressing beyond the front door was another matter entirely. After spending ten minutes with two inquisitive security guards, they were stalled again at the receptionist's desk.

"No, we don't have an appointment, but I'm sure if you explain to Reverend Scott that we're here, he'll be happy to talk to us."

The bubbly brunette kept her smile firmly in place. "I'm sorry. You must have an appointment."

"This is a homicide investigation." Alex leaned over the highly polished mahogany counter. "So, tell you what—I'm going to make a call and Reverend Scott can give us the answers we need down at the police station."

"And I'll call the press," Marcus added as he pulled out his cell phone. "They'll assume, of course, that Reverend Scott is being arrested. But misunderstandings like that are so easy to fix, don't you think?"

Her smile faltered a notch as she picked up the phone. "Just a moment, please."

A few minutes later, a suited man stepped out of the elevator. The hard eyes, the firm frown, and tattoos snaking up from the collar of his starched shirt reeked of crime, prison, and probation. "Can I help you?"

"No, we're here to see Reverend Scott," Marcus replied. "If you could just take us to his office, we can probably get this accomplished without bloodshed, pain, or someone being arrested."

The corner of the man's mouth quirked up a bit. "You think I'm here to hurt you?"

Alex planted her hands on her hips, which swept the corner of her jacket back far enough to reveal her holster. "We've spent the past half hour trying to get to our meeting with Reverend Scott, and I've seen less security at the Pentagon. Is there some reason he does not wish to help us investigate a murder?"

"A murder?" The man smiled, but wariness appeared in his eyes. "Why would you need his help?"

Marcus leaned in and said softly, "If I have to ask one more time, I'm going to lose my good mood."

The man took a step back, turned on his heel, and punched the elevator button.

"While we're here, maybe we should check out your alibi for the night in question."

The doors opened and the three of them stepped inside. The man punched the button for the third floor, and then just before the doors closed, he stepped out. "I was busy that night."

"We didn't tell you—" The doors closed behind him.

"That went well, don't you think?" Marcus said. Alex had that "fishy" look on her face again, but this time, he was inclined to agree with her. "Remind me to find out who he is and where he was the night of Cecelia's murder."

The Reverend Scott's office door was open, revealing a room with the hushed feel of a church during prayer. Classical music, soft and subdued, floated like a barely perceptible mist. Leather-bound tomes lined the walls. The ornately carved dark wood desk grew out of plush, dark red carpet. All tasteful and clearly expensive.

Reverend Scott rose from his chair to welcome Marcus and Alex. "Please, come in. Have a seat." After shaking both their hands, he retreated behind his desk. "I must admit, I am a tad confused. My receptionist said something about a homicide investigation?"

Alex took a seat. Marcus stayed standing. It was a small power play, but he needed every advantage he could get. He strolled over to the bookcases and glanced at the titles. From Shakespeare to Twain to theology and eschatology to Dean Koontz and Stephen King. "You have very eclectic taste."

"I like to read." Scott toyed with a gold pen. "I thought you came here to discuss a murder."

Marcus leaned against the bookshelves and crossed his arms. "How well did you know Cecelia Forbes?"

"Who?" The surprise act told Marcus what he needed to know.

"Let's try this one. How badly did you need to silence Suzanne Kidwell?"

Marcus saw the realization the moment it hit the pastor's eyes. He also saw serious discomfort.

"Ms. Forbes was the one found dead in Suzanne Kidwell's home, wasn't she?" Scott folded his hands, interlocking his fingers. Marcus couldn't help wondering if it was to keep his hands from shaking. "I didn't know the woman at all. If I've ever met her, I don't recall the incident. Ms. Kidwell, on the other hand, is a pariah feeding upon the lives of innocent people. But I neither murdered Ms. Forbes nor framed Ms. Kidwell."

Alex leaned forward. "Did you ask someone else to do the killing for you?"

"Me? Of course not!" He slapped his hands down on the desk. "I wouldn't know who to ask, even if I were capable of such a thing."

"Your bodyguard, Mr...." She let it hang there for a second, inviting Scott to respond.

"Bodyguard?" Scott looked from Alex to Marcus. "You mean Mac?"

"Mac?" Marcus strolled casually toward the desk.

"Aaron McGuffin. He's no killer, Mr. Crisp. And he's not my bodyguard. He's my assistant."

"An ex-con?" Alex asked as she jotted in her notebook.

Scott shifted in his seat. "I see where you're going, but no. Mac is not a killer. He was arrested for armed robbery. A liquor store. He attended a few of our Bible studies at the prison. We have a prison ministry, you know. Anyway, he became a Christian, and when he was released and had trouble finding a job, we hired him. Odd jobs at first, but he proved himself and now works as my assistant."

Alex looked up from her writing. "And what does being your assistant entail? Answering phones? Escorting investigators to the elevator before running off?"

Scott blinked. "Running off? I'm not sure what he would have done to give you that idea. He has nothing to hide. But to answer your question, he keeps track of my schedule, makes sure that I arrive where I need to be at the proper time. Things like that."

"And he's totally devoted to you, isn't he?" Marcus toyed with a crystal paperweight on the edge of the desk. "So, if he thought you were in trouble—maybe about to lose everything—he might step in to help you, right?"

Scott shook his head, his eyes wide. "He wouldn't do that. Yes, Mac is devoted to me, but he's a Christian now. He knows murder is forbidden."

"But stealing isn't?" Alex asked.

Alex had hit another nerve. "No one stole anything! Ms. Kidwell completely twisted an innocent story into something tawdry."

Alex made a show of flipping back a few pages as if she needed to review her notes. "You filmed a segment from a vacant piece of land, telling viewers that you needed five million dollars to build an amusement park for God and that you had the land all picked out. The owner of the property said all you ever did was rent it for the day to film your little plea."

Scott's face had turned an ugly shade of red. "This is all a misunderstanding. We didn't have the money to put down a deposit, so yes, we rented it for the day. But we had every intention of purchasing that land when the money came in."

"Did the money come in?" Marcus asked.

"Some. Not nearly enough. That's when we realized that it wasn't going to work out and we canceled the project."

Alex jumped in. "What happened to the money that *was* sent in?"

Scott ran one hand through his hair looking as if he'd rather be anywhere but where he was at that moment. "It went into other coffers. The prison ministry I spoke of. Orphanages we support. The nursing home ministry. The homeless shelter. It went wherever we needed it."

Marcus leaned down, planting both hands on the edge of the desk. "And did the people who donated to the amusement park know that the money actually went somewhere else?"

Scott nodded, shoulders slumping. "I promise you, they were notified of our intentions and told they could request their money back if they wanted. No one asked for any refunds. I didn't use that money to build my home."

Alex glanced over at Marcus before turning back to Scott. "And where did you get the money to build a five-million-dollar mansion?"

A touch of anger flared in his eyes. "Salary, investments, donations. All legitimate, I assure you. I did *not* bilk my flock to pad my own lifestyle." Scott stood up. "Listen, I need to prepare for my eleven o'clock meeting. If you have any further questions, please feel free to call. I'm sorry this is happening to Ms. Kidwell. Despite her attempts to hurt my reputation, I don't wish her ill."

Marcus stood. "One last question and we'll let you get to your meeting. Where were you Wednesday night between 10 p.m. and midnight?"

"I was at a conference in Philadelphia, and there are at least five hundred people who can verify that I was there."

"You talked to that many people in one night?" Alex asked.

"Yes," he replied. "I was the keynote speaker."

———

Suzanne gave the research notes for the upcoming show to her assistant. "Make sure you have the photos and film for the story ready to review at Monday's production meeting. And did we get that sound bite from the psychiatrist?"

"Randy is there now, taping it."

"Good. Let me know when he gets back. I want to make sure it's what I want."

"Yes, Ms. Kidwell."

As soon as her office door shut behind her assistant, Suzanne rubbed her eyes and then reached for her purse. She could feel a serious headache coming on. Just as she swallowed some Tylenol, her office phone rang. Setting her water aside, she wondered only briefly why her assistant hadn't picked it up.

She grabbed the receiver. "Suzanne Kidwell's office."

"Hello, Suzanne. Enjoying your freedom?"

"Who is this?"

"I just thought I'd let you know that we're just getting started. But how about this? My boss wants a certain briefcase. If you hand it over, he might be willing to let me kill you quick. Otherwise, well…torture is something that I truly enjoy."

Suzanne felt cold chills rush up her spine and explode as fear in her throat. "I told you before, I don't have a briefcase."

"Don't play with us, Kidwell. You're out of your league."

"Leave me alone!"

"Only after you're dead." His laugh was enough to send another rush of chills through her chest and she struggled to breathe. She hung up the phone and dialed another number.

On their way out to the car, Alex's cell phone rang. "It's Suzanne." She flipped it open. "Yes?"

"The guy who wants to kill me. He's been calling me."

"I told you not to answer your cell phone."

"He's not calling on my cell. He's calling my office."

"Okay. We're on our way."

"I need to get out of here. I want to go to the hotel, pack, and go someplace safe. I'm too exposed here."

"Then we'll meet you at the hotel. It'll be okay, Suzanne." Alex closed the phone and tucked it back in her pocket. "He's calling Suzanne at work now."

"Well, that didn't take long."

They arrived at Suzanne's hotel room about forty-five minutes later. She paced the room, making it no secret that she expected the killer at any moment. "We need to find a safer place."

Marcus pulled back the drawn curtain and looked out across the parking lot. "He's probably watching. We can't exactly walk you out the front door. He'll just follow us to wherever we take you."

"So that's it? You're just going to let him kill me?"

Alex touched Suzanne's arm. "First of all, we weren't hired to be your bodyguards. We were hired to find out who killed Cecelia. Second, Marcus is thinking out loud. Just sit down and take a deep breath."

Marcus let the curtain fall back into place. "Did you call the police?"

Suzanne snorted. "Like that would do me a bit of good."

"What about your attorney?"

"I called him, but he's in court today."

Alex sat down on the edge of the bed. "There's only one place we can put her that no killer can penetrate."

Marcus frowned. "You sure?"

Alex nodded.

He turned to Suzanne. "Okay, pack your bags." And then to Alex, he said, "You can handle this?"

She shrugged, her eyebrows lifting a fraction. "If it gets too bad, you'll be the first to know."

"Where are you taking me?" Suzanne asked as she shoved clothes into her suitcase.

"My condo," Alex replied, fishing out her cell phone. "We're going to need a little diversion."

"I'll call Razz."

23

Saturday, May 9

Merry curled in the corner of the cot as far as she could, her arms wrapped around her knees. Somewhere down the cement-block hall, another girl whimpered. But Merry was all cried out. She'd cried when she woke up in the back of a truck. She'd cried when two men with guns had taken her and two other kids down a long flight of steps into a dungeon—dark, cement walls, cold air, concrete floors. And she'd cried when she saw the cells.

She'd cried herself to sleep after some creepy doctor had given her a thorough examination and pronounced her healthy and clean. And then again when she was alone in the cell, watching the camera mounted in the corner.

For days, she cried until she had no tears left.

Now, another girl had been brought in and two had disappeared. Merry didn't want to think about where they'd gone. One girl said it was about organ transplants, but the horror of it was more than she could take.

There were so many things she still wanted to do. She wanted to see her mom and her brothers and sisters. She wanted to go to school and be invisible and be okay with that.

She wanted to live.

She wished there was a window so she could at least see the sun. It had to be sometime late in the morning, maybe even noon already. No, not quite noon. Noon was marked by the sound of the metal cart being wheeled in and food trays slipped under the bars.

She was going to die soon. She knew that. And while she wanted to accept it the way she'd accepted the cell and the camera that watched every move she made, she just couldn't.

———

Razz arrived barely an hour after Alex called. He sauntered in wearing black jeans, black high-top sneakers, a black and red striped T-shirt with a black and red leather belt, and his blond hair had red stripes throughout to match his outfit. He'd lined his eyes with black. A thick bullring looped through his septum, and he had a ring on every finger. When he slipped out of his black leather jacket, intricate patterns with black panthers and white tigers crouching in dense vegetation covered his forearms.

Suzanne stared at Razz with wide, confused eyes.

"You called for an extraction?" Razz tossed an oversized duffel on the bed.

Marcus gave a nod toward Suzanne. "We need to get her out

of here, make sure you're not being followed, and then deliver her to Alex's condo."

"We have eyes outside?"

Alex nodded. "More than likely, yes."

He turned his attention to Suzanne. "Dark hair, pregnant, and I could add a little weight to her face. Her own mother wouldn't know her."

"Do it." Alex grabbed her jacket and turned to Marcus. "We need to go. We are supposed to meet with Senator Sterling's aide in less than fifteen minutes."

Suzanne looked up at Alex. "How'd you get that meeting? I've been trying to do that for weeks."

"Well, you may have your press card, but we have actually made *friends* over the years."

"Fair enough," Suzanne said. "Well, why don't I come with you? With a disguise, he won't know it's me." Marcus knew the translation: *You're going to leave me alone with this freak?*

He couldn't hide his smile. "You don't remember Razz? The young man that works in our office?"

Razz whipped out a long black wig and blinked in feigned offense. "She doesn't like me?"

"She doesn't recognize you," Alex said. "And she doesn't know what to make of you."

Razz looked down at his clothes and then back at Alex. "What's wrong with me?"

"Nothing," Marcus replied.

Suzanne finally blinked. "This is that geeky guy with the black-rimmed glasses?"

Razz lifted both arms before dipping into a deep bow. "One and the same. The RazzMaster of disguise."

"Whatever. Either way, I'd like to join you. I'd like to be a part of this investigation."

"Sorry, Suzanne. You know better than that. If you show up, there's no chance they'll talk with us." Marcus turned to Razz. "Drop her off at Alex's condo and then meet us back at the office."

Marcus held the door open for Alex and then followed her out.

Suzanne stared at the closed door and prayed Marcus or Alex would come back and tell her this was all a joke. She felt uncomfortable alone with this weirdo. Even if it was only a costume.

"Okay, I need you to put this body suit on and then these on over it."

Staring at the maternity clothes hanging from his hand, a small shudder ran down her spine. Were they even clean? "Um, isn't there some other way to do this?"

"No."

After she was changed, Razz examined her disguise and nodded his approval. For the first time, she looked him square in the face. His eyes were the brightest green she'd ever seen on a person. Most likely contacts. But there was also a touch of contempt.

"If you want to live, come with me."

"You don't scare me."

"That was a line from a movie, not a threat." He looked her over. "Oh, one more thing." He handed her a pair of black rectangular-framed glasses. She slid them on and stood up to look in the mirror.

"Wow. I almost look good as a frumpy pregnant woman."

"That's the idea. But you can't wear those heels. They're a big no-no for a pregnant woman. Put on some flats."

Rolling her eyes, she took off her favorite black Manolos and exchanged them for a pair of brown sandals.

"Better. Now, I'm going to take your luggage down and put it in my van. Then I'll come back for you. Just sit tight and try not to mess up my work."

She studied herself in the mirror and had to admit, she looked terrifyingly different. He returned before she'd finished her scrutiny.

"Okay, let's go. Be sure to rest one hand on top of the belly. Pregnant women always walk that way. And waddle a little bit."

She wanted to slap him silly for his demands, but until she was safely ensconced at Alex's place, she'd have to put up with him.

"There's a man in a dark blue sedan about three rows back in the parking lot. He's been watching everyone going in and coming out. I'm thinking he's our tail, but so far, he doesn't seem too interested in us. Let's see if that holds."

———

Marcus and Alex arrived at the restaurant in Georgetown and found the senator's aide drumming his fingers and tapping his foot at a table toward the back of the room. As soon as he saw Alex, all the impatience fled from his demeanor and he smiled broadly. "Miss Fisher-Hawthorne. What a pleasure."

Alex knew Marcus would sit back and let her chat since this world—the world of politicking—was her territory. And it was a world that she knew aggravated Marcus beyond comprehension.

The aide looked to be in his early thirties. Prim, proper, and not a hair out of place, he wore his arrogance as confidently as he did that two-hundred-dollar tie.

"I'm sorry we're late. We had a little emergency," Alex replied as she sat. "One of our clients was being threatened."

"Oh. Sorry."

Alex draped her napkin across her lap. "What's good today?"

"Everything here is always good," the aide replied. "How is your father? We haven't seen him in Washington as much lately. He's greatly missed."

"He's fine. Busy." She folded her hands over the menu. "We expected to meet with the senator himself today. To what do we owe the pleasure of having you here instead? "

"He's out of town."

"And when did he leave?"

The aide frowned, narrowing his eyes. "I thought you wanted to talk to us about a campaign donation."

Alex went wide-eyed with innocence and looked over at Marcus. "Did you give him the impression I was looking to donate?"

Marcus shrugged. "Maybe."

"I'm so sorry. No, you see, we're investigating a murder and

what the senator really needs is an alibi, not a campaign donation."
She fluttered her eyelashes.

"This meeting is over." The man gripped the table and began
to rise.

Alex laid her hand over the aide's and gave a hard squeeze and
a sweet smile. "Okay, no problem. We'll just have the cops bring
him into their station. We can interview him there."

The aide settled back into his seat and sneered. "You aren't
cops. You're private investigators. And while the Fisher-Hawthorne
name may open many doors for you, it won't get the police to do
your bidding."

"No, but if I provide them with evidence that the senator had
means, motive, and opportunity, they *are* obliged to investigate."
She leaned in close and whispered, "And you and I both know how
messy it can be when the DC police get involved." The man
blanched and she continued, "Then, of course, the press finds out,
and *they* come running with their photographers and the nightly
news crews and the satellite trucks. It's all just such a circus."

"The senator has done nothing."

"Let's ask Gary Condit how being innocent worked out for
him when Chandra Levy went missing."

She could see the aide playing it out in his mind, weighing the
pros and cons of continuing the conversation a little while longer.
"He left Sunday evening."

"Now, that wasn't so hard, was it?" She smiled and sipped her
water. "So let's talk about the senator's partnership with Dr. Guy
Mandeville."

He stared at her as if she'd lost her mind. "What are you talking about?"

"They had this little partnership going. Well, until Dr. Mandeville was killed, that is. Now, here's the interesting thing—Dr. Mandeville wasn't the target. Suzanne Kidwell was. And she still is the target."

"The senator barely knew the man and certainly had no reason to want him dead."

"I'll take that as a denial. I'll be sure to let the senator know that you did your job admirably." She leaned forward. "He's going to need more than that, though. We know that he was in business with Dr. Mandeville. So you tell him he really needs to talk to us."

The aide sputtered, turning red in the face. "You are chasing the wrong dog, Miss Hawthorne." He stood up. "Now this conversation is over."

They watched him weave through the tables, his shoulders stiff. Alex turned to Marcus. "What do you think?"

"I think he's overpaid." Marcus pushed to his feet.

24

Saturday, May 9

Suzanne was bored. She couldn't stand to watch television. She'd tried, but it seemed as if every channel featured her story—how she was going to jail for the murder of Cecelia Forbes, how they were looking at her for Dr. Mandeville's death, and how she and Ms. Forbes fought over the affections of Guy.

All garbage.

"Please stop pacing," Razz said.

"There's nothing to do."

"Read a book. Watch *Oprah*. Listen to music."

Suzanne glared at him and walked over to the window. Pushing back the curtain, she looked out over the city. This was the kind of place she'd always dreamed of having. She bet Alex paid a cool mil and a half for it. Top floor. Fireplace in the living room. Two bedrooms. Hardwood floors. Stainless steel appliances. Jacuzzi tub in the bathroom. Balcony and a view of Washington. Doorman. Security guard. Security elevator.

"Get away from the window."

Suzanne spun around. "Will you leave me alone?"

Razz looked up from his laptop screen and rested one elbow on the edge of the dining room table. "Sure. But I want to warn you. I don't attend funerals and I don't send flowers."

"I'm perfectly safe here. I don't need you to baby-sit me."

"Can I tell you something that will end this discussion once and for all?"

"What?"

"That glass isn't bulletproof." He shook his head and went back to his work.

She quickly dropped the curtain and stepped away. "Oh, am I interfering with your video game?"

"Yeah. That's exactly what you're doing." He eased back from his computer. "That's what you see, isn't it? A streetpunk kid obsessed with video games and parties and drugs. No respect for people like you. No morals, no ethics, no desire for education or success in life, right?"

"Pretty much, yes."

"Which is exactly why you're in the position you're in. Because you see something, and you immediately make a judgment based on your own desire to be better than everyone else. You look for the worst, so you see the worst and condemn everyone you don't like."

"Where did Marcus find you? Some juvenile detention center? That's it, isn't it? You're one of his charity cases."

"Yeah. That's it. I'm some juvenile delinquent from the streets.

You might want to get off my case before I do something juvenile—like tie you to the chair and tape your mouth shut."

———

When they arrived back at the office, Alex checked their messages. "Hey, Holden called us back. Finally. Guess he made it out of court. I'm going to call him. Let him know where things stand."

Where they stood was nowhere. Marcus headed for his office. Too many people wanted Suzanne hurt, wounded, homeless, or dead. But none of their suspects so far seemed to be a clear stand-out for Cecelia's murder.

He turned on his computer and while it was firing up, pulled a bottle of water from his minifridge and settled in behind his desk

"Marcus?" Alex stepped into his office.

He kept on typing. "If it's another emergency, tell them to wait. I'm busy."

"But my arm is bleeding all over the rug."

His heart lurched as his head jerked up, and then he realized she was joking. "Funny. One of these days you really will be hurt and I'll ignore you."

"It'll never happen. You don't know how to ignore me. Listen, Holden said the DA is trying to rush this to trial."

Marcus leaned back in his chair. "No way."

"Way." She stood against the doorjamb with the "fishy" look on her face again, twirling a strand of hair around her finger.

"How fast?"

"Weeks."

"Well, I guess we start putting in overtime."

"That's what Holden said. Just in case."

"Has Holden gotten anything from the DA's case files yet?"

Alex shook her head. "He's promising to send his files over to-morrow or the next day." Her cell phone rang and she pulled it out of its hip holster. "Oh no."

"What?"

"It's my mother."

"Good luck."

Alex stepped back into her office as she answered the phone. "Hey, how are you feeling?"

"Furious. What are you doing? What could have possibly possessed you?"

"What are you talking about?"

"Senator Sterling. Are you actually investigating him for some sordid murder? My goodness, Alexandria, what *are* you thinking?"

"I'm thinking that he must have been fairly rattled to have called you within minutes of my meeting. I barely left his aide an hour ago." Smiling, she sat down behind her desk and started writing notes to herself. "How upset is he?"

"Extremely. Your father assured him there must be some mistake. To think, a daughter of mine would even *think* to accuse an

upstanding member of Congress. How can you believe he murdered some woman?"

"I merely asked if the senator was in business with someone.
But I never accused the man of murder."

She could almost hear her mother deflating. "Oh. I'm sure this
is all a misunderstanding then. He was quite upset. Your father
promised him we'd talk to you and clear up all this ugliness."

Which is exactly what the good senator intended. A little outrage
went a long way among the blue bloods and their cronies. And
then the daughter gets a call and politely told-but-not-told to back
off. "Now tell me how you're feeling."

"Tired all the time, but otherwise, I feel quite well."

"Is Father there?"

"Not at the moment, dear. He left a few minutes ago for the
club. A meeting with some stockholders, I believe. Alexandria, we
need to talk."

"About Father?"

"No. Considering my health, I believe you should seriously
consider moving back home as soon as possible."

"Why do I need to move home? You have Father, a house full
of servants, doctors that make house calls, and if you need full-time
nursing care, Father will arrange for it. What could I possibly do?"

"Your father met the nicest young man recently at the club.
Harvard graduate, I believe. Tall, blond, blue eyes. Just the type
you love."

"Mom."

"And he's single. I'm thinking of having a small dinner party. And it would be far easier if you lived here. I'm not sure commuting while dating is truly the best thing for a relationship."

"Mother, the only thing you need to be thinking about is getting better. Planning dinner parties or matchmaking is not restful or peaceful or good for your health right now."

"Well, I'm terribly sorry, Alexandria. I'm your mother. I simply want the best for you."

"I have the best."

"It's that man, isn't it? You're in love with him. And he's just not suitable. Can you honestly see him at the helm of Fisher-Hawthorne?"

"Hold on. First of all, I'm *not* in love with him. Second, he's never going to want to take the helm, the stern, or even the galley at Fisher-Hawthorne. It's not a matter for discussion."

"Well, if you're not in love with him, why do you stay there? You gave up a perfectly good law degree to go play detective, doing what? Spying on cheating husbands? Now, we understand that you've always been a bit headstrong and independent, but time is passing you by, Alexandria. You're getting too old for this nonsense. You have obligations here that you need to start taking seriously."

Alex closed her eyes and gritted her teeth, trying hard not to scream. After taking a deep breath, she dived in again. "I'm not taking over the company. How many times do I have to explain that, Mother? I don't want it."

"We understand that, dear. Which is why you must come home and marry the man who will take over and run it for you."

"Why do I have to marry him? Why can't I just hire him?"

"I'm sorry, Alexandria. I'm not feeling well. We will simply have to finish this discussion another time. I'm just too distressed at the moment."

Closing her phone, Alex tossed it on her desk and rubbed her eyes.

Marcus stared at his computer screen, his fingers resting lightly on the keys. Razz had ordered him a new monitor that was even larger than his old one, and he still couldn't be sure what was on the screen.

"I'm not in love with him."

Sometimes he wished Alex's office was down the hall, around the corner, or even on a different floor. He pushed her words aside and tried to concentrate on his work.

"Hey."

He took a deep breath, looked up at Alex, and smiled. "How's your mother?"

"Fine." She dropped down in the chair and stretched out her legs. "The senator called my parents."

"So they called you and politely told to keep your hands off."

"Something like that."

He could see the pain in her eyes and around her mouth, and he wished he could erase it.

"If he has nothing to hide, why would he go to all the trouble of calling my parents and having them call me like I'm some errant poodle that's wandered into his yard?"

"Oh, he has plenty to hide."

"I'm a grown woman with my own business, and still people feel the need to call my parents to come straighten me out and treat me as if I'm some recalcitrant child."

"You are a well-respected investigator, and you were a well-respected attorney. This isn't about you, partner. It's about a desperate man sinking to desperate measures because your reputation as a deadly combination of bulldog and hound dog is legendary."

She wrinkled her nose. "A bulldog–hound dog mix? Doesn't sound very pretty, does it?"

"It's not about pretty. The bulldog in you won't quit, and the hound dog in you will sniff out the truth no matter what—and nothing will stop you. Not even a call to your mommy, where her job is to turn you into a whipped puppy."

He saw the little telltale flare in the nostrils that he'd hit the right nerve.

"That's exactly what the senator wants, isn't it? For me to tuck my tail and sit in the corner. But I've got news for that man—he's stepped on this hound dog's tail and I'll be running him up a creek in no time."

"A tree, Alex. You'll run him up a tree."

"I thought it was up a creek. You know, without a paddle." She gave him a little smile and walked out.

One thing Marcus always admired about Alex was that she lacked that one feminine gene that fretted over windblown hair, chipped manicures, and smeared mascara. She could doll up like a runway model, walk into a room, whip out her gun, wrestle a suspect to the floor, and never mention that a brand-new five-hundred-dollar dress had just been ruined.

Until her mother stepped in. For some reason, that woman could twist Alex inside out and backward. Well, it was his job to set her back on course, and he'd done it enough times to be pretty good at it.

25

Saturday evening, May 9

Marcus pulled into his driveway a little before six. After fighting the usual crawl on I-270, he would have preferred to spend the evening watching a ball game on television. But that wasn't in the plan. Instead, he would get a quick shower, a change of clothes, and takeout for everyone at Alex's condo.

He and Alex had spent most of the afternoon tracking down Louis Barone—not an easy man to find. Of course, everyone on the street was willing to tell them where they saw him last, but no one could say for sure where he was at that moment.

Louis would more than likely find them.

Once inside, he turned on the lights and reached for the alarm box.

Something didn't feel right. A disturbance in the air. A presence.

He unzipped his jacket, eased it off his shoulders, and draped it over the banister.

As he made his way up the stairs and down the hall, he listened. No noise. No breathing. No footsteps. Nothing to indicate that he was anything other than totally alone.

Instinct screamed otherwise.

At the door to the master bedroom, he saw something out of the corner of his eye. He turned just as something slammed him into the wall. He swung, but his fist hit air. A punch in the back drove a spike of pain up his spine. Taking a deep breath, he pushed against the wall for momentum, spinning on the balls of his feet, ready to strike. But his attacker was gone.

Down the stairs. He took two steps forward and staggered as his vision began to swim. He reached for the railing, missed and crashed to his knees. Crawling on all fours, he slowly made his way toward the top step.

His cell phone. If he could just reach…

But his jacket was at the bottom of the stairs, not the top.

His muscles gave out and he dissolved to the floor.

———

Alex stopped just inside her door. Suzanne was curled up in the corner of the sofa, staring at the television, which wasn't even on. Razz was at the dining room table, working on his laptop. The silence could have crushed a truck.

Suzanne jumped up. "Thank goodness you're home. I thought I'd go crazy. Did you find out anything?"

Alex shrugged out of her coat and hung it in the coat closet near the door. "Nothing to speak of." She strode past Suzanne to join Razz. "What did you find out?"

Razz eased back from the table and stretched his arms above his head. "Merry wiped out her hard drive, but I was able to pull up her files. She was e-mailing back and forth with some guy named Paul."

Alex pulled out a chair and dropped into it. "Were you able to trace the IP address?"

"Dead end. It was one of those blanket addresses you can get at any library or Internet café."

"Were you able to find out anything? Where they were going? What they were planning?"

Razz shook his head. "Nothing. He invited her to come live with him, marry him—the usual lure for a young girl—but nothing concrete. He said he worked at an electronics store but never mentioned which one. Never said where he lived. More dead ends. This guy is smart. This isn't the first time he's done this." He waggled his eyebrows. "But I *was* able to hack into the doc's computer."

Suzanne hurried over. "You got into Guy's computer?"

Razz didn't acknowledge Suzanne's question, never taking his attention off Alex. "Some very interesting files. But I haven't finished going over all of them yet. A lot of patient files. Does the name Britney Abbot ring any bells?

Alex hiked her eyebrows. "Big ones. What does she have to do with anything?"

"She was a patient of his."

"I find that to be quite a coincidence."

"Check it out." He stood up, turned the laptop toward Alex, and stuffed his gear into his duffel. "Okay, I gotta run."

Alex stood up. "I'm so sorry, Razz. I totally forgot to ask. How's Mel?"

Razz shrugged. "Good days. Bad days. You know her. She won't complain, but I know the pain is getting worse now." He slung the bag over his shoulder. "I just take each day as a gift."

Alex pulled him into a hug. "Tell her I send my love and prayers."

"Will do. You need me tomorrow?"

"Please."

"Will do." He turned and, walking backward to the door, said, "Alex, you're not going to like what you read, so be prepared for the worst."

"It's bad."

"It's worse than that."

He left without a word to Suzanne.

Pressing her lips together, Alex sat down and starting reading over the files Razz had found. He hadn't been overstating it. "It wasn't about prostitution."

Suzanne pulled out the chair across the table from Alex. "Do I want to know?"

"Probably not. It was about black-market organ harvesting."

Suzanne lost what color she had in her face as her eyes went wide. "I thought he was evil for snatching those girls for sex, but organ harvesting? That is beyond evil."

"And it wasn't just girls. There are several boys mentioned." Alex pressed her lips together as she fought not to explode in a fit of temper. Instead, she let the tears stream down her face. "He was making a boatload of money selling clean, healthy organs to people who may not have survived the national organ transplant list."

"No wonder he's so desperate to get these files back."

Alex had to shut the laptop softly to keep from slamming the lid, picking it up and throwing it across the room. "You're sure that Senator Sterling was his partner?"

Suzanne nodded. "Cecelia told me that he was the biggest source of customers. I thought she meant men that wanted young girls. I had no idea. She said she had more to tell me, but she never got the chance."

Alex went into the kitchen. She opened the cabinets and pulled down plates. "Marcus and I are just going to have to find a way to connect him, that's all. Razz didn't have time to go through the whole computer. We may yet find it on there."

Suzanne folded her arms across her chest. "He's obviously a hacker."

Alex frowned at the tone in Suzanne's voice. "What happened between you two? People usually get along great with Razz."

"He's arrogant. And a punk."

Alex scooted past Suzanne and set the plates down on the table. Reaching behind her, she picked up three linen place mats from the credenza. "You have him all wrong."

Suzanne sniffed.

Alex looked over at her. "How old do you think he is?"

"I don't know. Twenty, maybe?"

"He's thirty-six. And a hacker? I guess you could call him that. He was pursued by the NSA, the CIA, and the FBI while he was still at MIT—where he got not one, but two master's degrees, by the way. He turned all the agencies down to freelance for a while and then came to work for us because it's a steady paycheck while he deals with a heartbreaking issue at home."

"Seriously? Well, genius or not, he's rude and selfish."

Alex turned on Suzanne and pointed to the door. "That rude and selfish man is on his way home to spend the next twelve hours taking care of his wife."

Alex walked past Suzanne and yanked open the silverware drawer.

"His wife? Why?"

Taking a deep breath, Alex looked over at Suzanne again. "She's dying of cancer. So if he didn't bow and scrape and wait on you hand and foot, it might be because he could have been doing those things for someone he truly cares for instead of someone that just insists that he does."

"I had no idea."

"That's because, as always, instead of bothering to have a conversation and maybe get to know him a little bit, you decided you knew what he was all about and dismissed him as beneath you."

"That's not fair!"

"Fair or not, it's the truth."

Suzanne just stared at her a minute. "I'm sorry."

"Don't tell me. Tell him." Alex glanced at her watch and frowned. "Marcus should have been here by now."

"I really am sorry about Razz." Suzanne hesitated. "Razz…is that his real name?"

Alex sat down on the sofa and stretched her legs out. "That would be a really good question for you to ask him."

26

Something was wrong. Marcus was very, very late, and he wasn't answering his cell. Alex refused to wait another minute.

"Where are you going?"

"To find Marcus."

"He's a big boy, Alex." Suzanne uncurled from the sofa with the grace of a Persian cat on a satin pillow.

"He's never late like this without calling. Something is wrong." She stopped for a second, then reached for her cell. "Come on, Razz. Answer."

"Why Razz?"

"Razz has a backup of Marcus's alarm system." She folded her phone and shoved it down in her pocket. "I have to go." She opened the front door. "Stay here and I mean stay inside. Don't let anyone in."

"Including Marcus?"

"Marcus has a key. You wouldn't have to let him in."

All the way up 270, Alex kept trying to call Marcus. No answer. A hundred scenarios tormented her, and each one ended with her never seeing Marcus alive again. It shook her as nothing ever had. Not having Marcus in her life was unthinkable. He was her best friend—the one person in the world she knew would never let her down.

She pulled up to find Marcus's driveway hosting two police cars, lights flashing. Her heart leaped straight up into her throat. Hands shaking, she ran to the front door. An officer stopped her. "I'm sorry, ma'am. You can't go in there."

She whipped out her badge and flashed it so fast she doubted he could have said whether it was gold or silver. "This is my partner's house. Nothing is going to stop me, short of a nuclear explosion."

Darting in past him, she ignored his call for her to stop.

"Alex."

Her boots skidded a little on the hardwood floors as she spun to a halt. "Lt. Mosley." She and Marcus had worked with Mosley several times over the years and had a good relationship with him. "Where is Marcus?"

Mosley lifted his eyes to the staircase where the EMTs were bringing Marcus down on a stretcher. "He's unconscious, but no apparent wounds."

She ran over to him, elbowing her way in to get close. "Marcus!" He looked so pale and still.

"Do you know if he was taking any medications?"

Alex shook her head. "Not that I know of. You didn't find any wounds?"

"Not so far. We'll be taking him to Frederick Memorial Hospital. You might want to meet us there and give them all the information they'll need."

"Sure. I'll be right behind you."

Mosley followed her. "Looks like he interrupted a robbery."

Marcus's leather bomber jacket hung on the post at the bottom of the stairs. She picked it up and held it close. "It doesn't look like a robbery."

Mosley pointed up the stairs. "His office is all torn up. You might take a look for us and see if you notice anything missing."

They climbed the stairs together. She stopped in the doorway and looked around. The desk had been swept clean. The file drawers were open and most of the files scattered on the floor. The pictures and plaques had been yanked from the walls and smashed. "It wasn't a robbery. They were looking for something in his files."

"How do you know?"

Alex pointed to the windowsill in the corner of the room. "The Bose stereo. They didn't take it. And Marcus's laptop is there on the floor. No, they came in here looking for something specific. Not to rob him." She clutched the jacket tighter. "But if they didn't shoot him or stab him, why he is unconscious?"

Mosley shrugged, shoving his hands into his pockets. "The hospital will find out, I'm sure. He'll be okay."

"They drugged him." She spun on her heel and headed downstairs.

"Wait!" Mosley came hard after her. "What are you talking about?"

"It's a case we're working on. They stuck her with a needle. Drugged her. It was over two hours before she woke up. I'll bet anything that's what happened to Marcus. Somehow they got the jump on him and rather than fight him, they just knocked him out with drugs."

Alex climbed in her car and backed out of the driveway.

———

Screams pulled Merry from a deep sleep. Groggy and disoriented, she almost yelled at her sister to shut up, but quickly realized that she wasn't home. And that wasn't her sister screaming.

Bolting up in her cot, she grabbed the bars and looked down the row of cells to where two men in white scrubs were trying to get the girl called Alice off her bed and onto a gurney. She fought them, clawing and kicking and even biting when she got the chance.

One of the men finally backhanded the girl hard enough to make her slump into the other man's arms. They quickly strapped her down.

Merry felt a cold chill run down her spine.

One of these days, it would be her turn. She'd be strapped down, wheeled out, never to return.

Two other girls and the one boy in the group all had their faces pressed against their bars, watching as intently as Merry. There were seven windowless cells, set inside a concrete-block room. Each cell was framed by bars on three sides and across the top.

Concrete floors slightly sloped toward a drain in the middle. The entire room felt like a basement—a little damp, a little cool, a little musty. It reminded her of the bomb shelters she'd heard her grandparents talk about.

One of the girls looked over at Merry and then quickly looked away. They were united against their fate, and at the same time, they couldn't bring themselves to reach out to each other. No one wanted to be the next one to go—and who wanted to become friends with someone while hoping they went next?

As the gurney passed, the girl looked straight at Merry. Her despair and pleading made Merry want to turn away, but if she were the one being wheeled out, she'd want someone to look her in the eye and acknowledge her life. And her death.

27

Someone was going to pay dearly.

Alex was on a tirade and even the emergency room nurses gave her a wide berth. She was finally permitted to sit with Marcus. She held his hand and gave up trying to be strong. She allowed herself to cry.

So far, he hadn't so much as flickered an eyelash. If it wasn't for the constant beeping of the machines, reassuring her that his heart still beat and his lungs still pulled air, she would have believed him dead.

He was so pale. She traced his cheek with her fingertips. "You aren't allowed to die on me, Marcus Crisp. You can't leave me. I'm going to call Suzanne and tell her we quit. She wasn't worth your heart then, and she isn't worth your life now."

She ran a finger over his lips. "Come on. Wake up and tell me I'm worried for nothing. Tell me what these people did to you. They're taking forever with the tox screen. I'm not sure they even believe me about someone injecting you with some drug. Please tell me I'm right and you're going to be fine."

Swiping at her tears, she leaned over and kissed his forehead. "You are the best thing that ever happened to me. There's never been anyone in my life that understood me the way you do. Or cared about me the way you do."

One of her tears dripped down on his cheek and she brushed it away. "Look at me. I'm a mess. I've never been so scared in all my life. Wake up, Marcus. Please."

Lt. Mosley stepped through the curtains. "How is he?"

Alex straightened her shoulders. "No change. Any word on the tox screen?"

"They said they found traces of chloral hydrate, carisoprodol and Rohypnol. A nice little knockout combination that won't give him much more than a groggy headache."

"They're sure?"

"Positive."

She sank down in the chair, unable to stop the tears. Mosley put a hand on her shoulder. "He'll be okay. I promise."

"I'm going to find the men that did this to him, and I'm going to seriously hurt them."

Mosley grinned as he squatted down in front of her. "Just don't tell me about it."

A little laugh erupted, surprising her. "Plausible deniability, eh?"

"I'd hate to arrest my favorite PI."

"Yeah. I'd hate that too."

"Does any of this have to do with the Kidwell case?"

"I'm pretty sure it has everything to do with the Kidwell case. We've had calls warning us off. They've broken into our offices and harassed Razz. Now this. Why is someone going to so much trouble to keep us from investigating?"

———

Suzanne's hunger finally forced her to give up on Alex and raid the refrigerator for something to eat. She passed on the tapioca and went for the roast chicken and asparagus. Leaving the dishes in the sink, she went through every cabinet until she finally found a few bottles of liquor. She settled on bourbon and, ignoring the fact that it had never been opened, grabbed a water glass out of the kitchen and settled on the sofa with the bottle and her laptop.

Flipping through the television channels, she bypassed the news to find an old black-and-white movie. Turning the sound down, she opened her laptop and worked on ideas for future shows.

And each time she found herself wondering if there would be any future shows, she would take another drink. Soon, the entire bottle was empty and she was staring bleary-eyed at the computer screen.

———

Alex walked into her condo to find Suzanne passed out on the sofa, snoring worse than a grizzly bear. Wrinkling her nose, Alex picked up the empty bottle and the glass and took them into the kitchen.

She heaved a sigh at the sight of the dirty kitchen. Alex never claimed to be the neatest or most organized woman in the world. The truth was she was a slob. But it bothered her when a guest left a mess for her to clean up. Or maybe it was just Suzanne that aggravated her. The least the woman could have done was toss the dishes in the dishwasher.

Too tired to deal with it, she tossed a blanket over Suzanne and headed for her bedroom. Sitting on the edge of her bed, she kicked off her boots.

Marcus had argued to be allowed to leave, but the doctors refused. One night for observation and then he could go home in the morning. Alex promised him she'd be there bright and early to spring him.

Sweeping the clothes she'd left on the bed to the floor, she stretched out. Marcus couldn't recall much except a shadow coming at him from the hallway. Everything after that was a total blank.

She didn't care what he could or could not remember. He was alive.

Closing her eyes, she hugged her pillow. She almost lost him. And it would have been her fault. She was the one that insisted they take Suzanne's case. Maybe she wanted to prove something to herself. Maybe prove something to Marcus.

Definitely to show Suzanne that Alex was firmly fixed in Marcus's life, and no one, including Suzanne, was going to replace her.

That bit of ego had nearly cost her more than she could admit.

———

Willard Mandeville slowly moved toward Bobby Carl. "I told you to find something for me, not put him in the hospital. Those drugs were only to be used on Suzanne Kidwell. You idiot. Don't you think they'll connect this to her now?"

Bobby wrung his hands as he backed up a step. He knew his boss enjoyed it when his employees were scared. And it only increased Bobby's fear. "I was just trying to do what you told me. I didn't expect him to come home. When I listened to the bug we planted in their office, they said they were heading to the girl's house, so I thought the coast was clear. I didn't plan on stickin' 'im with the needle, but he would have attacked me. I knew you wouldn't want 'im to be able to identify me."

Bobby backed up, as if that would save him. He knew he had made a huge mistake.

"You failed me," Mandeville said.

"It wasn't a big thing. I swear. Crisp never got a look at me. He doesn't know I stuck him. I'll make this up to you, I swear."

"It's too late. You've done too much damage. You may have blown my cover."

Bobby turned to run, only to realize that another man was standing behind him. He ran straight into the man's knife. He stared up at the acne-scarred face and felt himself babbling, but he knew it was incoherent.

28

Sunday morning, May 10

The sun streamed in through the sliding glass doors when Alex drew the drapes open. The sky was a brilliant blue, and puffy white clouds drifted lazily in a soft morning breeze. A light jacket would do. The weather report said it would reach a high of seventy-five by midafternoon.

Alex leaned down and shook Suzanne's shoulder. "I'm leaving now. Suzanne? Are you listening?"

"Quit shouting," she mumbled thickly.

Alex stepped back out of range of Suzanne's breath. "I'm not shouting. Razz can't be here today."

Suzanne opened one mascara-smeared eye. "You're leaving me here alone?"

"Well, I can't stay here to protect you."

Slowly sitting up, Suzanne held her head with both hands as if she were afraid it was going to fall off. "Let me go with you."

"Why would you want to do that?"

"I need to do something."

"If you want to do something, clean up the mess you left in the kitchen."

"I'm talking about the investigation, Alex. I need to do some more research into the senator, and you have my files."

Not once had Suzanne asked about Marcus. The woman was amazing in her self-absorption. "And what about the mess you left in my kitchen?"

"Don't you have a maid?"

She did, but that wasn't the point. "That was my father's bottle of bourbon you drank last night. You *will* replace it."

"Fine. Whatever. Let me go with you."

She didn't like it, but the woman was her client. If she wanted to help work on her case, she had the right. "I'm leaving in fifteen minutes. If you're not ready, I'm going without you."

Suzanne got up and slowly moved down the hall. At the speed she was moving, Alex would be going to work without her. Alex pushed up her sleeves and started rinsing the dishes and loading the dishwasher. Then she wiped everything down. When she glanced up at the clock, twenty-five minutes had gone by.

Grabbing her jacket, she headed for the front door. "I'm leaving now."

"I'm coming, I'm coming. You'd think you had to be there at a certain time. You own the place, in case you've forgotten." Suzanne ran into the living room, her hair still damp and her face without a lick of makeup. But she was dressed to impress with a designer suit and a pair of heels that made Alex's feet hurt just to look at them.

"I don't think so," Alex said pointedly.

Suzanne looked down at her outfit. "What's wrong with it?"

"Imagine someone shoots at us. We have to run. How far will you get in that tight skirt and those heels?"

Rolling her eyes, Suzanne disappeared down the hall and returned five minutes later in a pair of jeans, a red silk blouse, and leather flats. Shaking her head, Alex locked up the condo and headed for the elevator with Suzanne chattering mindlessly the whole way. It was not starting out to be a banner day.

While Suzanne used the vanity mirror to apply her makeup, Alex drove. It wasn't until Suzanne snapped the mirror back up in place that she realized they weren't anywhere near the office. "Where are we going?"

"The hospital." *And if you'd bother to think about anyone but yourself, you'd have already asked. Then again, you're probably too hung over to think straight.*

"Why?"

"To pick up Marcus."

"Marcus is in the hospital?"

Alex did a quick end run around a slow-moving car. "You may recall that Marcus was supposed to show up last night with dinner. We were going to work on your case. When he didn't show up, I went looking for him. Do you recall any of that, or were you already hitting the bottle?"

Suzanne shifted in obvious discomfort. "I didn't start drinking until long after you left."

"But you didn't stop to wonder what was taking me so long?"

Suzanne glared, her eyes all but burned with righteous indignation. "For all I know, the two of you were having dinner out. Or went to help someone. Or got caught up at the office. How was I supposed to know Marcus was in the hospital?"

The woman had a point, but Alex refused to acknowledge it. "Marcus was attacked last night when he got home. He was given a drug that knocked him out and left him a little fuzzy."

Suzanne's expression changed in a flash, lighting up with excitement. "That's exactly what happened to me. This is great!"

"It's great that Marcus got hurt?"

"No. Of course not. But it's great that he got the same drug I did because now they'll have to believe me."

Alex wanted to grind her teeth. "You never think of anyone but yourself, do you? Are you even capable of considering someone else, or was that left out of your DNA?"

The excitement faded and Suzanne's face went hard, her eyes curiously flat. "If you were facing life in prison for a murder you didn't commit, you'd be a little self-absorbed too."

"Not when it comes to Marcus," she replied softly.

"That's because you're in love with him. Do I care that he got hurt? Yes. Do I want him to be okay? Yes. Do I still think that this attack could help my case? Yes. If that makes me selfish, so be it." Suzanne shifted in her seat. "And you weren't hired to judge me or my personality. You were hired to find Cecelia's killer. Why don't you spend a little less time pointing out my faults and more time doing what you're being paid to do?"

Alex's smile came on slow until she was nearly grinning. "You are so absolutely right." She whipped the car over to the exit lane and pulled off at the Urbana exit.

"What are you doing?"

"My job and nothing more than that." There was a convenience store, a gas station, and a Waffle House. Alex pulled up in front of the Waffle House. Suzanne could sit and have some breakfast while she waited. "I suggest you call your attorney and tell him to come get you or send someone for you. I'm done taking care of you."

Suzanne's eyes went wide with disbelief. "This is a joke, right?"

"No. As you just so eloquently put it, I was hired to do a job. Now get out."

—

Marcus knew something was wrong the minute Alex stormed into his hospital room. "You ready?" she asked.

"Absolutely. But what happened?" The attendant began to wheel him out of the room and down to the elevator.

"I'll explain later."

When they reached the curb outside, Alex helped Marcus climb into the car. "I am not an invalid and I am quite capable of walking on my own and getting into a car. Will you stop hovering already?"

"Seems I can't do anything right today." Alex slammed the car door, muttering under her breath.

Marcus snapped his seat belt and waited for the storm to hit full force. She was on a tear, and until she got it all out of her system, there'd be no living with the woman.

He gave her five minutes and then started pushing. "Not talking to me today? Let me think. What did I do wrong?"

"Nothing. Let it go."

He shook his head. "Nope. No can do."

"Your little girlfriend helped herself to my father's very expensive liquor. And not for just one shot. Oh no. She drank the entire bottle. And that was after she trashed my kitchen. Then she wants—no, she *insists*—on coming to work with me today. Then when she finds out that you were hurt last night, does she ask if you're all right? No. She gets all excited because this proves she's innocent, and isn't that just the best thing ever?"

Marcus compressed his lips and tried not to smile. Not to speak. And to keep his face expressionless.

"I left her at the Waffle House. Let her attorney protect her, cart her around, and put up with her insufferable attitude. It's not in my pay grade."

He wasn't sure he was allowed to laugh or not, so he chose not to. "Alex, if she's killed at the Waffle House, we don't have a client to pay us."

"At this point, I don't care."

"Alex."

"Oh, fine. We'll swing by there and make sure she's okay. But I am not going to take care of her anymore."

"Works for me."

Ten minutes later, they pulled into the Waffle House parking lot and found Suzanne sitting in a booth having a cup of coffee. When she saw Marcus, she jumped up and tossed her arms around him. "Oh, Marcus. Are you okay? Are you sure you should be out of the hospital?"

When Marcus released her, Suzanne stepped back and then cupped Marcus's face with her hands. "I was just so upset when I heard about the attack. It's just so terrible."

"I'm fine." Marcus saw Alex's eyes narrow and knew Suzanne was walking a fine line between having a killer hunting her down and having Alex do the job for him. "Get your check and let's get out of here. We have a lot of work to do."

Suzanne flashed Alex a look and sauntered away. Marcus reached out and gripped Alex's hand. "You're the better woman, remember that."

"I'm going to kill her."

"Not until we get paid."

The trio piled into the car and headed over to Marcus's home so he could get cleaned up and changed. When they pulled into the driveway, a black sedan with tinted windows was sitting in front of the house.

"Were you expecting anyone?" Alex asked Marcus.

"No." He stepped out of the car.

The sedan's driver climbed out and opened the rear door. Louis Barone emerged, straightening his overcoat. "Marcus, my old friend. I heard you were hurt. I trust you are well now."

"I'm just fine, Lou. I'm touched that you'd come all this way just to see to my welfare."

Louis's smile was every bit as polite and false as Marcus's. "I heard you were looking for me." He spread out his arms. "And here I am. I felt if you were putting so much work into trying to locate me, it must be very important, no? I only wish to cooperate."

"You know what happens on the streets. Nothing is done that you don't know about. There is someone out there using an injection with several drugs, including Rohypnol and chloral hydrate, to incapacitate their targets. I need to find out who that is."

"And if I do this for you…" Louis grinned. "There is something you can do for me?"

"Depends on what you want."

"Tonight. You and Alex must visit the house on Spring Street. You know the one of which I speak?"

Marcus nodded.

"Perhaps you would care to take a few pictures that would be, as you say, secret? Of course, you will be escorted out, so you must do what you need to do quickly. You understand?"

"I understand."

"Around ten would be perfect."

"And what would I do with these pictures?"

"Merely send them to the man. You will understand. So will he."

Marcus thought about it for a moment and then nodded.

"There's a man named Bobby Carl. He lives in Wheaton." Louis reached to the inside pocket of his suit and pulled out a small notebook and a pen. He wrote down an address, tore out the paper, and handed it to Marcus.

Marcus nodded. "I understand. And I appreciate the help."

"I find it difficult to believe Bobby Carl would be a killer. He is, as you Americans like to say, a weasel."

Louis turned to Alex and for the first time, his smile was genuine and warm. He pulled a business card from his pocket and handed it to her. "If ever you should care to leave this man, I would give you a place of honor in my business."

"It'll never happen, Louis." Alex offered him a smile.

Louis nodded and turned away. His driver opened the car door and Louis folded himself inside.

No one moved until the car disappeared down the driveway.

29

Marcus stared at the documents Razz had printed from Guy's laptop. He slid each read page down the conference table to Alex while Suzanne sipped her coffee.

"This just keeps getting worse and worse." Alex grabbed her soda.

"This is beyond sick. Beyond twisted. It's just plain evil." Marcus ran a hand through his hair. "But why go after Suzanne?"

Suzanne smiled as if suddenly very proud of herself. "Because I was investigating two of the girls' disappearances. They clearly thought I was getting too close."

Marcus twirled his pen through his fingers and stared at the ceiling. "Doesn't play for me," Marcus finally announced.

"Why not?" Alex asked.

"Because she was off track. *Way* off track. She went after the principal of the school. She reported it as a sex thing. So why kill her? She was helping them by being wrong."

"And yet"—Alex lifted a finger—"someone tried to blow up her car, even *before* she had the briefcase."

Suzanne shook her head, her frown deepening. "You're right. It doesn't make any sense. I didn't know about any of this until after Guy was killed. And even then, I didn't have the full picture. We still don't."

"You knew something, whether you realize it yet or not," Alex replied.

"Okay." Suzanne looked from Alex to Marcus and back again. "I'm just more confused now. Guy is dead. He was the surgeon. Wouldn't his death put an end to it?"

"Good question." Marcus picked up his water bottle. "More than likely, Guy wasn't the only surgeon involved. And the senator would be the go-to man for the patients."

"But why teenagers?" Suzanne asked.

"Because," Alex interjected, "they're young and healthy and considered to be runaways. A lot of runaways disappear and are never seen again. That makes them a relatively safe pool to draw from."

"So we still need to prove that Sterling was partners with Guy in this."

"Yes," Alex replied. "Nothing in Guy's files does much more than prove that he was in touch with him on a regular basis."

"But what about the references to Sterling's calls about organs and blood types?"

"Still isn't proof enough," Alex told her.

Marcus placed his hands on the table. "First things first. We need to talk to this Bobby Carl."

"Well," Alex replied, "I've made some phone calls, and now we have eyes on the ground watching for him. As soon as he surfaces, we'll talk to him."

Marcus wasn't so sure. "*If* he ever surfaces."

"What makes you think he won't?"

"Whoever this guy is, I'd be willing to bet that he messed up last night. Giving me that shot was a huge mistake, and by now, whoever hired him knows that."

Alex nodded. "No argument. So you think he's dead?"

"If he's not, I'd lay odds he will be soon."

There was a quick rap on the door and then Razz eased it open. "Alex, I think I found something you need to see."

Alex stood up. "Excuse me a minute. If anything exciting happens, don't start without me."

She followed Razz back to his desk.

"Talk to me," she said, leaning over his desk so she could see his laptop.

Razz dropped down in his chair and swiveled it around. "I kept tracking that e-mail address in Merry's case. Over the past three years, he's used three variations of the same name. Guess where from?"

"Where?"

"An Internet café in Arlington."

"You are a genius."

"I know. And it gets better." Razz flashed her a wide grin. "I found two e-mails in his in box and was able to access them."

"Do I want to know how you did that?"

"I could tell you, but then I'd have to kill you."

She shot him a look and he grinned wider. "Tell me it was worth it."

"Oh yeah. Look at this. One is a confirmation of an ad he's placed on one of those dating Web sites. He claims he's eighteen, has his own apartment, is looking for marriage, loves dogs, long walks on the beach, candles, and romantic music."

"Geesh. He could be a little original, couldn't he?"

"Not if he's looking to attract desperate girls. The other e-mail was from a sixteen-year-old in Delaware. Says she, too, loves dogs and long walks on the beach, yadda yadda."

"Can you put those back so that he doesn't know we read them?"

"Already done. He'll be none the wiser."

"Monitor his mail. I want to know if he makes arrangements to meet her and if so, where. I want this guy. Can you track his outgoing messages?"

"Sure. I responded to his ad with a keystroke bug. He opens the e-mail, and I have him."

Alex gave him a pat on the shoulder. "That's why we pay you the big bucks. Give me the address of this café."

"What are you going to do now?" Razz asked.

"I think Marcus and I will take a drive out there and look around. He has to be setting up close by. I want to check out the café. Maybe we'll get lucky."

30

Suzanne stayed in the conference room after Marcus and Alex left for the coffee shop. She toyed with the files spread out in front of her. Each folder represented an acclaimed exposé; only some of the people weren't as guilty as she had made them out to be.

But that was the nature of the business. Why didn't anyone understand that? People wanted sensationalism. They wanted to see people fail and fall. They wanted to watch the humiliation of bullies and tyrants.

She flipped open one of the files. The principal she'd accused of taking those two girls. The ratings had gone through the roof every time she updated the public. She had been so sure of him. Talking to that police officer, she had been so positive of the principal's guilt.

But in the end, he'd been innocent.

He'd been fired.

Reviled by the community.

Branded a pedophile and a killer.

And so he'd committed suicide.

It nagged at her. Maybe she should have checked with the detectives actually handling the case. Maybe double-checked the officer's story with the police chief. Maybe held off on filling in missing details.

But his death wasn't her fault. Not really.

Right?

Suzanne winced and pushed the folder away. No sense in worrying about it now. Nothing could be done.

So why do I still feel so much regret?

———

Marcus and Alex located the Internet café right away. But that was the only easy part of the day so far. None of the employees could tell them anything about the person who had used that computer.

"Do you have any idea how many people come in here and use these?" a cashier asked. "Unless they're in here every day and make a point to say, 'Hey,' we don't pay much attention."

The customers had even less to offer.

Once outside, Marcus shrugged. "Well, we didn't actually think he'd be sitting there waiting for us with a sign on his chest, did we?"

Alex fisted her hands on her hips as they stood on the sidewalk.

"I know, but all this time, I've been thinking they'd just run away—that I'd find them holed up in some drug den or sitting in an alley, wishing to go home. Instead, they've been dead."

"You don't know that."

"No, but the truth is, I don't hold out much hope."

———

Suzanne paid the cab driver and stepped over to the sidewalk beside a tiny house with broken shutters and barely-there lawn. She leaned down to talk to the driver. "You'll wait for me?"

"How long?"

"Ten minutes, maybe fifteen."

"Meter will be running, lady."

She nodded. "I understand. Please wait."

Stepping over a broken skateboard, she slowly climbed the stairs and rang the bell. She didn't hear it ring inside, so she knocked.

When the door opened, a young woman stared up at Suzanne with a trace of impatience. Suzanne watched the realization creep into her eyes. "You."

"Please. I just want to apologize."

"Apologize?" Peter Fryer's widow practically spit the word at Suzanne. "A little late, aren't you?"

"Yes. I am." Suzanne licked her dry lips. "I never meant for this to happen to you."

"My husband tried to tell you. You just wouldn't listen. You just wanted the ratings. The hype. The glory of bringing a good man down."

"I didn't know."

"You didn't *want* to know. Women like you never do. You paint a picture and then you look for the facts to match what you want everyone to believe. Doesn't matter if the facts are actually factual."

"I came here to apologize. And to see if there was anything I could do to help you."

"Help me?" The bitterness in the woman's voice forced Suzanne back a step. "I think you've done enough. Now get off my porch and don't come back."

The woman slammed the door in Suzanne's face. *And doesn't that say it all.*

Suzanne turned and walked down the steps. And discovered the taxi was gone.

"No!" She stomped her foot.

"Need a ride, miss?" A man stepped out of a dark sedan at the curb. "This neighborhood can be a dangerous place for a lady like you."

He was tall, clean-cut, with a disarming smile. But the man behind the wheel was a different story. Something about him made Suzanne want to freeze and flee, all at once. When he unfolded himself out of the car, he was even bigger and more sinister.

"Ms. Kidwell," the first man said, stepping toward her, "you don't have a choice in this."

"Why are you doing this?"

"Because it's our job. Our boss says, 'Go get this lady,' and we go get her. Coming back without you is not an option. Now, please. I really must insist—get in the car."

31

Sunday afternoon, May 10

When Marcus and Alex returned to the office, Razz was on his way out.

"The nurse just called. Mel's taken a bad turn. I have to go."

Marcus squeezed Razz's shoulder. "Go home. Stay there as long as you need to."

"I don't know if I can handle this."

"You will." Alex told him. "You're one of the strongest men I know. And we'll be there for you every step of the way." She looked around quickly. "Where is Suzanne?"

"Don't know," Razz tossed over his shoulder as he pushed open the door. "She took off right after you did. Wouldn't tell me where she was going."

Alex turned to Marcus. "Where would she go?"

"Home?"

"I doubt it, but I'll try calling and see if she answers." Alex started to pace. "That woman. I knew we shouldn't have taken this case. I'm going to go call Holden and let him know his client is AWOL."

Marcus went into his office and started calling the local cab companies and hit pay dirt on the second one. A woman had called for a pickup there and was dropped off in Langley Park.

He wrote down the address and then stuck his head in Alex's office. She was just hanging up with Holden. "Ted is righteously annoyed. Says he'll call us if he hears from her."

"I know where she went. Let's roll."

Alex opened her desk drawer, pulled out her gun, and holstered it as she followed him out.

Sunday traffic was light, but even so, it took them nearly an hour to get over to Langley Park. Marcus parked the SUV at the curb. There was no sign of Suzanne. "I'll check the house," Alex told him and ran up to the house.

The front door opened, revealing a tired-looking woman. Alex flashed her badge and asked, "Did you happen to get a visit from a Ms. Kidwell? Tall, blond—"

"She was here. I told her to leave. She did." She started to shut the door.

Alex put her hand out and caught it. "When was this?"

"Around eleven thirty."

"Did you happen to see how she left? A taxi?"

"Didn't notice; don't care."

This time when she went to shut the door, Alex allowed it. She rejoined Marcus down at the curb. "No help. Suzanne was asked to leave right after she showed up, which I would assume means she left shortly after the cab dropped her off. The woman said she didn't notice how Suzanne left, but surely she would remember an idling cab in front of her house."

Marcus looked around. "Maybe someone else around here was paying better attention."

But none of the neighbors had seen anything either. They finally gave up and headed back to the office. "Why would she take off like this?" Alex asked. "She knows her life is in danger."

"Don't ask me to figure out how a woman thinks."

"Hmph. Definitely not that one." Alex's cell phone rang and she pulled it out. "Talk to me."

"Alex?"

The sound of Razz's voice broken and full of tears alarmed her. "Razz? What's wrong?"

"Mel. She's gone."

Alex closed her eyes. "Oh, I'm so sorry. At least her pain is over." Alex's throat burned as she strained to speak over the lump of grief. "She's dancing on streets of gold."

"I know." Razz sputtered. "I know. I have to make a few more calls. I just wanted to let you know."

"Thanks. If there's anything we can do, you call us."

Alex closed the phone. "You heard?"

Marcus pulled up to a red light and stopped. "This is going to be so hard on him."

"I know."

"We'll be there for him as much as we can."

Marcus's cell phone rang as they pulled into the office parking lot. Alex answered it for him. "Marcus's phone." She switched over to speaker phone. "We're both here."

"Hey, it's Ted Holden. I just wanted to let you know that we found Suzanne."

"Where is she?"

"In jail."

Alex looked over at Marcus. He parked the car and turned off the engine before asking, "Why?"

"Her bail was revoked. A couple of thugs jumped her father this morning. Beat him up pretty good, and then threatened his wife if he didn't withdraw his bail guarantee. So he withdrew it. The bondsman had no choice but to send a couple of his fugitive agents out after her."

Alex frowned. "Is her father okay?"

"Shaken, bruised, broken wrist, but otherwise okay."

"What do you want to do, Ted?"

"There's not much I can do. I'm not going to put my money on the line for this. And there's no one else with those kinds of funds. Honestly, it may be the best thing for her right now."

"I can't disagree with that. Okay, we'll keep plugging along here."

"Keep me in the loop."

"Will do." She ended the call and handed Marcus his phone. "What now?"

32

Sunday evening, May 10

Suzanne pressed her hands over her ears as her cellmate—a tiny old woman with more wrinkles than brain cells—paced and muttered to herself. Incessantly. Why didn't someone come by and force her to quiet down?

"Judge not, lest ye be judged. You have no excuse. When you say they are wicked and should be punished, you condemn yourself, for you do the very same things. Judge nothing before its time."

"Please stop talking," Suzanne moaned.

The old woman ignored her and continued shuffling from one side of the cell to the other, fingers flying as if she were working an invisible puzzle.

"He that judges is the Lord. Smooth words hide a wicked heart. You are whitewashed tombs—beautiful on the outside but dead on the inside. You teach others; why don't you teach yourself?"

Suzanne grabbed the meager excuse for a pillow and tried to cover her head.

A guard stepped into the cell. "Kidwell? You have a visitor. Let's go."

"Gladly," Suzanne replied, scrambling off the cot. "If I spend one more minute in here with her, I'm going to need a strait-jacket."

The guard led her down to a private room. Ted Holden waited for her in his full lawyer mode—expensive suit, sharply pressed white shirt, and power tie.

"Ted! Thank goodness." She sat down at the table across from him. "How soon can I get out of here?"

"Unless you know someone with a lot of money they're willing to give you, no time soon."

"But my parents guaranteed my bail. I don't understand."

While he explained, she sat in disbelief, trying to take it all in.

"I hope you can see why they felt they had to comply."

"I do." All hope of release drained away. Something heavy settled down over her. "I'm going to rot in here. Everyone will just go on about their business and forget that I even exist."

"Suzanne, that's not going to happen. I'm working overtime preparing for your case. Marcus and Alex are tracking down every lead. We're going to prove your innocence. You'll be released."

She heard the encouragement in his voice and understood it. Nevertheless, she brushed it aside. "What if someone would rather kill me in here than let that happen?"

"You're in a special wing, not general population. Don't be melodramatic."

"Ted, the people after me clearly have a lot of power. Paying off a guard is no big deal to them."

"Well, the only option is bail. Do you know anyone else that might be willing to post?"

She thought for a moment. The station wouldn't do it. And Elizabeth couldn't, even if she were willing to consider it.

Only one place she could go.

She really didn't want anyone to call Will Mandeville and ask him for money. But did she have a choice?

Sure. Sit here in jail until someone killed her.

Suzanne sighed. "Willard Mandeville. You can call my secretary and get the number from her. He might be willing to help."

Ted wrote the name down and closed his notebook. "I'll give him a call. But you'll probably spend another night or two in jail."

"Ask him to hurry, Ted. I have a really bad feeling about staying here."

"Suzanne." Ted stood up, grabbing his briefcase. "Everyone in this prison has a bad feeling about staying here."

33

Sunday night, May 10

Large, stately homes lined Spring Street, flanked by towering oaks and cherry trees; turrets and balconies from the Victorian era jutted and curled; boxwood hedges divided the properties, some tall enough to deter prying eyes. To most of the world, it looked like a quiet, upscale neighborhood of lawyers, doctors, and stockbrokers. But most of the homes hid brothels, private clubs, and the safe houses of murderers and thieves in thousand-dollar suits. Alex couldn't understand why the authorities didn't just execute a zip code–wide search-and-destroy mission.

"Busy night," she remarked as she watched a Town Car pulling into the drive of the house they'd staked out.

"Probably like this most nights."

"Everyone knows what goes on in that place and yet the police never bother it."

"Too many high-powered clients. The police chief probably has free access to whatever he wants in there."

"I understand how it works. Doesn't mean I have to agree with it." Alex shook her head as she toyed with the camera. "So why would Louis want us to expose Michaelson?"

"Offhand, I'd say it's because he doesn't want to kill him, but he wants the DA to know how close he is to getting a bullet in the head."

"You'd think Michaelson would have been smart enough not to get in bed with Louis."

"I don't think it's Louis that Michaelson wants in his bed."

"Funny." Alex smacked Marcus on the arm. "I just have my doubts about this."

"It's no different than when we pay snitches for information."

"But Louis isn't asking for a twenty."

"Heads up, partner."

Alex raised the camera and shot several pictures of the district attorney's car as it slowed down and then turned into the drive. "Got the license plate. Perfect."

Marcus zipped up his coat and cut the engine, tucking the keys deep in his pocket. Alex double-checked her SIG and then climbed out of the SUV. Her job tonight was strictly backup. Marcus had the lead, wearing a tiny camera disguised as a bolo tie clasp.

The guard at the front door looked over, nodded, and walked away for a smoke. "I guess Lou really did clear the way for us," Alex said softly.

"Looks that way."

In spite of that, Alex was wary. Anything could await them on the other side of that door. Could be a few men like the DA having a good time. Could be six armed brutes, ready to mow them down as soon as they stepped over the threshold.

Marcus entered and Alex stayed at his elbow.

Smoke, alcohol, and perfume saturated the air, making Alex's nose twitch as she searched the room for the DA. It didn't look as she expected. No gilded mirrors or red velvet. She could have been in any living room in Washington, except for the mahogany bar along the far wall.

Marcus spotted Michaelson first. "Two o'clock." Alex's gaze moved slightly right.

The DA stood near the bar with a blond woman wrapped around him and a redhead kissing him. Trusting Marcus to be catching all the action in brilliant color, Alex watched the guards. The beefy crew seemed to take in everything except the investigators. Finally one of them—a burly black man with arms the size of small countries—nodded at Alex.

She tapped Marcus. "Hospitality hour is over. We need to go."

"We're good."

They stepped back out of the room as quietly as they'd entered. The guard met them at the door with a tiny smile. "You must leave now."

"No problem. Thank you."

He nodded and shut the door firmly behind them.

Marcus zipped up his coat. "I don't know if that redhead was told to plaster herself all over him or not, but I'm grateful. She gave me some great material."

"Stop right there." Two men stepped out of the shadows. One was a tall blond with military hair. The other was just as tall and twice as broad with dark hair and dark complexion.

"We were asked to leave. We're leaving," Marcus responded.

"And we're ordering you to stay where you are."

"By whose authority?"

"None of your business. Raise your hands."

Alex could tell by the way Marcus shifted his feet that he didn't plan to talk his way out of a confrontation. The dark one neared. "Would you mind opening your coat?"

"Why?"

"I'm not going to ask you again."

"Good. Then if you'll excuse us."

The man lunged at Marcus, and Alex whipped out her SIG and pointed it at the blond as he reached for his weapon. "I wouldn't if I were you."

Marcus swept his leg and caught his attacker on the side of his knee, buckling it. As the man stumbled, Marcus made three quick moves, leaving him sprawled unconscious.

Alex sighted the gun a little higher. "I suggest you take that out of the holster and toss it over here."

"Now, little lady, you need to be careful with a big gun like that. It might go off and hurt somebody. Or you could break a nail." He cackled at his own joke.

Alex frowned. "Really? Oh my, I never thought of that. Are you going to shoot me now?"

He reached for his gun. She didn't hesitate to pull the trigger. The man yelped, dropping his gun and grabbing his ear. "You shot my ear off!"

"Nah, just put a nick in the lobe, but don't you worry. I didn't break a single nail." She holstered her SIG, then picked up his gun and handed it to Marcus. "The next time you consider drawing on a woman, you just touch that ear."

The man fell to his knees. "You're gonna pay for this. When I get done breaking every bone in your hand, you'll never hold a gun again."

Marcus stepped closer. "Did I just hear you threaten my partner? I did, didn't I?" Marcus grabbed the man's right hand and slowly began to twist it. The man tried to wriggle away, but his efforts seemed to intensify his pain. Leaning down, Marcus whispered in the man's good ear, causing him to lose what little color he had left before passing out.

"What did you say to him?" Alex asked as they climbed back into the SUV.

"Just let him know how short his life would be if he tried to hurt you."

She snorted softly. "No kidding. I'd have to seriously hurt him."

"No. I told him what I would do to him. Slowly and painfully."

Alex opened her mouth to protest and then snapped it shut. If he wanted to play hero, let him.

"Not buying that my menacing persona could cause a man to faint? Fine. I may have *accidentally* hit a pressure point too. But it was mostly the threats that overwhelmed him."

Alex smirked. "So what's our next move?"

"Go back to the office, upload the pictures, send copies to Michaelson. And I want to send copies to Holden, just to be safe."

"You think that's a good idea? Wouldn't we be wiser to send it anonymously?"

Marcus pursed his lips as he appeared to think it over. "You just gave his bodyguard a .45-caliber ear piercing. How anonymous do you think we can stay?"

"Good point. But there could be a serious backlash."

Smiling, Marcus reached over to pat her hand. "Not to worry, partner. I think Louis has a solution for that."

"Why are you not concerned about this? I don't trust Louis."

"I don't either, but he came to us. Even if he has something up his sleeve, it's not going to hurt us."

"And just how can you be so sure?"

"Because Louis doesn't want us coming after him. In case you haven't noticed, he has always kept a respectful distance."

"Ivan breaking your ribs is a respectful distance?"

"Absolutely. He could have killed me."

———

Suzanne pulled the pillow tighter over her ears, but the old woman in her cell would not stop. She just kept ranting the same things, over and over. "Shut up or I'm going to shut you up, I swear."

The old woman ignored Suzanne's threats. "You judge others but cannot see your own sins. You will be judged just as you have judged. You condemn yourself with your accusations. Beautiful on the outside but dead on the inside."

"Shut. Up."

"You need to stop judging by mere appearances and make right judgments. If you are without sin, be the first to throw a stone."

Groaning, Suzanne rolled over to face the wall.

"Why don't you judge your own faults? You teach others; why don't you teach yourself? A false witness offers nothing but lies and will perish and whoever listens to his lies will be destroyed forever. For out of that corrupt heart comes nothing but lies and slander."

Of all the people to be locked up with, it had to be some old loon who didn't like her show. Okay, she had made some mistakes. She got that. And she'd accused a few innocent people of wrong-doing. She got that too. But how many times would she have to hear about it? When were people going to get over it and just move on?

———

Willard Mandeville poured two fingers of bourbon in a Waterford glass and slowly walked over to take a seat in one of the leather chairs in front of the fireplace. While he appreciated the convenience of gas, he missed the smell of wood burning. The pop and crackle and the occasional collapse of embers and ash.

Setting his glass down on the coaster, he opened the small humidor and pulled out a cigar. He didn't light it right away—there was something so soothing about rolling it between his fingers.

Patiently, his right-hand man stood by, hands in his pockets, waiting to find out why he had been summoned.

The man lit the cigar, puffed a few times and then exhaled. "It's time for the next stage."

The lackey nodded, his acne-scarred face expressionless. "Right away, sir."

Picking up his glass, the man took a long sip. While little showed on his face, inside he was humming with excitement. Just a few more days. Ah, the irony of it. Instead of *Judgment Day with Suzanne Kidwell,* it would be Judgment Day *for* Suzanne Kidwell.

———

Alex leaned over Marcus's shoulder as they reviewed the snapshots on his computer. "Cut this one," she said, pointing to the third photo in the collection. "It's a little blurry."

Marcus clicked the picture with his mouse and hit delete.

"I think that narrows it down enough." Alex straightened and stepped back. "Why do I feel a little sleazy?"

"I don't care much for this either, but we're not going to call the reporters and make sure this is tomorrow's headline. It's for his eyes only. Just a warning. No harm, no foul." Marcus pushed back his chair, folding his hands across his stomach. "But if you don't want to do this, we won't. Regardless of what Louis is after, I want

Michaelson to know that we have him dead to rights. If he is behind Cecelia's murder, he's going to panic and make a mistake."

Alex nodded her assent. "Okay, but answer me this. Why do you think Louis wanted these pictures taken?"

"Honestly? I think Michaelson crossed a line somewhere—maybe even Cecelia's murder—and Louis is smacking him down."

"I still don't understand why he used us. Why not have pulled Michaelson aside, let his goons rough him up a little, and be done with it?"

"Michaelson could have turned on Louis. Have his men arrested, or worse. No, Louis wants that one degree of separation."

"Okay, but we better not get burned on this, Marcus. Or I'm going to take Louis apart by more than one degree of separation."

"Which is exactly why I don't think Louis will double-cross us." He grinned up at her. "Even I know better than to get you mad, and Louis is every bit as smart as I am."

"Just not as ethical."

34

Marcus had barely rolled out of bed before the phone started ringing. He picked it up on his way down to the kitchen to start the coffee. "What?"

"Good morning to you too," Alex replied. "Turn on the news."

"Why?"

"Just do it."

He detoured over to the television and turned it on. Then continued to the kitchen and the coffee maker. "What am I going to see?"

"The district attorney resigning."

Marcus spun around on his bare feet and headed back to the living room. "Are you serious?"

"Deadly. The pictures, Marcus. Somehow they ended up on the front page of the newspaper. And they're being shown on every news channel. How did that happen?"

How, indeed? Marcus had only sent them to the private e-mail accounts of two people. "That is a very good question."

"We are in so much trouble, partner."

"Why? We didn't leak them to the press."

"No, but we took the pictures. How did this happen? No way would Holden do something like this."

"No. But I'm going to call him anyway. Maybe something went wrong on his end."

He hung up with Alex and dialed Ted Holden's cell. Ted answered on the second ring. "Tell me you didn't send those pictures out to the press."

"You don't even have to ask. You didn't either?"

"No. So how did they get out?"

"I have no idea. I assumed you and Alex had released them."

"No. We were very careful to only send them to you and Michaelson."

"Something went very wrong."

"No kidding."

"How did you get those pictures?"

"Louis Barone arranged—ah, geez." It hit him with all the force of a punch to the gut, knocking the breath out of him. "We were set up. I gotta go, Ted. I'll call you later."

———

Suzanne was surprised to wake up and find her cellmate gone. "Thank you, God."

"What?" the guard responded as she unlocked Suzanne's cell. "Nothing."

"Then let's go. Breakfast is getting cold."

Suzanne slipped into her jail-issue flip-flops and followed the guard down to the cafeteria. Thick cold oatmeal, thin cold toast, weak cold coffee, hot powdered orange juice, and overripe bananas. But since they weren't going to let her call her favorite restaurant for delivery, it was all she was going to get.

She sat down at a table by herself and picked at her food. At this rate, she'd lose twenty pounds before the trial even began.

"You need to stop judging by mere appearances and make right judgments. If you are without sin, be the first to throw a stone."

Suzanne closed her eyes and pressed her fingers to her temples, trying to push the old woman's words out of her head.

"A false witness offers nothing but lies and will perish, and whoever listens to his lies will be destroyed forever. For out of that corrupt heart comes nothing but lies and slander."

Now the headache spread down her spine. She nibbled at her toast, wishing the coffee was hot.

When she looked up, her guard was gone. That was unusual. The woman haunted Suzanne's every move like a ghoul. She couldn't even shower alone.

Suddenly, she felt someone behind her. Then something sharp pressed against her neck. "He wants you to know that he can get to you anytime, anywhere. You aren't even safe in your cell. Sleep with your eyes open, Kidwell. He is far from done with you. But one piece of good news—you'll never get to trial."

Then the pressure was gone, and her guard returned with a cup of steaming coffee. A flicker of something in the guard's eyes chilled Suzanne's blood.

They were going to kill her before she ever reached a courtroom.

———

Alex watched as Marcus hung his coat on the rack in his office and settled behind his desk. "I can't believe I didn't see it coming."

"It's not your fault, Marcus." Alex stood in the doorway, arms folded.

"Oh, it's my fault. You tried to warn me, and I wouldn't listen. I was so positive Louis was dealing square with us, and I wanted to slow Michaelson down in his race to convict Suzanne. That clouded my judgment, and Louis used it."

"Okay, self-flagellation time is over." Alex pushed off the doorframe and dropped down in the chair across from his desk. "What do we do?"

"I don't know. If the e-mails were forwarded to the press and they have our names as the sender, I expect the police will be breathing down our necks here shortly."

"I thought they don't reveal their sources."

"Depends on whether or not they want to protect us." He pinched the bridge of his nose. "I can't believe this."

"Okay, let's assume we're in trouble. What happens to us?"

"I don't know. I called our attorney to ask that very question, but he hasn't called back. We'll find out when he does." Marcus cupped his tea, elbows braced on his desk. "Do you get the feeling everything in this case is blowing up in our faces?"

"Not at all," Alex told him.

"No?"

She shook her head. "Seems to me, someone is playing a game and we're just pawns. Every time we think we're on to something, everything changes and we're off running in a new direction. And getting nowhere."

He slapped the arms of his chair and stood up. "For now, let's pretend this Michaelson debacle hasn't happened and continue our investigation."

They both stepped into the conference room and stopped short. Alex gasped. "Razz."

Dressed in jeans and a gray sweatshirt, he was disheveled and subdued. No color in his hair. No jewelry in his ears, nose, or lip. Just a dialed-down Razz, working on his laptop.

"What are you doing here?" Marcus walked over and touched Razz gently on the shoulder.

"I needed to be here. I had to get out of the house. Away from all the—funeral arrangements. Put my thoughts somewhere else. I hope you don't mind."

"Not at all," Marcus told him. "We definitely need you. I'm just so sorry about Mel."

Razz nodded and went back to typing on his laptop. "I just sent some pictures to the printer. I found them in an encrypted folder on the doc's laptop. Also, I found this document." He leaned back so that Marcus could see the screen. "It looks like a list of people that he received money from, and the amounts."

Marcus whistled low. "Half a mil. Two point two million. He wasn't selling anything cheap, was he? Can you print that out for me?"

Alex set the pictures on the conference table. After they were all lined up, she studied them, going from one to the next. In addition to several pictures of Guy with friends and business associates, there were several of kids ranging from about thirteen to one that looked to be about twenty-two. Male and female. Black and white and Hispanic and Asian. Young people who should have had their whole lives ahead of them. She recognized Britney and bit her lip as she studied the picture of the young girl sitting in what looked to be a cell, looking lost and afraid.

"Is that Britney?" Marcus asked, looking over her shoulder.

"Yes. I wonder if she's still alive?"

Marcus didn't have a chance to answer. The phone rang and he picked it up. Then he tapped Alex on the arm. "We'll be right there," he said and hung up. "We have Bobby Carl."

They met the caller in the parking lot of an abandoned grocery store a few blocks from Bobby Carl's apartment. The man, dressed in jeans, sneakers, and a T-shirt, had a beautiful black Doberman at his side. The dog was alert, but didn't appear to be aggressive. Then again, Dobermans were known to be smarter than their prey.

Marcus eyed the thin leather leash with a wary eye. One good lunge and that leash was history.

The man said something to the dog, which immediately lay down, resting his nose on his massive paws. "You said to call if I seen him, right? And I get money?"

Marcus nodded as he strode over to Bobby Carl's old Chevy. "When did you find him?"

"'Bout an hour ago, maybe. Was walking the dog and saw his car. Called you right off." The excitement on his face morphed into greed in the blink of an eye. "How much do I get?"

Alex reached into her pocket and pulled out a wad of bills. She peeled off two fifties and handed them to the man. "Here you go."

The man's eyes lit up as he snatched the money. "Thanks. I can go now?"

"Did you touch anything?"

The man shook his head. "Just called. That's all you said to do."

"You can go. Thanks."

Marcus leaned over and looked into the car, shaking his head. "Bobby, you must have been a very bad boy."

Bobby Carl was stretched out in the backseat. His face looked like some prizefighter had used it to practice for a couple of hours. One kneecap had been shot through, and both hands looked to have multiple breaks. But the death blow was a knife to the throat.

Alex glanced into the car and then looked away. "They weren't kind to him, were they?"

Pulling out his cell phone, Marcus shook his head. "Nope." He dialed 911. "I need officers at the old A&P store on Red Birch Road. And we need the coroner."

"Now what?" Alex asked.

"Back to square one."

35

Monday afternoon, May 11

Ted Holden was at lunch when he got the call from Lt. Mosley about Bobby Carl.

"We found several of those hypodermics filled with the same drug that Marcus Crisp was hit with," Mosley said. "The coroner also confirmed that Suzanne Kidwell's tox screen came back and she was injected as well. We also found several credit cards that belonged to Cecelia Forbes in his wallet. At this point, it looks like we found our killer."

"How soon will the charges against Suzanne be dropped?"

"We're waiting on something from the Assistant DA's office. He's in charge until Michaelson is replaced."

"Call me as soon as you know something, will you? I want to be there when Suzanne is released."

"Sure thing."

Ted ended the call and dialed Marcus. "Did you hear about Bobby Carl?"

"We were the ones that found him and called the police," Marcus told him.

"Well, good job. Looks like we're done here. They're going to release Suzanne."

"That's it? It's over?"

"I'd say so."

"But who hired Bobby Carl?"

"I don't know," Ted said, matter-of-factly, "and frankly, that's for the police to worry about. Our job was to get the charges against Suzanne dropped, and we've done that. Case closed."

"But did you see his file? His record is long but not exactly evil genius–type stuff. Bobby didn't do this alone. He didn't think this up. He was the puppet in a bigger play."

"It's no longer our problem, Marcus. Suzanne is free. That's the end of our involvement."

Ted ended the call and went back to his lunch. He should feel good. His client was going to be cleared of all charges.

So why did he feel as if this case was anything but closed?

———

"Wait a minute." Alex set her soda down and leaned over, bracing her arms on the edge of the conference table. "That's it? Case solved?"

"As far as Ted's concerned, it is. They're charging Bobby Carl with the murder, and they're releasing Suzanne."

Alex shook her head. "And isn't it convenient that Carl shows up dead, with the drugs and Cecelia's credit cards, so it can be all over, real tidy-like."

"A little too convenient, if you ask me, but Holden's right. It's up to the police to head down that road. We're done." He started scooping up all of Suzanne's files and shoving them down in the boxes, watching from a safe distance as Alex began to pace the room.

"And the senator wins? That stinks. He kills Cecelia, he kills Bobby Carl, he breaks into our office and your home, torments Suzanne, and he walks away, free as a canary. And what about those poor kids?"

"Free as a bird," Razz interjected.

Alex whirled on him. "A canary *is* a bird."

"But it's not a free one. It lives in a cage."

"Well, that's exactly where Sterling needs to be." She turned and pointed at Marcus. "We have to finish this. We need to prove Sterling was behind all this. We can't let him get away with it."

"The police will do that."

"Hah! You know as well as I do that the senator can block them even easier than he blocked us. They'll never be able to touch him."

"Then what makes you think we can?"

"Because we have right on our side. We can't be bought."

"I could maybe be bought," Razz said..

"We can't be intimidated."

"How about unsettled? Would it be okay if some things un-settled us?" Razz asked.

Marcus kicked Razz's foot, but Alex clearly wasn't listening anyway.

Alex slapped her hands down on the table. "I'm not done with this case. Not as long as he's getting away with murder."

"Um, guys." Razz looked up from his screen.

"We don't know for a fact that he's behind any of this. Strong suspicions, yes, but no clear proof."

"Yo, guys. Seriously." Razz snapped his fingers.

"The senator wouldn't be deflecting us every which way from Tuesday if he were innocent."

"You think this is the first time a politician will have gotten away with murder?"

Razz stood up. *"Hello!"*

Marcus and Alex turned toward him. "What?" they said in unison.

"That guy. He's made contact with the girl in Delaware. He's meeting her tomorrow night at the bus station."

"Oh no," Alex whispered.

36

Monday afternoon, May 11

Suzanne took a deep breath as she looked over the sea of press. Ted touched her elbow. "They want a statement. Be careful what you say."

Laughing at him, she patted him on the arm. "Relax."

She couldn't recall the last time she had been this happy. When they came to tell her the charges had been dropped, she didn't believe them. Now, she just wanted to laugh and cry and jump and dance. It was over.

Stepping up to the bank of microphones, she smiled out at the crowd. "I'd like to thank all of those who believed in me and fought so hard to prove what was obvious all along. I am innocent."

"Ms. Kidwell! Will we see you on the air next week on *Judgment Day*?"

"I don't know." Frank had scheduled a couple of reruns to cover for her while she cleaned up the mess in her life, as he put it. But now it was time to get back behind the wheel. "I'd like to."

"Suzanne, Suzanne! If you don't go back to *Judgment Day*, what will you do next?"

"I haven't really thought about it. Is your job available?"

The reporters laughed, and Ted pulled her away to a waiting car.

Suzanne sank down in the seat and laughed out loud. "I am free. No more jail. No more murder charges. I can go home, right?"

"You can go home."

She sank down in the seat. "Have Marcus and Alex been able to connect this Carl person to the senator?"

"I have no idea. I told them the case was over."

"Over? Ted, this isn't over."

"My job was to get you out of jail. You're out."

"Then take me home."

———

"There is something about this one that bothers me." Alex picked up one of the photographs they'd printed from Guy Mandeville's laptop. It showed four men on a charter fishing boat. "I feel like I've seen this before."

Marcus unwrapped his lunch. "Is it possible it was one of the pictures that we had before? The ones that were stolen?"

Alex shook her head. "I don't think so."

She stood there, staring at it. It was like a song that you knew but the words and the melody wouldn't come.

Her cell phone rang. She pulled it off her hip and answered it without looking at it. "Crisp and Hawthorne."

"Alexandria?"

"Father? What's wrong?" She stepped away from the pictures, totally focused on the call.

"Your mother is worse. She's on the way to the hospital now. I just thought you might want to know."

She felt the flutter of panic run all the way down to her toes. "I'm on my way."

"I've already put the plane in the air for you. It should land in Frederick in about an hour."

"I'll meet it there." She hung up the phone. "I have to go. It's my mother."

"Go," Marcus replied. "Stay in touch."

———

Suzanne took a long, hot shower, dressed in her favorite satin lounge outfit, straightened up the mess the police left, and had a couple of drinks while going through the mail. It was so good to be home. While she wanted to believe the worst was over, she knew that Sterling was still out there and she still had a target on her back. It was more imperative than ever to expose him for the evil fraud that he was.

And when she exposed him—when the story was released, maybe she'd demand a raise, or a better time slot. Maybe other job offers would pour in. She'd be even more famous. The big star falsely accused of murder, the district attorney fired, and a senator arrested for black-market organ harvesting. It was perfect for a movie of the week. Or a book deal!

She'd be able to sell it to the highest bidder. Name her own price. Maybe a two-hour special.

One letter addressed to her caught her attention. No return address. She ripped it open. There were just four words typed in bold letters across the page:

It isn't over yet.

37

Alex stepped off the plane and into a limo waiting for her near the hangar. The driver placed her one small bag into the trunk and then climbed behind the wheel.

"Welcome home, Miss Fisher-Hawthorne. I believe I am to take you straight to the hospital."

"Yes, thank you."

Closing her eyes, she leaned back, dreading what the coming hours might bring. She'd been trying to push the reality of her mother's condition behind Suzanne's case and those missing girls. But now, the sorrow and fear threatened to consume her. What if this was really it? What if she had to say good-bye?

She wasn't ready.

The hospital corridor was hushed except for the occasional squeak of a nurse's shoes and the steady bleeps of machines.

Alex found her father sitting sentry over her mother in their private room.

"How is she?"

Her father looked up, his face haggard and drawn, almost gray with misery. "Holding her own. She just fell asleep half an hour ago. I think she was trying to stay awake until you arrived."

Alex reached down and kissed her mother on the forehead. "What do the doctors say?"

"Days. Weeks. It's hard to be sure." He stood up. "Take a walk with me."

The walk took them down the elevator and into the cafeteria where they settled into a booth with coffee. "I want you to move home, Alexandria."

"I know. And I've told you no."

"But things are different now. Your mother needs you. I need you. I can't go through this alone."

Guilt wrapped around her and squeezed tighter than a python. "We've had this discussion before. I don't want to move home."

"So you don't care what's happening to your mother?"

Alex shifted in her seat and stared down at the now-lukewarm coffee. "I care very much. I can fly back and forth on weekends and some evenings when I don't have a critical case in front of me. But I don't have to move home to show that I care or to be there for either of you."

"I'm barely at the office anymore." He ran his hand through his perfectly cut salt-and-pepper hair. "I can't run the business and be with her as well. It's too much. I need you to take the helm."

"Father—"

He leaned forward, placing his hand over hers. "Promise me just one thing."

"What's that?"

"That you will think about it. Long and hard. Consider every angle. Weigh the pros and cons. Discuss this with Marcus. Then make your final decision."

He gently sipped from his cup and stared out the window, as if in a trance. After a few moments, he shook his head and broke whatever spell the glass had cast. "Why do you despise all that I have to give you? Was I such a bad father to you?"

A bad father? Where in the world did he get that idea? "No. You were a wonderful father. But some of the ways that made you so special to me are at the root of our problems today."

"Can you explain that to a very confused old man?"

She smiled. "Old, my foot. That nonsense doesn't work on me." She took a deep breath. "You remember all those wonderful parties you and Mother would host when I was little?"

"Yes. And you would always sneak out of your room to spy on everyone. You were so afraid you were going to miss something."

"I would wander through those rooms, invisible to everyone the way a small child always is. These beautiful, glittering people would gush all over you, telling you how wonderful you were. How smart. How successful. How brilliant. But the minute you were out of earshot, those same people would rip you apart." She saw the frown burrow between his brows and pull at his lips. "I don't mean to hurt you."

"You aren't. I am not so blind or seduced by compliments to misunderstand how it works. I am just sorry you had to hear such things. But not all wealthy people are like that, Alexandria."

"But could you see me in a board meeting with creeps like that? The minute one of them snapped at their secretary because their water wasn't cold enough, I'd be inclined to whip out my Glock and shoot a notch in their earlobe."

Her father chuckled, setting his cup down. "Will you allow me to offer a different perspective?"

"Go ahead." She sipped her cold coffee, even though it tasted like nail polish remover.

"Maybe you could wield your power instead of a Gluck."

"Glock."

He winked at her. "You could make a difference in the lives of a great many people, Alexandria. Be a breath of fresh air in a smoky old room."

She let the silence fall between them, comfortable enough to let his words sink in and attempt to put down roots. There was no guarantee that it would flourish and change her mind, but she respected her father enough to allow him the right to try.

When his cell phone rang, he frowned before answering it. "Hello?"

Alex gazed around the room, ignoring the phone conversation. A few minutes later, her father hung up. When Alex saw his face, she was immediately concerned.

"Father?"

"I need a moment to digest this."

"Digest what?"

"A heart has just become available for your mother."

———

Marcus looked down at his notes and then out the window at the storm clouds roiling in the distance. Something had to connect the senator to Dr. Mandeville. So far, everything they'd found pointed directly to Guy Mandeville and ended there.

A knock on his doorjamb pulled him from his thoughts. "Michaelson?"

The former DA wasn't the last person Marcus expected to see; the man hadn't even made the list. Marcus stood up. "Come on in." Then he turned to Razz. "Could you excuse us?"

"Sure." Razz gathered up his laptop and notepad and scurried off.

"Have a seat."

Michaelson settled down in one of the visitors' chairs. "I didn't mean to barge in, but I needed to talk to you."

"I'm listening. Would you like something to drink?"

Michaelson shook his head as he unbuttoned his suit coat. "No, thank you."

Marcus sat down. "So how can I help you?"

A twisted smile appeared on Michaelson's face. "Odd choice of words, wouldn't you say?"

Marcus didn't bother playing dumb. "Suzanne didn't kill Cecelia Forbes. There was no love triangle. The evidence was planted, and she was framed. You either knew or suspected, and yet you still went out there on the air and made sure everyone believed that Suzanne was guilty. Why?"

"And for that, you destroyed me?"

"I didn't destroy you. I sent the photos to you personally, not the press. That was someone else who wanted to see you brought down. I merely wanted you to stop and think about what you were doing to Suzanne. It's your job to convince the jury that someone is guilty. Not the public. Who put pressure on you?"

"How do you know someone did?"

"If not, it means you knew all along who killed Cecelia Forbes and that you were in on it."

Michaelson stood up, shoving his hands into his pockets, and walked over to the window. "How do you know I didn't?"

"Because Louis Barone would have gone out of his way to protect you. Right now, you frequent his girls, but that's nothing compared to the leverage murder would give him. You could be a lot of help to him in the DA's office. Yet he made sure you had to resign. So I think you did something that upset Louis, but it didn't have anything to do with Suzanne Kidwell."

Michaelson turned from the window and leaned back against the windowsill. "So why do you want to know who put pressure on me to go after Suzanne? It's over. She's cleared."

"She's cleared, but the man behind all this is still walking free. And this goes far deeper than you know."

"How deep?"

"Black-market organ harvesting."

Suzanne tried to call Marcus, but there was no answer. She tried his cell. It went right to voice mail. "Marcus, call me when you get this. I think I know how we can bring Sterling down. I'll be up for several hours, so if you and Alex want to drop by, feel free."

She had an idea she wanted to run by Marcus. It was simple, really. She should have done it before, but she was so sure she was going to find the proof she needed. Well, that didn't happen. So they could doctor some of the documents and make sure there was proof. By the time the senator realized he was in trouble, he'd be in jail. It was the answer to all their problems.

It wouldn't be the first time she'd done it. Sometimes the ends justified the means.

Pacing the living room, she started planning which document would be the easiest to doctor to make the greatest impact.

The doorbell rang.

Marcus? Setting her wineglass on the coffee table, she hurried over and yanked the door open.

She took a step back as Will Mandeville stepped in with another man, gun drawn. "What are you doing?"

"Forgive the pun, Suzanne, but it's your judgment day."

38

Late Monday night, May 11

Wake up, Suzanne."

She was cold. And she was sleepy. She managed to slowly open her eyes, but the light made her head hurt worse.

As soon as she closed her eyes, he hit her across the face. "You don't get to sleep right now, Suzanne. I want you to think about where you are and why you're here."

Suzanne squinted up at the man, wondering why he was in her bedroom, why he was waking her, and why he was so angry. "Go away," she whispered roughly.

"Wake up!"

Before she could reply, she was yanked up by the arms and slammed against a concrete wall. Her eyes flew open as lights exploded in her brain. The pain jarred her memory as she slid to the floor. He had come into her home. He had hit her. Several times. Then she had passed out.

She looked around. This wasn't her bedroom. And it wasn't her house. "Where am I?"

He smiled and snapped his fingers. Another man, even larger, grabbed her arms and lifted her up, tossing her onto a metal table hard enough to make her teeth rattle and cut her tongue.

"You are in the last place you'll ever see."

She took in the white concrete walls and floors, the surgical equipment along the wall, the bright lights overhead. The drain on the floor. Horror slammed into her.

"Do you like it? Quite a comedown for the high and mighty Suzanne Kidwell, isn't it?"

"You're going to kill me." The words sounded hollow coming out of her own mouth as if someone else was speaking her thoughts without her permission.

"I've been trying to tell you that, but you haven't been listening."

She tried to roll off the table. To run. Escape. Her bare feet hit the floor for a mere split second before she was picked up and slammed back down on the table, causing her to bite her tongue again. She tasted blood. "Why are you doing this to me?"

He leaned over so close, she could smell the cigar and coffee on his breath. "Because you had my son's briefcase, and you wanted to destroy me with it. Didn't work out quite the way you planned, did it?"

"You're wrong!" she cried out as he cuffed her wrists to the metal table.

"You always underestimated me, Suzanne."

She kicked out as he tried to grab her ankles. He punched her in the face. Pain radiated across her head as the man secured her ankles. Jail hadn't been the worst of it after all. "You did all this, didn't you? Pretending to be my friend. The adoption agency story. The lawsuits. In and out of jail. Charges pressed and charges dropped. You were just playing with me."

He smiled broadly, and for the first time, she saw the evil and madness glittering in his eyes.

"You're crazy," she said softly without realizing she'd said it aloud.

"Where is the briefcase?" He slapped her across the face. "I'm not playing anymore, Suzanne. I know you were with Guy for only one reason. You knew about the transplants. You wanted to destroy him. Destroy all of us. Where are your notes?"

She ran her tongue over her lip and tasted more blood. "What notes?"

The door opened again and a man in a white lab coat entered. A doctor. Could he save her? Why was he here? "Help me!"

The man tipped his head down and looked at her from over the top of his wire-rimmed glasses. "Not yet, my dear." He opened one of the white metal cabinets and withdrew syringes, blood tubes, and needles. He set them on a metal tray and pushed it over next to Suzanne. She tried to twist and turn to keep him from tying off her arm. "The more you fight, the worse this will be."

He swabbed the inside of her elbow.

"How can you do this? Don't you care about all the kids you're killing?"

The man in the lab coat inserted the needle and began to draw blood. "They're going to die anyway. They run away from home. Get involved in drugs and prostitution and worse. They get STDs and then expect the taxpayers to pay for their medical attention, food stamps, and welfare. Why waste time, waiting for them to kill themselves slowly? I make it easier on everyone. And get obscenely rich in the meantime."

He capped off the first tube and started another.

He pulled out the needle, swabbed her arm, and released the rubber tie-off. Gathering up his equipment, he said, "I'll run these samples right away."

Her captor waited until the doctor had left the room. "Anything else you'd like to say, Suzanne?"

"You have this all wrong."

"Do I? Well, let me tell you something I *don't* have wrong. You're going to die here. You wanted to expose all this? Well, why not experience it firsthand?"

Cold fear slid down her spine.

———

Alex and her father managed to spend a few minutes with Alex's mother before she was wheeled away to surgery. A nurse led them to a waiting room and offered them coffee, which they both declined. And the long wait began.

"How could this happen so quickly?" Alex asked.

"They said a heart just became available at this hospital and location carries a great deal of weight in deciding who gets it. Your mother is critical and the heart is here."

She couldn't help wondering how much the generous Fisher-Hawthorne donations had factored into the decision.

Her father reached out and clasped her hand. "It's probably those prayers."

"Most likely."

Over the next few hours, they napped, talked, drank coffee, and occasionally hit the vending machines for candy bars and chips.

When the doctor finally came in and reported that her mother had come through the surgery quite well, both Alex and her father let the tears of relief flow. After the doctor excused himself, her father pulled Alex into a hug. "I promised your mother that as soon as she's strong enough to travel, the three of us are going to take a nice little vacation. Maybe we'll rent that house on the beach in Bermuda that you both loved so much. Do you remember that?"

"A little. Mostly I recall the beautiful beach and the fact that I was so sick during the entire flight."

He smiled and sank down in a chair. "Oh yes. Poor thing. It was years before you would eat shrimp again. But you felt just fine by the time we reached the house. I don't think you even bothered to unpack before you were off looking for the young men in the area."

"I was not," she retorted with a touch of embarrassment. The memory hit her with all the force of a hammer between the eyes. She dropped into the chair next to him. "I knew I had seen him before."

"Who?"

"The pilot." She half turned in her seat. "The pilot that flew our plane to Bermuda. He worked for you, what? Ten years, maybe?"

"I don't know what you're talking about."

"He made a big deal of teasing me about being airsick. I didn't like it. When you sold the extra corporate planes—remember? Because you found out some of the executives were using the planes to take their families on trips without permission? He was one of the pilots that was let go. He was tall, blond, had a mustache, and he wore a black onyx stud earring."

Her father stroked his chin, his brow furrowed. "Oh yeah. I hated that earring. Told him more than once that it wasn't professional."

She jumped to her feet and started pacing. "His name? What was his name?"

"I don't recall, honey. Why does it matter?"

"Because he was in a picture with Dr. Mandeville and Senator Sterling. I knew I had seen him before. That picture kept bothering me, but I couldn't figure out why. I need his name."

"I can call the office in the morning and find out."

"Can we find out where he's working now?"

"I doubt that I would have that information. But you should be able to find that out easily enough. Pilots are licensed."

Her cell phone rang before she could respond. She looked at the screen. "It's Marcus." She answered the call. "Hey, what's going on?"

"Suzanne has disappeared."

"As in taken and gone?"

"Exactly. I'm at her place now. She left a message on my cell. But she's not here, and there are definitely signs of a disturbance. Her purse and cell phone are here on the table, door unlocked, but she's gone."

"I'm on my way."

"It's getting late. I just wanted to let you know. There's really nothing much we can do until morning."

"I'll meet you in the office bright and early." Slowly she ended the call and then looked over at her father. "Our client has disappeared, and it doesn't look good for her. I need to get home right away."

Her father sighed as he nodded. "I'll call and have the company plane waiting for you. There's no need for you to fight the airport and the airlines at this hour." He pulled out his cell phone and dialed. "And I'll call you with the pilot's information when I get it."

"Thank you."

"Kevin? I need the Gulfstream gassed up and ready to go in forty-five minutes."

39

Tuesday morning, May 12

Marcus was already in his office working when Alex came rushing in. "I got here as soon as I could."

She stopped in her tracks when she saw Buddy—the owner of the security company that installed the office system—working his electronic magic. Marcus nodded toward her, and they left the office without saying anything more until they were outside.

"Why is he here?" she asked.

"Our offices are bugged."

"What?"

When they reached the sidewalk, they stopped. Marcus leaned against the maple tree that separated the sidewalk from the parking lot. "They knew when we had those files in the office. And then they knew we had another set of copies. And they knew we moved them to my house. From there, they didn't know we moved them, but they hit my house looking for them."

"So you called Buddy?"

Marcus nodded. "First thing this morning. He confirmed we're bugged. He'll have us clean in a little while."

"What about Suzanne?"

"Nothing so far. The police are brushing this off. They don't believe she's been taken against her will. I don't know how much time we have. If any. He may have killed her already."

"I don't think so."

"Female intuition?"

"Because he promised he was going to make her suffer before he finished her off. Because he's going to want those documents back. And because he needs her alive to force us to hand them over." She glanced up at the building. "Where are all the pictures Razz found on the laptop?"

"Locked up in the storage closet. Why?"

"I recognized someone in one of them. He used to be a pilot on one of my father's corporate jets."

"I don't get the connection."

"Follow me on this. I talked to my mother's doctors about the procedure for an organ transplant. In addition to things like blood type and tissue compatibility, there's also a little matter of location. The closer the patient is to the organ, the better. Organs are usually packed up and flown to the patient. On very rare occasions, the patient is flown to the organ."

Marcus's expression sobered. "Oh, Alex. I forgot to ask. How is your mother?"

"She's good. Came through surgery with flying banners, and I was even able to talk to her for just a bit before I flew back."

"Colors."

"What?"

"She came through with flying colors. Anyway, I'm glad she's okay."

"Me too."

"Okay, I get that the senator and Mandeville would benefit from having a private plane to ferry organs and patients back and forth, but how do we know that this pilot in the picture is working for them? Maybe he's just a friend."

"I doubt very seriously that a pilot like this guy would be running in that social circle unless he was of use to them."

"And you think this pilot can lead us to Sterling?"

"It's worth a try. My father is going to call me as soon as he gets the guy's name. He says from there, we can track the pilot's license to find out where he's working now."

"Or for whom."

Alex smiled. "In the meantime, we have an early lunch date."

"With who?"

"Senator Sterling."

"How did you pull that off?"

"My father's feeling bad for something he said he shouldn't have done, but he wouldn't tell me what it was. He just said you would understand. You gonna tell me what that's about?"

"I don't think so."

She stared at him for a moment. There wasn't much he kept from her, but she wasn't the type to push him on things he felt he needed to keep to himself. So she let it go. "He made a luncheon appointment with the senator, who believes he's meeting with my father but will be meeting with us instead. We're going to ambush him."

"My kind of lunch meeting."

They arrived at the restaurant a few minutes before Sterling and waited in the back bar until he had been seated. As soon as the waitress delivered his drink, Marcus and Alex swooped in.

"What are you doing here?" he asked.

"Meeting my father for lunch. Didn't he tell you that we'd be joining you?"

The senator's knuckles turned white around the stem of his wineglass. "No. I don't believe he mentioned it."

"Oh, well, now you know." Alex picked up the menu. "What do you recommend?"

"Enjoy your lunch," Sterling said as he set his napkin on the table and started to rise.

Marcus reached over so casually, no one other than Alex would have seen it for what it was. But his grip on the senator's arm was hard enough to make Sterling wince and slowly return to his seat.

"Do we understand each other?" Alex asked softly, meeting the senator's angry glare with a calm and steady gaze. "Now, if you want this over quickly, we can do that. All you have to do is tell us where Suzanne is."

"I don't know what you're talking about."

"Oh, Senator. I had so hoped you would just be honest with us, but I guess we're just going to have to do this the hard way."

Sterling turned to Marcus. "Do you allow her to do all your talking for you?"

"Yep. She does it so well, don't you think? Now me, I'm not much of one for talking. I'd just as soon take you in the alley and beat the information out of you, but she insists on being civilized about this." Marcus smiled, his eyes dark and flat with barely contained rage. They reminded Alex of a shark's. "But don't push me too far, Senator, or I'll be inclined to overrule her."

"I don't know what you want."

"Tell us where Suzanne is."

"I have no idea."

Alex lowered her voice. "We know all about the organs and the teenagers you're snatching off the street. We know you and Guy Mandeville were partners. We know about the pilot. Do I need to keep going?"

Senator Sterling's eyes darted around the restaurant as he sipped his wine. "I've never heard anything so outrageous."

"And you don't know about Suzanne being missing?"

"No."

"And Marcus and I are completely wrong about this."

"Yes." His hands were shaking now. "This conversation is over."

"Oh, that's right. You're above the law. I had forgotten." She leaned in closer. "You may have managed to evade justice in some of your little schemes, but this isn't one of them. This is cold-blooded murder."

"I—," he boomed, and several nearby patrons snapped their gazes toward him. He adjusted the volume of his voice to a growl. "I don't know what you're talking about."

Alex rolled her eyes and sighed. "This is getting monotonous. Let's try another one. Remember all those things I just ticked off? We have documented proof for all of them."

His face drained of all color and his eyes widened. Good. She was finally getting through to him. "Now, Suzanne—she thinks this is all about you. Marcus and I? We're starting to get the impression that you just aren't smart enough to be the brains of this operation. So why don't you just tell us who is pulling your strings and we'll go away."

He wiped the sweat from his brow, dabbing at it with his handkerchief. "I can't...I can't help you."

Alex waited until the senator looked over at her before she smiled slyly. "Oh, it's okay."

She pulled a slender tape recorder from her pocket and set it on the table. Glancing over at Marcus, she winked at him. He winked back. He looked so relaxed, arms folded across his chest, leaning back. He totally trusted her to pull this off. She looked back over at Sterling. "Here, allow me." She hit the play button.

Her father's voice spilled out. "Senator Sterling came to me with a scheme to confiscate the property of private citizens so that he could turn it over to me for commercial development. Then I was supposed to pay his wife millions in consulting fees."

Alex picked up the recorder and shut it off.

The senator sputtered. "I never did that."

"Well, actually, you did. And my father is willing to testify. As are several of his key people. You're finished. Now, I might be willing to lose this tape and ask my father to forget about this if you tell me where Suzanne is and who has her."

"How can you do this to me?"

His self-absorption rivaled Suzanne's, Alex inwardly marveled. Or maybe it was nausea. "This isn't about you. It's about Suzanne. Where is she?"

He twisted the napkin in his lap. "I don't know. I swear. He's out of control. You have to understand. I did try to stop him."

"Sure you did. And I'm sure it was for all the right reasons. Who has her?"

Marcus leaned forward. Alex wouldn't have thought he could look any more lethal, but he managed to harden his face enough to make Alex glad she wasn't on the receiving end of his temper. "Yes or no. Someone else was running this show besides Guy Mandeville."

The senator's eyes darted around the room, and Alex wasn't sure if he was looking for an escape or just making sure no one overheard. "Yes," he whispered.

"Who?"

The senator snorted. "Some detectives you are. He was right under her nose the whole time. Playing like he was her friend. Like he cared about her."

"Who?" Marcus asked.

"He toyed with her. Like with a mouse. Arranged for her to move so he'd have the keys and the alarm codes. It was all a game to him. Pumping her for information. She told him everything. Every story she was working on. Every shortcut she was taking. She made it easy for him. It was all about setting her up."

"Who?" Then a moment later, said softly. "Will Mandeville."

Senator Sterling nodded slowly. "Give the man a prize."

"Where do you think he'd have her?" Alex asked again.

Sterling shook his head and then gulped down the rest of his wine. "Honestly, I don't know. It could be anywhere."

"It has to be a place where no one would hear her scream."

Alex thought the senator now looked as if he might toss his brownies. She scooted back from the table a little, just in case. "I don't know," he whispered. "I warned him this was going to destroy my career, but he wouldn't listen."

Sterling managed to pour himself another glass of wine. He gazed into the maroon depths and his face softened. Almost a look of relief. "Guy was the same way. Obsessed. He'd only been dating Suzanne for a couple months and was totally convinced she was going to marry him. He even ran the engagement notice before proposing. He was so sure, so obsessed with her. His father is that way. Totally obsessed with blaming Suzanne. But it was his own fault. He was so determined to get Suzanne out of our lives. Convinced that she was getting inside information from Guy." Sterling sighed and raised the glass to his papery lips. Drank and blotted his mouth. Met Alex's gaze with glassy hazel eyes. "He put the bomb in the car. But he can't see how he started all this."

"Give us something, Senator," Marcus finally asked. "He's planned everything so well up to now. He'd have made sure to pick a place no one could find."

Senator Sterling shook his head. "I swear, I have no idea. None. He could have her anywhere."

"Where does he keep the kids he snatches off the street?"

He swallowed hard. "I don't know. I didn't want to know."

Alex looked over at Marcus and he nodded. They were done here. Standing up, Alex leaned over and tapped the recorder with her finger. "Because what we did was a bit underhanded, I'm not going to turn this over to the police. But rest assured that when this is finished, they're going to come looking for you. And it will be your own fault."

He merely nodded, not even looking up at them as they took their leave.

———

For hours, Suzanne had been trying to find a way off the table. Her wrists were raw and bleeding. She finally gave up, staring up at the ceiling, crying. How could this have happened to her? One day, she's on top of the world, and then suddenly everything comes tumbling down. She had trusted Will. Believed him when he said he cared because Guy had loved her. And the whole time, he was plotting her death, looking forward to destroying her.

Alone and afraid, Suzanne's self-pity gave way to thoughts of the old woman in her cell. At the time, she had driven Suzanne to distraction, but now her rants began to make sense. Everything she'd said was close enough to the truth to hurt. Suzanne hadn't given a second thought to the people she'd hurt along the way. She hadn't cared about the truth. All that mattered was that she got what she wanted. And now she was in the hands of a man that didn't care about her as long as he got what he wanted.

Ironic, really.

Stupid. She was so stupid.

Instead of a national award for outstanding investigative reporting and the top show on cable news, she would die in obscurity.

When had she stopped caring if the story was true or not? When she'd come to Washington. When she suddenly realized she may have bitten off more than she could handle. When she realized she wasn't nearly as talented or ready for the show as she'd convinced herself she was.

Why was it so hard to earn respect? Or love? What was so wrong with her that her mother had to constantly berate her? She wanted to be one of those people like Alex, who didn't seem to care what people thought of her. People respected her. And Marcus loved her.

The sound of footsteps scraping along concrete and a door being unlocked interrupted her thoughts. Choking back a scream, she twisted her head, trying to see who it was. The doctor was back? Was it time to cut her open and take her heart? Her lungs? Her kidneys?

Would anyone even miss her when she was gone? Who would come to her funeral?

The door opened. Mandeville.

"Hungry?" he taunted, waving a brown bag in front of her face. "And I imagine you need to take a bathroom break." He signaled for his bodyguard to untie her.

It took her a few minutes to work the circulation back in her limbs and stop the tingling. Tentatively, she stood up. Her legs felt like rubber, but they held.

"I'm sorry about Guy. I swear I didn't know he would get hurt when he took my car."

He backhanded her across the face, sending her sprawling backward, smacking her head against the concrete wall.

"You do *not* get to talk about him! He was my son and you killed him."

Hot tears streamed down her cheek, and she slowly crawled to her feet. "I didn't. I had no idea."

"You were using him and you know it. Pumping him for information so that you could build your career."

"No. I didn't know anything until after he died. I swear."

He shook his head, eyes brilliant with hatred. He wasn't hearing her. He was beyond that now. "You led him on. You made him think you were in love. You got him so twisted up, he couldn't think straight. Did you get off on that? Did you feel powerful?"

She shook her head and whispered, "No."

"Liar!" he screamed. He used his fist this time. Something in her nose gave way under his knuckles, and blood, warm and sticky, gushed down her face and the back of her throat as she doubled over. Pain beyond anything she'd ever experienced radiated out, worsened with each passing moment.

He grabbed her by the hair and yanked her face back. "She doesn't deserve to eat."

Suzanne whimpered as she was hauled to her feet and slammed down on the table. She was too busy fighting the urge to pass out from the pain. Then again, maybe it would be best just to let go. She wouldn't feel anything. And maybe, mercifully, he'd kill her while she was unconscious and she'd never know.

———

Alex hung up with her father and handed Razz the note. "His name is Kenn Riley. Find him." She glanced down at the picture of the pilot. "I knew it was him."

"I never doubted you for a minute, partner."

"Got it," Razz exclaimed. "Kenn Riley. He left Fisher-Hawthorne and went to work for Mandeville Industries. Still employed with them."

Alex slowly stood up. "He doesn't work for the senator?"

Razz shook his head. "Nope."

"Relax, Alex. It was a strong lead. So he was hired by Guy Mandeville. That shouldn't be that great a shock to us."

"I guess not. I was just hoping that this was going to be the straw to break the llama's back."

"Camel, Alex. Camel's back. And this isn't over yet. Why don't we have a little chat with the pilot and see what he can tell us."

——

Senator John Sterling felt his ambition melt away with each passing moment. He was going to be hauled out in handcuffs. Humiliated in the press. His career eviscerated. His family attacked. His name stomped into the mud and ruined. His finances destroyed.

When he'd called and insisted on meeting, he hadn't told Willard why. Only that it was imperative that they meet. Willard had chosen this filthy no-tell motel for discretion. Not that Willard had much to worry about in that arena, but Sterling surely did. He was still half expecting to see the press congregating in the parking lot.

Questionable stains on the bedspread quelled his desire to sit. He paced the tiny room. He had to talk Willard out of this madness. There had to be a way to get through to him. This wasn't going to work; it was all crashing down on them.

Two short taps on the door. Sterling breathed a sigh of relief and opened the door. Willard stepped in and looked around. "Well, this is certainly depressing."

"You suggested it. Look, we need to talk."

"No one knows you're here?" Willard peeked into the tiny bathroom.

"Of course not. I'm not an idiot. Look, this has to stop here and now. Those detectives? They know. They know you're behind everything—the runaways, the organ transplants, the Kidwell woman. They're trying to find out where you have her."

"Are they? And what did you tell them?"

"Nothing!"

"Of course you didn't. You know if I go down, you go down."

"Then stop this now. It's gone too far. It's over. You can't get away with this."

"Of course I can." He stepped on a cockroach as it scuttled from under the bed toward the bathroom.

"They're closing in on you!"

"And of course you told them that you're just an innocent bystander."

Sterling wiped his brow. "You don't get it, do you? They *know*. All of it."

"They don't *know* anything. They suspect a great deal."

"No. They have all the documents."

At that, Willard lifted an eyebrow. "Is that what they told you?"

"That's it? That's all you have to say?"

Shrugging, Willard lifted a corner of the curtain and looked out over the parking lot. "Knowing you, you gave them more than they expected to get. You never were a strong man, John. A puppet is never as good as the man pulling the strings. And that's all you've ever been. And not a very good one, at that. You've tried to think for yourself too many times to count. I've had to run around and fix the messes you got us into. Frankly, I'm exhausted."

Sterling was too stunned to even respond. This was a waste of time. He headed for the door.

"I don't think so," Willard said, pulling out a gun.

Disbelief stopped Sterling before he'd taken three steps. "You can't be serious."

"Oh, call it 'tying up loose ends,' or some such drivel. The truth is, you've become a liability. If you haven't told them everything yet, you will. Eventually. You'll spill your guts in the hopes of cutting a deal. I can't allow that. Why do you think they even started looking at you?"

"You set me up?"

"Of course. Everything points to you. I'm horrified at what you've done, of course. Never realized you were so twisted."

Shaking his head, Sterling backed up a step. "Willard. You don't have to do this."

"Yes, actually. I do." He fired twice.

The first shot found Sterling's chest and lifted him off his feet. He felt the impact, the burn, but before the full brunt of pain, the next shot hit him and he felt nothing at all.

———

They found the plane at a small airfield outside Manassas, but no one knew where to find Kenn Riley. "He's in and out," one pilot told them. "If he has to fly, we see him; otherwise, I don't know where he would be."

Alex showed him a picture of Senator Sterling. "Ever see this man on the plane?"

The pilot shrugged. "Maybe. Can't say for sure. Not like I pay a lot of attention."

Alex walked out of the hangar. "Well, that was a bust."

"Let's try the control tower," Marcus said.

"Sure," the man in the control tower told them. "I know Kenny. Been to his place a couple times for cookouts. The man knows how to put together a party."

"Can you give us his address?" Alex asked. "It's important that we talk to him."

"No problem." He wrote it down and handed it to Alex.

Marcus plugged the address into the GPS and pulled out of the airport. It took them nearly half an hour of wandering down rural lanes, passing one farm after another, to reach the pilot's home.

Like the neighboring homes, it was set back from the road and surrounded by cornfields. Marcus drove past it and then pulled over to the side of the road.

As they climbed out, Alex double-checked her SIG. "I didn't see a car out front."

"He might have his car in the barn." He reached under the driver's seat and pulled out a Walther PPK .380. He checked the magazine, chambered a round, and stuck it in his coat pocket along with two extra mags. "I'm going around the front. You take the back." He looked over at her. "And be careful."

She rolled her eyes and jogged over, staying low. Marcus watched her for a long moment and then headed toward the front of the house. He wished he could shake his deep sense of foreboding.

Staying low, he peeked through one of the dirty windows. Furniture was bare and minimal. A couple of beer cans on the coffee table, a pizza box on the sofa, a jacket slung over the back of a chair. The television played some game show.

He moved down the front porch to the door and eased the screen door open. He gave the door three hard raps then listened for footsteps or someone calling out.

Nothing.

He knocked again. Still nothing.

He tried the doorknob. It turned.

This was too easy.

Pulling out the gun, he slowly stepped through the doorway and into the living room. He strained to hear footsteps, breathing, anything to indicate that he was not alone.

But his nose found it first.

Walking carefully so as not to disturb anything, he pulled out his cell phone and called 911. "I need to report a murder."

Alex appeared in the kitchen. "Did you find anything?"

"He's over here on the floor. Doesn't look like he's been dead very long."

"One step ahead of us, as always." She holstered her gun.

"We're getting closer," he replied as he took one more step.

And heard a tiny click.

A bomb.

"Alex!" he barked. "Run!"

As long as he could stand still, the bomb wouldn't explode, but he could feel the sweat breaking out across his forehead. It was probably no more than four or five seconds before he heard Alex go out the back, but it felt as if it had been minutes. He took a deep breath, counted to three, then pivoted on one foot and jumped through the window, shattering the glass. He hit the ground and rolled. Kept rolling. The heat swept over him a split second before the explosion launched him forward.

40

Suzanne was awake. And alive. She waited, listening, but didn't hear anything. She slowly opened her eyes. A chill settled in, and she shivered.

Her face throbbed. Her arms hurt. Her head had given up on pounding and now existed as one huge ball of excruciating torture. It all but made her hunger irrelevant.

How long was he going to drag this out?

"I'm going to torture you for days before I kill you."

His threat echoed through her mind, making her head hurt even worse.

"I want you to feel all the pain you've forced other people to feel."

So far, he seemed to be keeping his promise.

"By the time I get done with you, you'll beg me to kill you, just to end the torment."

She was nearly there. But not quite. She wanted to live. She wanted to escape this and live.

But there was no way out. None. He had her right where he wanted her. And it was just starting.

Slowly, painfully, she eased up on the cot. She was in a cell now instead of strapped to the metal table. No one knew where she was. No one would care. She cursed every show she'd ever done. She cursed every man she'd ever dated. She cursed every desire for attention and success. And she cursed Willard Mandeville most of all.

Crying only made her head hurt worse, especially her nose. It was more than likely broken.

"Are you okay?"

The soft feminine voice startled Suzanne. She turned to see a young girl sitting cross-legged in the cell next to hers. "Who are you?"

"Merry Christopher."

"Is it just you and I?"

Merry shook her head. "There were more of us, but they took one yesterday and one today. That's Adam down there in the end cell."

"How long have you been here?"

Merry shrugged. "I don't know. Without clocks or sun, you lose track after a while. I've tried to keep count by how many dinners I've had, and I think it's been maybe five days."

When the door swung open, she tensed. He was back. Along with that hulking brute that never talked and seemed to take such delight in her pain. The big man opened the cell door, and Mandeville strolled in like a celebrity on the red carpet.

"Hello, Suzanne. How are you feeling? Is your nose still bleeding?" He leaned over her. "No, it looks like it stopped. But I bet it still hurts."

She didn't bother giving him the satisfaction of an answer. What was the point?

Gripping her jaw with his fingers, he grinned at her. "Does it hurt, Suzanne? Do you think it hurts as bad as it hurt Guy when he hit that windshield?"

Wincing, she tried not to cry out.

"Aw, look how brave she's trying to be. What? No whining? I'm surprised at you, Suzanne. I didn't think you knew how to do anything except complain."

She glared up at him, wishing she had something she could say that would hurt him as badly as he'd hurt her. "How long are you going to keep this up?"

"Are you ready to beg me to kill you yet?"

"No."

"Then we're not done yet. I'll be back later."

———

Covering his head, Marcus curled into a tight ball. Glass, fire, and wood rained around him.

He thought he heard his name, but his ears were ringing and it sounded so far away. And then Alex was hitting him on the back and pulling at his arms.

Marcus rolled to his feet and ran with her back toward the barn. There she stopped and turned around. "Are you okay?"

Nodding, he bent over and braced his hands on his thighs, breathing heavily. "That was way too close."

"What happened?"

"There was a trigger under the rug. I tripped it. As soon as I stepped on it and heard the click, I knew the place was rigged to blow." He lifted his head. "Why were you hitting me?"

"Putting out the fire on your back."

"My jacket is burned?"

She grimaced with a shrug. "Sorry, partner."

"Oh, well. Could have been worse."

She tilted her head and frowned. "Gee, ya think?"

"Yeah. I lost your gun."

"My Walther?"

She looked totally devastated and it made him feel bad. "I had it in my hand and used it when I went through the window to help break the glass, but then I dropped it when I hit the ground."

"Well, let's go look. It might be easy to find."

She took one step and a bullet hit the barn, just inches from her head. Both of them dove to the ground. Alex lifted the leg of her jeans and pulled out her backup weapon, tossing it to him.

"We have to get out of here." Three more bullets came at them.

"You go first and I'll cover you," Alex insisted. She pointed to a small shed on the other side of the now-burning house. "They're in there. Go to the cornfields. Stay low. And when you're in position, start firing."

There was no time to argue. "Be safe."

"Be fast," she replied and turned her attention to the shed.

Marcus took a deep breath and then bolted, zigzagging to the cornfield. He hit the ground, rolled over and around, and then aimed his gun at the shed. Sure enough, as soon as Alex stopped shooting, he saw movement and then gunfire. He aimed and fired. Kept firing.

And ran out of bullets a split second before Alex slid to the ground next to him. "I'm out."

"That's because you weren't taking enough time between shots. Never mind. Let's go."

They started running through the cornfield, changing from row to row, trying not make an easy target.

Marcus, with his long legs, jumped the ditch along the edge of the road where the SUV was parked. Alex wasn't so lucky, having to go halfway down the ditch before making the jump. She'd just made it to the other side when Marcus waved her back.

"What's wrong?"

A bullet hit the windshield.

"They slashed the front tire."

She pointed across the road. "That way. The woods."

Crossing the road meant no cover at all, but she was right. The woods would be better in the long run. Trees could stop bullets a whole lot better than corn.

Bullets chipped at the blacktop as they ran. "These guys just don't give up," Alex panted as they ducked behind the trees and took a moment to catch their breath.

"They are determined, no doubt."

"Which way?" Alex asked.

"East," Marcus replied.

"Lead on," Alex instructed, then slammed backward as a bullet ripped into her.

41

Suzanne couldn't stop shaking.

"Judge not, lest you be judged."

The old woman's words had been replaying in her head. She had made a good living judging others, never stopping to wonder how she would feel if she were on the receiving end. Closing her eyes, she desperately wanted to cry, but she had wrung every tear out of her system. Nothing left but numbness.

"You teach others; why don't you teach yourself?"

Because she kept busy pointing out everyone else's faults so she wouldn't have to look at her own.

She wiggled her toes, trying to work some semblance of heat into them. *Someone help me, please. I don't want to die. Please. Don't let me die.*

"Here." Merry was pushing her blanket through the cell bars. "We can share."

Suzanne snatched the blanket and wrapped herself in it. "Thanks."

"You're welcome. You're that reporter, aren't you?"

"Suzanne Kidwell. Yes."

"My mom likes your show."

Suzanne shifted so that she could see Merry a little better. "But you didn't?"

The girl shrugged. "Are they going to kill you too?"

"Yes." Suzanne let her forehead drop to her knees.

Merry's voice dropped to a whisper. "I don't want to die."

Suzanne lifted her head. "Neither do I."

———

"Alex!" Marcus caught her as she went down. Blood oozed from her shoulder. Another shot hit a tree just a few feet away. *No time.* He lifted her into his arms and jogged through the leaves, dodged trees, scraped through the brush. He came to a small creek he couldn't jump with Alex in his arms. He didn't hesitate, running through it, soaking his boots.

"Marcus," Alex whispered. "Put me down."

"You're hurt."

"I think it's just a graze. I can walk. Put me down."

He found a large locust tree and knelt, setting her down as gently as he could.

"Stop fussing." She reached up and touched her shoulder,

wincing. Looking at the blood on her fingers she held them up. "See? Almost stopped bleeding. I'm fine. Honest."

"You scared ten years off my life."

"Sorry. Forgot to duck."

"Yeah, well, don't do it again." He helped her climb to her feet. "Sure you can walk? No dizziness?"

"I'm good." She looked over her shoulder. "You think they've given up on us?"

"Maybe. But without the SUV, we need to find a way out of here."

"Call Razz. Tell him to GPS us and pick us up wherever he thinks we'll come out."

"Give me a sec and then I'll carry you again. I don't want you falling on your face."

"I'm not going to fall."

Stubborn woman. He dialed the office. He really didn't like that wound. "Razz? Long story, short: Alex and I are on foot. Our tires have been slashed. We're in the woods, heading east, and Alex has been shot. I need you to track the cell phone and get over here and pick us up."

"I'm there." He could hear the Razz tapping away feverishly on the laptop. "Want me to send an ambulance?"

"Yes." Alex would throw a fit when she found out, but he wasn't going to take any chances. Not with her life.

"Done. I've got you. You need to head more southeast. You'll come out on a two-lane road. Hold until I get there."

———

Suzanne must have dozed off because when she opened her eyes, Mandeville and his goon were back. Mandeville was watching her with a smarmy grin. It made her skin crawl. He was actually going to kill her. And torture her with knowing the exact moment it was going to happen.

"Where did you get the blanket?" He glanced over at Merry's cell and frowned deeper. "I see. Made a mere child feel sorry for you, didn't you? Your selfishness never ceases to amaze me."

"I could say the same of you."

"Do you know what bothers me about torturing you this way? That you know you're going to die." His expression changed, and she didn't like the way his mouth was twisting. "Of course, my poor son didn't have that, did he? He didn't know that he had so little time left. He thought he had his whole life ahead of him. I had big plans for my boy. And you took all that away from him. And away from me."

"I told you, I'm sorry."

The smarmy grin twisted into a sneer. "You make a living out of getting men to fall for you just so you can have the pleasure of tossing them aside. Does it make you feel good? Or is it just that you can get people to love you but you're incapable of loving them back?"

That shot hit closer than she would have expected.

"That's it, isn't it?" He leaned over her and she tried to pull away. "You are so stone cold you don't know how to love anyone but yourself. And you don't even like yourself very much." Laughing, he straightened. "Think you can figure out how to like yourself? I don't. I don't think you have a heart."

"You are a bitter waste of a man."

She knew he was going to slap her. Braced herself for it. And was surprised when he didn't. She opened her eyes.

"You think that bothers me? What someone like you thinks about me? I've killed dogs with more value than you."

"I'm not sure why that doesn't surprise me. That you'd kill an innocent animal and never think twice about it. And you say I'm cold."

He looked at her as if she were little more than a bug pinned to a board. Something to pick at. And if it died, you just got another bug.

"You know my wife died the day our son was buried. Oh, she's still breathing, but her heart just died with him."

"Married to you, it's surprising she didn't—"

He backhanded the words right out of her mouth. "You don't talk about my wife, my son, or my life. Watch that tongue or I'll cut it out."

——

"I do not need to go to the hospital," Alex insisted.

"Then don't go. But let the EMT clean the wound and check it. That's all I ask."

"Fine, but it's nothing. All I need is a Band-Aid."

While the EMT cleaned her wound, Alex listened to Razz talking to Marcus.

"I've been monitoring that e-mail account. The girl still plans on coming in tonight. He's supposed to pick her up at the bus station at seven. She said she'll be wearing a red hoodie and jeans."

"We need to be there," Alex interjected. "*Ouch.* That *hurts.*" She glared at the EMT.

"You get shot and insist you're fine. I put a little antibiotic cream on it and you cry like a baby." Alex offered a small laugh before the EMT continued. "You lost a lot of blood. You should go to the hospital."

"Not happening."

The man taped a bandage to her shoulder and handed her a tube of cream. "Fine. Put this on twice a day."

———

Suzanne closed her eyes, burrowing deeper under the thin blanket. She had tried to give it back to Merry, but the girl refused. Now, as Merry slept, Suzanne's thoughts tormented her as deeply as Mandeville's punches.

Her life was almost over. Who would show up at her funeral? Her parents. It would be expected. And her sister with her fiancé. Marcus and Alex would just because that's the type of people they were. But she had a hard time thinking of anyone else.

Unless, of course, it turned into a major media event. Then there would be hundreds of people there with cameras in tow. But they didn't really count because they didn't really care and they certainly wouldn't mourn her.

It would be an empty casket, of course, because her body would never be found. It might be months or even years before they gave up looking and declared her legally dead.

She thought of her parents. Would they insist on a long search or would they give up? Then again, they'd probably just chalk it up as inevitable and console themselves with loving Elizabeth all the more. Suzanne had always been such a disappointment to them.

Alex and Marcus. They might search for a while and then just move on to a new case.

Suzanne heard a cell phone ring and her hopes jumped. Had someone come for her?

Mandeville's voice.

This nightmare was never going to end. No one was coming for her.

She was surprised to discover that as the thoughts came and went, they lost the power to pull her down to that same level of self-pity that they once could. She had regrets—plenty of them—and given the chance, she'd more than likely do things quite differently with her life, but she was enough of a realist to know that there would be no going back.

Mandeville came in with his man and sat down in a folding lawn chair a few feet from her bed.

"Eleanor and I wanted more children. Guy should have had brothers and sisters, but it simply never happened. Before we knew it, Guy was a teenager and we just gave up. Of course, we assumed there would be plenty of grandchildren. You took that away from us."

She didn't want to hear about Guy anymore. She licked her cracked lips before asking, "Did you…kill Cecelia?"

Confusion hazed his features for a moment and then cleared. "Cecelia. Well, I had her killed. It was the perfect setup, don't you think?" He shifted in his chair, warming to the conversation. He practically cackled. "After that, the rest just clicked into place. Pure genius."

Pure madness. "You are sick. And crazy."

"I'm not crazy. I'm just making sure you have your judgment day."

"Who are you to judge me?" As soon as the words were out of her mouth, she could hear the echoes of her victims asking her the same thing. Who had she been to judge them?

"Oh, look who is getting indignant, Roger."

"Can I do it now?" Roger asked eagerly as he pulled out a knife.

Mandeville laughed. "He loves to play with his knife. Sure. Go ahead."

Roger's grin was even worse than Mandeville's. She could understand Mandeville to some degree—he was just insane. But this goon, he was just in this for the fun of it.

He pulled up a handful of her hair, yanking hard enough to force a scream out of her as he began sawing it off. There was a time when she would have been completely horrified, but at this point, she didn't even care about her hair. He could have it if he wanted it. Who was ever going to know anyway?

He nicked her scalp, and she knew he'd done it on purpose.

Then he stabbed her.

Suzanne screamed.

42

Marcus walked into Alex's office. "Hey, just heard on the news that Sterling was found dead in a motel. Shot."

"Mandeville's cleaning up all the loose ends."

He watched as Alex loaded her SIG and shoved it down in her holster, then loaded the Glock and stuck it in the small of her back. She double-checked the clip in the Beretta and gave it to him. "Take this."

He handed Alex a pain pill. "Take this."

"I'm okay."

"If I hear you say that one more time, I'm going to leave you here. I can see the pain all over your face. Now take it."

"You really want me altered *and* packing?" Rolling her eyes, she took the pill from him and set it on the table. "Later. I will take it later. Satisfied?"

"Yes." He stuck the Beretta in his belt. "You ready to go?"

"Ready."

Razz ran down the hall with his duffel.

"Where are you going?" Marcus asked.

"With you, and don't argue with me. You may need some backup."

"You aren't licensed to carry a weapon. How can you back us up?"

"*You* don't carry a gun," Razz pointed out, then noticed the Beretta sticking out of his belt. "Usually, anyway. Look, I'm going. We'll take my van. I'll need my equipment." He tossed his keys to Marcus. "You drive."

Marcus let Razz lead the way out of the building. After stowing their gear in the back, Marcus climbed behind the wheel, adjusted the mirrors, and turned off the radio. He glanced over at Alex as he pulled out of the parking lot. She was pale and obviously hurting. Probably had a headache. But trouper that she was, she wasn't going to let it slow her down. Eyes closed, she leaned her head back against the seat.

"You okay?" he asked. "What about ibuprofen?"

She opened her eyes and looked over at him, not saying a word.

"Okay, got it. You're fine. Perfect. Couldn't be better."

"I'm just wondering what Mandeville has in store for us next."

Marcus eased to a stop at a red light. "He does seem to anticipate our every move."

"Which means we have to change our tactics. Think like him."

"There's a scary thought."

"I'm just saying—know your enemy."

The light changed and Marcus hit the gas. "But our enemy is usually a corporate thief, an embezzler, insurance fraud—the sort of thing we can at least vaguely understand. This time, our enemy is so far out of his mind, I'm not sure it's possible to know him."

Alex's cell phone rang. "Hello? How bad?"

Marcus gripped the steering wheel a little tighter as he saw what little color she had drain from her face. Then he saw the tears glistening in her eyes.

"Call me if anything changes. I love you too." She hung up.

"What's wrong?" he asked.

"Mom's body is rejecting the heart."

"So what happens now?"

"She either gets a new heart or she dies."

"You want me to take you back so you can fly home?"

Alex shook her head as she looked out the window. "There's nothing I can do there. But there's something I have to do here."

———

Mandeville peered down at Suzanne. "Have you made peace with your Maker yet?"

One of her eyes had swollen shut and the other wasn't much better, so she could only see a blurry figure standing over her. She licked her dry, cracked lips. Her throat seemed reluctant to form words. "Have you?"

Mandeville laughed. "Still a little fight left in you. Good. I want you to go to hell and resist it the whole way."

"Right back—" She licked her lips again. "At ya."

"I don't know what my son saw in you."

"He...believed the...lie."

"So you admit it. You lied to him. Finally! Progress."

"I...lied to every...one." *I made them think I was so smart, so talented, so important, so wonderful, so much better than they were. And it was all a lie. I was so scared the world would see past the facade. See me for the phony I really was. I rejected them before they could reject me. I despised them before they could despise me. And—God forgive me—I hurt them before they could hurt me.*

"Look, Roger. She's finally admitting what she did to my son. She's finally taking responsibility for killing him."

No, not killing him. I may have hurt him, but I didn't kill him. Not that it matters now.

"Beg me for your life, Suzanne. Tell me how much you want to live."

"No point." She swallowed hard, trying to lubricate her dry throat. "You'll still...kill me."

"Well, of course I will, but I still want to hear you beg."

"Don't always get...what you want...in life."

"Or in death, eh, Suzanne?"

She closed her eyes.

"It's almost time for the next phase, Suzanne. Just hold tight." And with a jerk of his head, he walked away and Roger followed behind him.

Suzanne turned her head to the wall. *God, if You're there, I'm* sorry. I don't have the right to ask anything of You. I know that. I've ignored You the way I've ignored everyone else in my life. And I don't know if You can do this, but could You let my parents know how sorry I am? They really did try to do right by me and I just couldn't see it. I let them down. I've let so many people down.

43

Tuesday evening, May 12

When they arrived at the bus station, Marcus parked across the street.

Alex opened the van door. "I'll be right here, but I need to make a call."

Closing the door, she leaned against the van and called her father. "How's Mother?"

"It doesn't look good, Alexandria. I don't know what to do. I can't lose her."

"She's a fighter. Don't give up on her."

"I'm not. I just got a call from a friend of mine. He knows where I can bypass the donor list to get a heart for your mother. It's expensive, but I don't care. I'll pay anything."

It took a moment before Alex could truly assimilate what her father was saying. "Whoa. Wait a minute. You're talking about a black-market organ."

"No, of course not. It's just that it isn't going through the donor list."

"You can't do this!"

"Alexandria! How can you not want your mother to live?"

"I *do* want my mother to live. I want it very badly. But not if someone has to be killed for it."

"That's not the case, Alexandria."

She began to pace with agitation. "Listen to me. Do you know where I am right now? I'm in the middle of trying to save the life of a young girl who is about to be killed so that some men can harvest her organs for people like you."

"Now, Alexandria, I hardly think this—"

"No, that's exactly what this is. For you to get a heart at a moment's notice for a great deal of money? Please don't delude yourself. Someone has to die, and people don't die on command, Father. They die because someone kills them so that you can have their heart."

"I don't believe that's what this is about. My friends would not condone such a thing."

"Father, listen to me!"

"I have to go. The doctor is back."

"Father!" But he had ended the call.

She climbed back in the van.

"Everything okay?" Marcus asked.

"Not in the least," she responded. Then Alex sat up a little straighter. "I see a girl with a red hoodie, but she's not with that guy."

Razz stuck his head between the seats and stared out the windshield. "That's her. She looks just like her picture."

"But she's with another girl."

Marcus turned the key and fired up the van. "We follow them anyway."

Alex opened the van door. "Let me follow on foot. I'll stay in touch."

"We can follow them in the van," Marcus insisted.

Alex looked back at him over her shoulder. "They're walking, Marcus. How long before they figure out there's a van creeping along behind them?"

Darting across the street, Alex fell in behind the two girls, keeping her pace the same as theirs. Until a scruffy guy stepped in front of her. "Hey, sweet thing."

Hands shoved deep in her pockets, she flipped the coat back so that he could see she was armed. "Get lost or get dead."

He threw up his hands and skittered sideways. "Just trying to be friendly."

"So am I. Keep walking."

The two girls stopped and went inside a hamburger joint on the corner. Alex glanced back over her shoulder and then entered the restaurant, taking a place in line behind the girls.

"Why don't you go wash up while I get the food and get us a table?" the one girl said to the girl in the red hoodie. She nodded and headed off to the rest rooms. Alex watched the girl with the tray move to the drink station. Alex stepped out of line in time to see her drop something into one of the cups.

Stepping outside, Alex called Marcus. "They're drugging the girl here. My guess is that the guy is nearby and waiting to pick them up."

"On my way."

When Marcus pulled in and parked, Alex climbed in. "They're going to eat their burgers and most likely start walking again. I'd say he isn't more than three or four blocks away."

"Did you manage to keep her from drugging the drink?"

Alex shook her head. "It would blow everything. I have to go by faith that it's just going to knock her out for a little while."

"It's probably the same thing they gave Suzanne and me."

"While we're here and so we don't look suspicious, can I get you guys any food?"

Razz shrugged. "I could eat."

———

Suzanne didn't feel the cold anymore. Maybe her body had just gotten used to it.

She looked over to see Merry pressing her face to the bars of the cell again. "You awake, Ms. Kidwell?"

"Yes."

"If you make it out of here, will you let my mom know what happened to me?"

The slight tremble in the girl's voice pulled at Suzanne's heart. The kid was trying to be so brave. So strong. But underneath that tough exterior, she faced something no one should have to endure.

She had so much life yet to live. Suzanne wanted to give her some hope, but Merry was too smart to believe a lie. "I won't be leaving here alive, Merry."

"I know he keeps threatening to kill you, but you're famous. People would miss you. Not like me."

"Your mother misses you. And your brothers and sisters. Being famous doesn't mean a thing. People will say it was sad, and then within days they'll forget all about me. That's the way it works."

"That can't be."

"Really? Name three famous people who died last year."

Merry stared at her, and then her shoulders slumped and she returned to her cot.

The door scraped open and Mandeville strutted in with the doctor and two guards maneuvering a gurney. "So sorry to interrupt your chat, but we have a customer that needs a heart right away."

Suzanne sat up slowly, but her heart jumped like a jack rabbit on speed.

Mandeville stopped and looked from Suzanne to Merry. "Now, here's my dilemma. Both of you have the right blood type. Which one of you should I take? Dear me, dear me. Which one, which one?"

Suzanne eased to her feet. "Take me."

"My, haven't we become the generous one. I fully expected you to cower in the corner and beg me to take the kid."

"I prefer not to give you the satisfaction of enjoying yourself at her expense."

Mandeville looked over at the guards. "The girl."

"No!" Suzanne lurched forward and grabbed the bars. "Take me. Leave her alone."

"It's not your decision, Suzanne. Maybe I prefer to let you suffer a little longer."

One of the guards grabbed Merry by the arm and yanked her to her feet. Merry jerked away. "I can do this myself. You don't have to manhandle me."

Mandeville looked over at Suzanne with a slimy grin. "Such pride. I almost hate to kill her."

"Then don't. Take me."

Merry shook her head at Suzanne. "Don't beg for me, Ms. Kidwell. My life was never anything much anyway. I was stupid and put myself here." She eased up on the gurney and stretched out.

"Stop," Mandeville barked. "Get off."

Confused, Merry hesitated before slowly sliding off the gurney.

"Take Suzanne. Now. I'm done playing this game."

Suzanne could feel her body shaking from the inside out, but she refused to give Mandeville any edge over her. If Merry could go with her head high, so could she.

———

When the two girls came out of the restaurant, Marcus started the engine. Alex shoved her fries into the bag and set it on the floorboard. "Razz, quick. Do you have any hats in here that I can wear?"

"How about the fedora? Or the Stetson?"

"Give me the Stetson."

She took the beat-up old cowboy hat and shoved it down on her head as she climbed out of the van.

"Testing," she whispered softly.

"Loud and clear," Marcus replied in her earpiece.

She and Marcus had hooked up their wireless mikes and earpieces while the girls ate. Now she wouldn't have to call him if anything happened.

The girls walked for two blocks and then the girl in the hoodie began to falter, stumble, and weave.

"I was right, Marcus. The girl is drugged. She's barely able to stand now."

"Stay close. It won't be long now."

A moment later, the other girl took her arm and veered off the street.

"There's an alley, halfway down this street. They just went in there. Drive by and see what's going on."

"Done," Marcus replied.

Alex held back and waited as Marcus drove past. "He's lifting her into the back of the van," she whispered. She turned and stared into a shop window. "Pull over and park. As soon as they pull out, we'll follow them."

"Affirmative."

She glanced over as Marcus pulled to the curb, then she turned her attention back to the store window. A moment later, a dark blue van pulled out of the alley. She made a show of barely glancing over, but she saw enough of the driver to memorize his face.

The van passed Marcus, and Alex started running. She jumped into her seat. "Go."

—

Suzanne stared up at the bright lights above her while the doctor bustled about, preparing her for surgery. "You won't feel anything, I assure you. I'll put you under anesthesia, and then I will operate on you—the unfortunate victim of an accident. You'll die on the table, of course. At which point, I will harvest your organs and within minutes, they will be in flight to their recipients. All neat and clean."

"Illegal. Immoral. Ruthless. Deplorable. But neat and clean."

He chuckled. "He's going to kill you anyway, why not let someone benefit from your death?"

He hung the IV bag on the metal hook attached to the gurney and with quick efficiency, inserted the needle into her arm. "Any last words, Miss Kidwell?"

"Rot in hell."

"Someday, I probably will, but in the meantime, I will enjoy my life very much."

Suzanne wanted to rail at him, cursing him from one end of this life to another, but her eyes grew heavy and it suddenly seemed impossible to speak.

"Good-bye, Miss Kidwell."

44

Tuesday night, May 12

Marcus followed the blue van out of the city, west on Route 66 and then on to Lee Highway, maintaining several cars between them. The scenery slowly changed from downtown to suburban to rural. The number of cars on the road dwindled. Marcus frowned. Razz was on his computer in the back of the van, keeping Marcus apprised of the terrain.

"We're coming up on another small town in about two miles."

Marcus looked in the rearview mirror. "I would prefer updates that included things like how many guns they have and how much danger we're facing when we arrive."

"And whether we're all going to get out alive," Razz added.

Marcus glanced back at him again. "You're a big help."

"I'm just saying," Razz muttered under his breath.

"Razz?"

"Affirmative."

Marcus rolled his eyes. "I'm going to assume that all the jokes and sarcasm are your way of dealing."

"Better than falling apart and crying."

Alex pointed. "He's turning."

Razz went back to the computer. "It's another fairly major road leading into a different town. We're not far from Fredericksburg."

Alex tensed. "Almost go-time."

Marcus scanned his mirrors. "No one else is turning. Let's hope he doesn't notice us."

"Map shows no turnoffs for at least four miles. You can drop back a little."

Marcus eased off the gas and let the van pull ahead. "Do we know any police officers in this area?"

Alex stretched. "Not local. But we know Rusty and Mitch from the state police."

"We might need their help."

"I'll call when we know where to send them."

Marcus spent twenty minutes yo-yoing distance before the blue van signaled a right turn. Razz clapped his hands. "Okay, up ahead on the left, there's a small shopping center. Across the street is a hotel. And a mile further down is—wait for it, wait for it, drumroll, please—an airport."

The van pulled into the shopping center and disappeared behind it.

Marcus pulled into a parking space. "Now what?"

"Grocery store, card store, Chinese restaurant, sports bar, and veterinarian." Alex looked over at Marcus. "I'm going with the vet. Medical facility notwithstanding, it's the perfect cover."

"I'll agree."

"It's Mandeville," Alex hissed, pointing.

Marcus watched Mandeville and his bodyguard climb out of a sedan and head inside the vet's office.

"Get down." Alex said between clenched teeth, pulling out her gun.

Marcus grabbed her arm. "Don't shoot him. We need to see which way he goes."

"I wasn't going to shoot him. Yet. But we need to go through the back."

They eased out of the van. Marcus led the way, staying low behind parked cars. Alex followed behind him with Razz trailing her, his duffel slung over his shoulder.

At the rear door, they found a locked metal door and a keypad. The van was parked a few feet away, but no one was in it.

"Okay, now what?" Alex whispered, gingerly twisting the doorknob just in case.

Razz stepped forward and set his bag down. "Move aside and let the genius work his magic."

Razz connected several wires from a small box to the keypad next to the door.

"Another second," Razz whispered.

A snick.

"And bingo. We're in."

Alex eased the door open. She nodded at Marcus and slipped through, gun drawn. Razz disconnected his equipment, picked up his bag, and followed her with Marcus taking up the rear.

The door opened into a long, well-lit hallway. It ended and turned right into another hall with three doors.

"Which one first?" Alex asked.

"Take your pick," Marcus responded.

Before they could move forward, one of the doors opened. Alex retreated a step, her arm extended to hold Marcus and Razz back. Then she eased her head around to look down the hall. A guard walked away from her. He opened the door at the end of the hallway and went in. The door closed behind him.

"Okay," Alex whispered.

They moved to the first door. Alex gripped the gun tightly in one hand and grabbed the door handle with the other. "On three."

She threw the door wide and quickly stepped in, sweeping the room. Empty of personnel, but full of computer monitors and security setups.

Razz moved up and examined the active monitors. He pointed to one. "Those are holding cells. Looks like a girl and a guy are in them."

"Merry," Alex breathed. "She's alive."

"I don't see Suzanne," Marcus replied.

"Guys," Razz whispered. Alex glanced over at Razz. "This monitors the door we came through," he said. "I think they know we're here."

"Very astute," someone said from behind them.

Alex whipped around to find a gun against Marcus's temple. A large man shook his head. "Drop it, or I kill him first."

She slowly bent over and set the gun down on the console.

The man jerked the gun. "Move away. Over there. Next to your smart friend."

"Where's Mandeville?" Marcus asked.

"It's none of your business, but if you must know, he's helping the doctor dispose of Ms. Kidwell."

Marcus stared hard at Alex, sliding his eyes left and back to center. She blinked once slowly. "I assume she's the next organ donor?" Alex asked.

"You're astute as well, Miss Hawthorne."

"Can I assume we're next in line?"

Just then, Marcus flipped his head back, hitting the man in the face. He stumbled back. Alex took the opening and dove for her weapon. Razz knelt and stayed low. Marcus twisted and hit the man across the side of the neck. The chop drove the man to the ground, but he rolled and returned to his feet far quicker than Alex expected.

Marcus dove on him and the two went down in a flurry of arms and legs. Alex grabbed Razz. "Let's go."

"But Marcus—"

"He has it under control. Let's go." Alex led him out of the room and down the hall to the last room. She opened the door and went in low, again sweeping the room with her drawn weapon.

Cells. Empty cells.

"Someone moved the kids."

Alex walked down the center, checking all the cells anyway. "Where did they take them?"

Razz looked forlorn. "I wasn't watching the monitors, Alex. I'm sorry."

"It's not your fault." She blew out a deep breath. "Let's check the other room."

As they went to open the door, Marcus stepped in, a trace of blood on his lip.

"You okay?" Alex asked, holding back the instinct to reach up and wipe the blood away.

"Fine. In better shape than our guard." He looked around. "They moved them already?"

"Kept us distracted while they did."

"The other door leads to an examination room. No help there."

"Then they've either taken them out and driven them away, or they're still here somewhere."

"I vote we keep searching."

The door to the exam room opened before they reached it, and a guard stepped out and lifted his arm. Marcus grabbed Razz and pulled him to the floor. Alex went down on one knee, aiming her SIG at the man. "Drop it and hands up! I said drop it!"

He took a step forward, and Alex squeezed off a shot. He spun around and hit the ground, screaming. Marcus sprinted forward, Alex at his side.

She stopped, legs braced, the pistol gripped in both hands, and sighted the man's left nostril as Marcus reached down and spun the man around.

He was screaming, holding his ear. "You shot me."

"I told you to drop your gun and put your hands up. Don't you listen?"

Marcus retrieved the weapon, then asked, "Why were you going to shoot us?"

"Ordered to."

"Where did he take the boy and girl that were in the cells?" Alex asked.

He hesitated. Marcus stepped on the man's knee. "Downstairs."

Marcus took his foot off the man's knee. "And Suzanne?"

The man pressed his lips together.

"Man, don't you get it?" Alex re-aimed for the man's knee-cap. "I have the gun. You have the most to lose. Shall we test the theory?"

"It's too late, don't you get that? You can't save any of them."

"I can save you. Just tell me what I want to know."

Fear contorted the man's face. "They're all downstairs."

"See how easy that was? Where is Mandeville?"

"He left as soon as he saw you come in."

"Where?"

"I don't know. I swear!"

Marcus bent over and hauled the man to his feet. "I'll lock him in one of the cells."

"We'll wait for you in there," Alex pointed to the exam room. "Don't be long."

They found the door to the stairs right off one of the exam rooms. Once again, Razz stepped in and quickly managed to override the security. They descended the concrete steps, and Marcus caught up with them at the bottom. "Go easy," he whispered.

Alex nodded, biting her lip.

"You hurt your shoulder, didn't you?" Marcus shook his head.

"I'm fine. Just a little sore."

She stepped out of the stairway into the hall. And found herself staring down two barrels attached to two large guards.

"Mr. Mandeville said you might be good enough to make it this far, but this is the end of the road."

While one guard kept his gun trained on them, the other relieved Alex and Marcus of their weapons. The young boy, that had been driving the van was dead on the floor, shot twice through the chest. "Why did you have to kill him?" she asked.

"Through that door," the armed guard instructed, ignoring her question.

Inside, they found three teens—Merry, a young boy and the girl that had drugged the girl in the red hoodie—huddled side by side, tied to the arms of the chairs they sat in. The girl in the red hoodie was strapped to a gurney.

Alex recognized Merry and desperately wanted to run to her,

scoop her up, and take her to her mother. All in good time. First she and Marcus had to figure out how to get their weapons back. Tricky proposition.

Movement pulled Alex's attention toward a huge window. She gasped as realized she was looking into the operation room where Suzanne lay on a table, a white sheet pulled up to her chin, machines beeping and chirping as a nurse and doctor scurried about.

She stepped toward the window.

"Fascinating, isn't it?" One of the men asked her.

"Not exactly the word I would use."

Glancing over at Marcus, Alex tried to read his expression. He had a plan. Was he waiting for her? It was hard to tell. *Come on, Marcus. Talk to me.*

Finally, Marcus returned her gaze and nodded. She understood. Time to move.

"So what now?" Alex asked as she casually strolled over toward the window, positioning herself closer to one of the guards.

"Just waiting for the boss to call that he's safely away."

"And then what? Save us for this operating room?"

"Nah. Boss said to just dispose of you. You'll end up in a landfill somewhere."

"How comforting." She slowly turned as if she didn't have a care in the world when she was actually angling her bad shoulder away from him. "There's just one small problem with that."

"And what might that be?"

"I don't want to be disposed of."

The guard laughed. "Hear that, Ray. She don't want this."

"Too bad for her," Ray responded.

Marcus struck as silent and as quick as a rattlesnake—a round-house kick that would have made Chuck Norris smile. As Ray flew back, the other guard lunged toward him. Alex picked up a chair and swung it, hitting the man in the back.

She swung again, this time hitting him in the back of the head with the leg of the chair. His gun dropped and skittered. Alex dove for it, but not fast enough. The guard dropped on top of her and wrestled her for the gun.

Biting back a scream as he bore down on her bad shoulder, she could barely breathe under his weight. She jerked her elbow back, trying to hit the man in the face. She missed.

He growled something in her ear, but she focused on getting free. His hand closed around hers. She knew she had to do something fast. Suddenly the man stiffened and then collapsed, pressing her into the floor. She writhed to roll him off. When she flipped sideways, a man loomed above her with a big smile on his face and a huge needle in his hand.

Razz.

No time to ask questions. She whipped around on her knees, aiming the gun toward the other guard. No need. Marcus had him in a hold that was slowly rendering the man unconscious.

Climbing to her feet, Alex turned to Razz. "What was in that needle?"

He shrugged. "I didn't ask. But don't be surprised if he wakes up and starts barking."

Alex hurried over to Merry. "We're here to help. Your mom

sent us. I just need you to stay here a few more minutes. We'll be right back for you, I promise."

Merry nodded weakly.

Marcus picked up his gun while Razz gathered up the guards' guns and shoved them into his duffel.

"We gonna tie these hombres up now?" Razz said.

"With what? Gauze?"

Razz dug into his duffel and pulled out lock ties. "Or I brought these."

"By all means, then, cuff 'em up."

—

Marcus barged into the operating room with his gun drawn. "Nobody touches her. Understand me?"

The nurse tried to block his access. "Sir! You can't be in here!"

Marcus noticed the doctor hadn't said a thing and was sidling down the wall toward the door. Marcus aimed at the nurse. "Take Suzanne off these machines."

The doctor squared his shoulders. When all else failed, use bluff and bluster with a touch of arrogance. "Who are you? Why are you here?"

Marcus turned the gun on him. "You're not operating on Suzanne today. That's all you need to know. Now unhook her."

Marcus edged closer. The doctor stared at him a minute and then his shoulders sank. He walked back over to Suzanne and began to remove her tubes and wires.

Marcus couldn't believe it was really Suzanne. Her hair had been cut off to bare inches—and not even that in some spots. Her scalp was nicked and bloody. Her face was a mass of bruises. Her eyes swollen shut. Her lip cut. Her nose obviously broken.

Razz joined him and gasped. "What did they do to her?"

"Tortured her. I want these people cuffed."

The doctor tried to run. Marcus clipped him on the back of the head with the butt of the gun. "Oh no you don't."

Marcus kept the gun out until Razz had secured them both. Then he handed his gun to Razz.

He folded Suzanne in the bedsheets and lifted her gently. "We need to get her to the nearest ER."

"I'll call for an ambulance," Razz replied.

45

Thursday, May 14

It is always difficult when we lose someone so young, so beautiful. A woman with her whole life ahead of her. It's hard to understand what God was thinking when He took her away from
us." The pastor looked down at the casket and then out at the
crowd. "But we have to see beyond the here and now and realize
that there is a world beyond this one. A life more beautiful than
the one we know. A purpose higher than we can ever understand."

Marcus bit his lip. Alex leaned over and whispered. "You
okay?"

He nodded.

"We rest in this assurance—God is faithful to keep that which
is entrusted to Him." With a nod, the pastor stepped aside to let
everyone come forward and place a rose on the casket.

Marcus stepped in line behind Alex. Except for the bright
white bandage peeping out from the collar of her shirt, you'd never
know that she had so recently come close to death herself.

Alex placed her rose in the pile and then stepped back. Marcus reached out and gently did likewise.

He was surprised when Alex took his hand, walking beside him away from the grave site. "It was a beautiful service."

"Yes."

She glanced up at him and then fell quiet. There was no need to talk.

Razz waited for them at the curb. He stepped into Alex's arms, holding her for a long moment before stepping back and looking at Marcus. "Thank you both for being here."

"We wouldn't have missed it," Marcus told him.

"How's your mom?" he asked Alex.

"Her condition has improved. They put her on some different medications, and her body isn't rejecting the heart anymore. It looks positive right now." Her father had called her just two hours after they rescued Merry and the other teens to tell her that he'd thought long and hard about what she'd said. He had talked it over with the doctor, who informed him that Alex was right.

"Good. Any word on Suzanne since this morning?"

Marcus shook his head. Just hours after being admitted into the emergency room, Suzanne had insisted on being released. Her parents came for her, taking her back to her home and staying with her while she recuperated. "Haven't heard anything, so I'm assuming all is well."

"And Merry?"

"Home with her mom and happy to be there," Alex interjected.

"What about Mandeville?"

Marcus shoved his hands into his pockets. "The police said they've had no luck finding him so far. But they're looking. And they found all the evidence they need in the doctor's files to be able to identify a good many of the missing teenagers. Families will be able to find a little closure."

"What about Britney?"

Alex looked away as Marcus answered for her. "They found her records."

"So, she's not going to be coming home?"

Marcus shook his head. "I'm afraid not."

"Those poor families. Well, I'm glad we were able to at least bring Merry and Adam home. What about that other girl? Kathi?"

"In jail."

Alex touched Razz's shoulder. "We couldn't have done it without you. We can't thank you enough."

Razz took a deep breath as he looked up. "I needed you guys as much as you needed me. It's all good. I see my dad waving at me. I gotta go. I'll see you two later, right?"

"Count on it."

Alex watched Razz walk over to his family and his father drop an arm over his shoulder. He was a strong man and had a strong family. He'd be okay.

"You ready?" she asked Marcus as she turned and started walking away.

"Yep."

"You want me to drive?" Alex asked as they approached the car.

"No. I'm good."

The drive to her condo was a quiet one. She stared out the window, leaving Marcus to his thoughts while she fretted over hers. Was she wrong in wanting to stay with Marcus? To own her own business and make her own way in the world without the Hawthorne money and power? Or was she just fooling herself? She still used the family jet. And the vacation home on Cape Cod. And when she needed a favor, didn't she always go running to her father? Who was she kidding? She was a Fisher-Hawthorne, and running off to Maryland and opening up a little private investigator's office wasn't going to change anything. Maybe her parents were right and it was time for her to stop acting like a rebellious teenager and step up to her responsibilities.

"Be careful."

Alex looked over at him, her brows pulling together. "What?" She looked around and realized that they were sitting in front of her building.

"Mandeville is still on the loose, and when he discovers that we got Suzanne out, he's going to be furious. So be careful."

She unsnapped her seat belt. "I'm in one of the most secure buildings in Washington. If anyone needs to be careful, it's you."

"I'll call you later."

When she entered the building, she turned and watched him pull away. Where was Mandeville? And what was his next move?

———

Alex was just falling asleep when her cell phone rang. She debated for a moment and then reached over to pick it up. "Hello?"

"Alex? It's Razz."

"Razz? What's going on?"

"I don't know if it means anything, but I got home and found my computer beeping at me."

"Well, that's nice. I think."

"No. You don't understand. It's Marcus's alarm. I modified it after the last break-in. Someone bypassed it. They're in his house. And it wasn't Marcus. According to this readout, it occurred while we were at the cemetery."

Alex already had her feet on the floor and was reaching for her jeans. "Did you call Marcus?"

"I did. No answer."

"Okay, thanks. Call the police. I'm on my way."

"Already did."

If he said anything after that, she didn't hear it. She ended the call and tossed the phone on the bed as she raced to dress, hopping across the floor as she jammed her feet into her boots. She opened her gun safe and pulled out her SIG and an extra clip.

Five minutes after Razz's call, she rode the elevator to the parking garage. *If that madman touches one hair on Marcus's head—if he puts one mark on him—it'll be more than his ear that will suffer.*

She used her remote to unlock her car and jumped in.

The passenger door opened and Mandeville leaned in, pointing a gun at her. He smiled. "Hello, Alexandria. Now, I want you to slip that nice gun of yours out of the holster and hand it to me. Grip first, if you please."

Slowly, Alex lifted the SIG and handed it to him.

"Very nice." He slid into the car, keeping the gun trained on her. "Now drive."

"Where are we going?"

"Well, to see your partner, of course."

———

Marcus unlocked his front door and stepped inside, tossing his coat across the chair. He punched in the code for the security alarm and started for the stairs. But the panel didn't change colors. He reset and tried again. No response. And too late, the hairs on his neck stood up.

"Just raise your hands and turn around, nice and slow."

Marcus complied, turning to stare down the barrel of Alex's Walther. "I see you found my partner's gun. She'll be thrilled to have it back."

"She'll be here soon enough." The man waved the gun. "Have a seat in that chair right there."

He was a big man, easily six-two and two hundred and thirty pounds of muscle. Pockmarks and scars covered his face and neck. "You're Mandeville's bodyguard. You have a name?"

"Roger."

"So is Mandeville here too?"

"Not yet."

"Then he has Alex."

"Yep. They're on their way."

Marcus eased down in the chair. "So what now?"

"We wait. My boss has business with you and your partner."

"I see. And what do you get out of all this?"

"My boss's gratitude."

Marcus kept his eye on the gun. "Sure. Sure. But one problem. You realize that you're a liability, don't you?"

"Nonsense."

"Oh? You know everything that man has done. You know where all the bodies are buried, so to speak. You think he's going to allow you to live? Not likely."

"He won't hurt me. He needs me."

"Yeah, sure."

"Just shut up."

"The police are on their way. Just thought I'd let you know."

"He thought of that."

Marcus tensed when he heard car tires on the gravel drive. Roger backed over to the window and looked out. "They're here."

"Let the fun begin."

Roger shot him a look and his hand tightened on the gun. "What's that supposed to mean?"

Marcus shrugged. "Just an innocent remark. Whatever plans your boss has, I'm sure he's going to have fun. And you look like the type that enjoys hurting people."

Alex was pushed through the door. Mandeville stepped in behind her. He looked more disheveled than Alex did. His suit was wrinkled, he needed a shave, and his white shirt had a few streaks of dirt on it. Guess being a wanted man on the run will do that to a guy who isn't used to living on the edge. Probably missing his fine brandy and Cuban cigars.

"Any problems?" Mandeville asked.

Roger shook his head. "Not a one."

"Then let's get this done and get out of here."

Roger grabbed a rope he had on the floor and approached Alex first. "Turn around."

"You have to tie us up to kill us?"

"We're going to leave you here to burn with the house. Rope burns. Bullets don't."

Alex glanced over at Marcus as she turned around. "Seems a shame to burn down this old house."

"I know," Marcus agreed. "I don't think I'm too fond of that idea."

"Well, then, let's tell them no."

"All right."

They both moved at the same time. Alex whipped around and dropped down low, diving into Roger's legs, knocking him off balance, and drawing Mandeville's attention. Marcus braced his arms on the chair as he swung out with his leg to hit Mandeville's hand, knocking the gun free.

Then Marcus pushed himself out of the chair and into Mandeville.

Alex shifted, putting all her weight on her upper back as she kicked out at Roger's face. Then she drew one leg around and back, grabbing for her ankle holster. Roger roared and came at her, grabbing her by the throat.

Marcus rolled over on top of Mandeville, who was reaching for the gun that lay inches out of reach.

Alex lowered her chin, trying to block Roger from getting a good grip on her throat as she struggled to get her pant leg up far enough to get to the gun. Her lungs began to burn as she struggled to breathe, and her throat felt like he was breaking it in half. If she didn't move quickly, she wasn't going to be able to move at all. She brought her free hand up and gouged Roger in the eyes. He screamed and reared back, giving her just enough clearance to pull the gun.

She brought it up and pulled the trigger. Roger reflexively reached for his wounded leg then teetered and fell back.

Before she could take aim at Mandeville, she caught movement from the corner of her eye and heard two shots.

Mandeville froze and then went slack. Marcus rolled away and stared up at Lt. Mosley. "About time you got here."

Mosley smiled as he waved in another officer. "Sorry about that. You two okay?"

Alex slowly climbed to her feet. "Sure. Marcus?"

He stayed sprawled out on the floor. "The next time one of my old girlfriends calls with a problem, tell them I'm out of town."

"Happy to," Alex replied. "Just how many old girlfriends are there?"

"I've lost count." He frowned. "You opened up your wound. It's bleeding."

Alex looked over at her shoulder as she swayed. "I hesitate to mention this, but I think I'm going to pass out."

46

Friday, May 15

Suzanne woke up just as her mother entered the room. Despite her tiptoeing, the smell of food had pulled Suzanne from a warm slumber to wide awake in a matter of seconds.

She was starving.

Her mother wrinkled her nose. "I didn't mean to wake you. I hadn't realized you were asleep."

"Perfect timing, trust me. What did you make me?"

"Chicken and dumplings. You always loved it—until you were more concerned about your figure than eating."

"Thanks, Mom. But if you give me two minutes to get up, I'd rather eat in the kitchen. I'm tired of being in bed."

"Are you sure?"

"Positive."

Her mother shuffled out, closing the door behind her.

Suzanne stared after her for a moment. She couldn't have been more surprised when she woke up in the hospital to find her mother hovering over, fretting like a mother hen with a wounded chick. At first, Suzanne just let her mother take over, smothering her with attention and love. She'd wallowed in the attention. After a while though, she had to ask her parents what had changed. Why they were showing her love. Their answer stunned her.

"We've always loved you. You just never seemed to need or want our love. It hurt us to think that you didn't love us, but when we realized how close we came to losing you forever, well, it doesn't matter whether you love us or not. We love you and that's that."

When they asked to stay for a few days, she eagerly agreed, even offering to let them take her bed. They refused, taking the guest room even though the bed was smaller. Her sister called, and for once they didn't snip at each other. Suzanne wasn't sure whether her family had changed or the changes in her were helping her see everything differently. Either way, she was happy for the first time in years.

After washing her face, brushing her teeth, and wrapping a scarf around her head, she stared into the mirror, studying the bruises, the black eyes, the bandages over her nose. She looked like she'd gone fifteen rounds with Evander Holyfield. But she was alive. And for the first time in her life, that mattered more than what she looked like. Of course, the station was telling her to take all the time she needed to heal before she came back to work, but they just didn't want someone that looked like her in front of the camera. Not that she blamed them. And not that she intended to go back to *Judgment Day* anyway.

She ambled down the stairs and took a seat at the kitchen table. "I'm in heaven." She picked up the spoon. "Where's Dad?"

"He just went down to the store to get us some groceries. He'll be right back."

Suzanne was sprinkling a bit of salt on the food when Alex and Marcus arrived with a big bouquet of bright flowers. "Oh, how pretty," Suzanne exclaimed, standing up. She gave Alex a hug.

"How are you feeling today?" Alex asked.

"A thousand percent better." She turned to Marcus. "My hero." She wrapped her arms around his neck. "You saved my life. I'm never going to forget that."

"Alex did too. And Razz."

She smiled up at him, her arms still locked behind his head. "And I so appreciate everything the three of you did. I owe you everything."

Marcus awkwardly eased her arms away, holding them at her side. "You look better."

"No, I don't, but you're sweet to lie to me."

Marcus pointed to her food. "You need to eat."

"Well, I am hungry, if you don't mind. So tell me the latest." She sat down, never taking her eyes off Marcus.

"Mandeville is in the hospital. But soon enough, he'll be serving a very long prison term."

"Although his attorney is claiming an insanity defense," Alex added with a touch of bitterness.

"Either way, he'll never be a free man," Suzanne pointed out. "He killed a senator. They frown on things like that. Not to mention all the runaways."

"True." Alex crossed her legs. "Razz sends his regards."

"Oh, how's he doing?"

"Pretty good, all things considered. I think the nights are the toughest for him. Going home to an empty house. But he's spending most of his time at the office, making himself invaluable."

Suzanne's father stepped into the room carrying grocery bags. "Oh, hi. I didn't realize we had company. I could run back to the store and get more food."

"We can't stay long," Marcus told him. "But thank you anyway."

"I'm glad you came." Suzanne shoveled another forkful of food into her mouth.

"Suzanne got a call from Frank," her mother said. "He wants her back to work as soon as she's feeling better."

"Really?" Marcus replied. "That's great."

Suzanne shook her head and swallowed. "I'm not going back."

"Why not?" Alex asked.

Suzanne set her fork down. "It's hard to explain, but I did a lot of soul-searching when I thought I was going to die. I realized some things about myself, and one of them is that I really don't want to do that kind of work anymore. I'm thinking maybe I'd like to try my hand at reporting for a local station. Maybe doing some special-interest stories. Hometown heroes. That sort of thing."

"Well, that sounds pretty exciting," Alex replied. "What about the Mandeville story? It needs to be told."

"And it will be. But not by me."

Marcus nudged Alex. She stood up. "We need to run, but we'll talk soon."

"I hope so. I'm thinking of starting my new career with a story about the two of you."

"You can't," Marcus said with a slight smile. "You signed an agreement." He winked. "Nice try, though."

She reached up and cupped his face with her hands. "I really can't tell you how much I appreciate everything you did for me. You didn't have to come after me, but you did. I owe you my life. If there's ever anything I can do for you, don't hesitate to ask."

Marcus just nodded and slipped out the door.

Suzanne shut the door and then peeked out the front window.

"Suzanne, what are you doing?" her mother asked.

She smiled. "Just checking to see if my plan worked."

They were barely out the door, but Marcus knew he was in deep trouble. The stony expression on Alex's face could have been placed on Mount Rushmore. "Do I dare ask what you're upset about?"

"Nothing."

"Nothing," he repeated softly. "Why don't I believe that?"

She turned on him, her eyes narrow, her lips practically snarling. "Did you like it, Marcus? When she threw herself at you? The big hero, all warm and fuzzy."

He stared at her a minute, trying not to laugh, and trying to separate logic from emotion.

"Oh yeah, you enjoyed it. Look at you, grinning like a monkey on banana boat."

Forget logic.

He took her face in his hands and slowly, softly, kissed her lips. She leaned into him, and he heard that soft little flutter in the back of her throat.

He lifted his head. "Now, that makes me feel warm and fuzzy."

"Yeah?" she whispered with a smile.

"Absolutely." He kissed her again.

"What took you so long?"

HE'S ABOUT TO FACE
THE HUNT OF A LIFETIME...

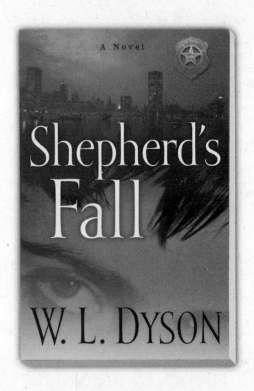

Bounty hunter Nick Shepherd is juggling financial problems, an angry ex-wife, a rebellious daughter, and siblings who are battling their own demons. But when his daughter is kidnapped in the midst of pursuing a fugitive, Nick must face his doubts about God as he risks everything to save his daughter.